through
the green door

lies a world of mystery pleasure . . . literate entertainment for fans of such great writers as Rex Stout, Simenon, the Lockridges, J. J. Marric, and many others . . . the suave delights of expert detection . . . the terror of death . . . the plots of master criminals . . . the excitement of the chase.

green door mysteries

are a new series of reprints of the best in mystery fiction—famous authors, favorite detectives, superb stories—all discriminatingly selected for exacting readers.

MANNING COLES

is a pseudonym for the collaborative team of Adelaide Oke Manning and Cyril Henry Coles. Besides joining Miss Manning in the production of the Tommy Hambledon thrillers, Mr. Coles was for many years a "Hambledon" himself, in the service of British Intelligence.

A GREEN DOOR MYSTERY

Night Train to Paris

manning COLES

▲ **PYRAMID BOOKS**   **NEW YORK**

To Jimmy Russell, of Cook's

*"The vagabond, when rich, is
called a tourist."*
P. RICHARD

NIGHT TRAIN TO PARIS

A PYRAMID BOOK—Published by arrangement with Doubleday & Co., Inc.

PRINTING HISTORY

Doubleday & Company edition published March 1952
Second printing, March 1952

Detective Book Club edition February 1952

Pyramid edition published April 1962

Library of Congress Catalog Card Number: 52-5534

Copyright, 1952, by Doubleday & Company, Inc.   All Rights Reserved

Printed in the United States of America

PYRAMID BOOKS are published by Pyramid Publications, Inc.,
444 Madison Avenue, New York 22, New York, U.S.A.

Contents

1

AT SEA

THE BIG CABIN CRUISER rushed on through the darkness, the faint glimmer from the binnacle lamp showing nothing but the face of the man at the wheel like a mask hung upon a black wall. The sky was overcast though occasionally a rent in the clouds showed for a moment a few stars covered again at once as the hurrying rack streamed across. The sea was getting up; the steady hiss of the bows cutting through the water was more and more frequently interrupted by the heavy spatter of spray upon the deck.

A second man entered the small wheelhouse and bent over the binnacle to see the time by his wrist watch.

"No sign of her yet?" said the helmsman.

"Of course not. Much too early."

"Sea's going up. What was the last weather report?"

"More gale warnings," said the man with the wrist watch.

"Going to be a real blow, Alton."

"What did you call me?"

"Sir."

"That's better," said Alton smoothly, and walked away.

"Thinks he's still in the ruddy Navy," said the helmsman to the floating compass which immediately slewed several points to port as a vicious cross sea caught the little ship abeam. "Come up, you cow. Glad it isn't me goin' to be picked off a ship on a night like this."

Nearly an hour later he saw a distant light and opened his mouth to shout, but before he could speak a strong light awoke in the bows of the cabin cruiser as Alton switched on the searchlight and swung it vertically upwards. He shouted down to the second engineer to come on deck and then came himself to take the wheel.

"Go and lend Dick a hand, Johnny. Fender's out on the portside."

The ship came on, showing first the green starboard light and then a row of lighted portholes. She was visibly slowing down; the cabin cruiser turned to meet her and then swung round in a wide circle to starboard. Dick at the searchlight brought it down until the side of the ship was bright in the glare of it; faces looked over the rail and a long rope ladder fell down the ship's side, unrolling as it came. The ship was rolling heavily; the end of the rope ladder was dipped in the sea, snatched out and dipped again and again. The cabin cruiser, slowed down till she had only just steerageway, was being thrown about like a toy. They drew nearer together, a rope was flung from the steamer, missed, and flung again. This time Johnny caught it.

A short stout figure began to climb slowly down the ladder with occasional stops to look down at the sea. The ladder swung out from the ship's side and smacked back again while the man clung frantically and shouted something.

"Come on!" bellowed Alton. "Come on!" He brought the cabin cruiser close alongside and Dick ran to the foot of the ladder, but it was snatched from him by a roll of the ship.

The man on the ladder came down almost to the end and hesitated, as well he might. The roll swung him out towards the waiting boat and Alton yelled to him to let go and jump. He left it just too late, let go as the return roll started and fell headlong into the sea between the ship's side and the hull of the cabin cruiser.

He was dragged out gasping, crowing and spitting sea water; Johnny brought him to the wheelhouse while the line was cast off, the cabin cruiser turned away from the ship and the engine revolutions speeded up. The searchlight clicked out, the ship's lights retired into the darkness of the night and were surprisingly soon lost to view.

The passenger, sea water pouring off him, clung to the side of the wheelhouse and said in English with a strong German accent that he was wet, very wet. And cold. He was also, rather unexpectedly, clutching the sort of brief case which businessmen carry to the office.

"Take the wheel, Johnny," said Alton, and gave him his course. "You come below and have a drink," he added, addressing the passenger, "you'll be all right. Sea water never hurt anybody except by drowning. This way."

The small saloon was warm and stuffy; merely to be out of the tearing wind was a relief, and the lines of strain began to fade out on the passenger's face. Alton poured out a handsome tot of rum, the stranger drank it straight off and managed to smile.

"Now that my teeth stop chattering," he said, "I introduce

myself. Doctor of Physics Ignatius Muntz, formerly of the University of Heidelberg." He bowed.

"My name is Alton and I am in command of this large ship," said Alton, with a friendly smile. "You want to get those wet clothes off. Just a minute."

He called up the companion ladder and the second engineer came running down, a young man in the very early twenties with sandy hair and eyebrows and a freckled face always ready to grin. It was his first trip with Alton and he was very anxious to please; he was an odd contrast to his black-haired skipper whose lean frame and sallow skin with deep creases running from nostrils to mouth made him look older than his twenty-eight years. His eyes were dark, deep-set under heavy brows and a little too near together, and his mouth shut into a thin line with the lower lip slightly protruding. Dr. Muntz looked from one to the other.

"Dick," said Alton, "Dr. Muntz is soaked to the skin and I think you are the only man with a spare suit on board."

"Certainly, I'll get it. And vest and shirt. Anything I can do——" He opened a door at the far end of the saloon and went out.

"Have some rum," said Alton. "Finest thing in the world to stop a chill from developing." He poured out a second tot and Muntz drank a little of it.

"Strong," he said. "Very strong. Ah! Now I remember something, something most important——"

He put his brief case upon the table; it was attached to his left wrist by a short length of cord which he began to untie.

"In case I drop it coming down that ladder," he explained.

"I did wonder how you had managed to keep hold of it," said Alton.

"If I had not, if it had gone away in the sea, I might as well have gone with it."

"So important as that," said Alton.

"So important as that," agreed Muntz, opening the case. There was a little water in it which he tipped out on the floor and then drew out a flat package wrapped in oil silk with rubber bands round it. He slipped them off and opened the package, which contained several sheets of paper closely folded; he unfolded them carefully. There were scale drawings of some long cylindrical object, so much was obvious at a glance ,but there were also immensely detailed drawings of complicated mechanisms and fittings which conveyed nothing whatever to Alton.

The second engineer returned with an armful of clothes.

"Sorry to have been so long, sir. Couldn't find any socks."

Muntz was too busy examining his papers to take any notice. "A little damp here, a corner where the water has entered," he complained.

"They will soon dry down here," said Alton. "Let's get those wet clothes off you. Finish your rum first, you're shivering."

Muntz drank it off and submitted like a child to having his soaked clothes pulled off him, being rubbed down with a rough towel and dressed again in Dick's dry garments. The process was awkward in the extreme as the space in the saloon was very cramped, the cabin cruiser was apparently trying to stand on her head and roll at the same time like a dog which has just been bathed, and Muntz seemed to have lost any sea legs he ever had. Evidently the rum was taking hold upon him, for his face became flushed and he talked without ceasing.

"I am obliged to you so very much for all your kind acts," he said. "I knew if I to England could get I should among good friends be, and it was true, for here I am on an English ship and the so-kind friends are here before me. Also the papers, my impossible-to-be-overestimated papers. I thank you from the bottom of my heart. Others also. Your Mr. Churchill will thank you. Your Government will thank you. Your people, when they of it come to know, will selephade—salunade——" He abandoned his English and continued in a flood of German which was only terminated when, at the awkward moment of putting him into Dick's trousers, a salmon-like leap of the cabin cruiser hurled all three men into a heap by the door.

The shock seemed to sober Muntz temporarily and he helped to dress himself in a thick jersey and a coat. He sat down at the table, folded up the papers which were not really damp enough to hurt them, and wrapped them again in their oil-silk cover. He slipped on the rubber bands and patted the packet affectionately, while the other two men stood round the table watching him.

"Better lie down for a bit," suggested Alton. "You might be badly hurt falling about."

Muntz looked up and his eyes were glassy.

"This packet," he said thickly, "the Russians would give one million pounds sterling for this packet. One million pounds. Sterling. But they shan't have it." His eyes focussed with difficulty upon the second engineer.

"That's right," said Dick consolingly. "They shan't have it, then. You take it to London and give it to Winston Churchill yourself."

Some other thought took possession of Muntz, an over-powering and unpleasant thought. He yawned suddenly, changed colour, and sweat broke out upon his forehead.

"Hot in here," he said, "very hot." He rose slowly to his feet, holding the edge of the table.

"He's going to be sick," said the second engineer, and dived into the next cabin for a suitable vessel. But Muntz did not wait; he staggered towards the door with the packet still in his hand.

"Fresh air," he said. "Be all right on deck." He opened the door and in doing so dropped the packet, which Alton picked up for him.

"Give it to me," said Muntz.

"I've put it in your pocket," said Alton, pushing his hand well down into the pocket so that Muntz could feel it. "That's quite safe. Up you go; hold on with both hands, I'll help you."

With Alton pushing behind they arrived at the top of the companion ladder and the wild night sprang at them like an animal. Muntz was whirled, staggering, to the lee rail; Alton, at the head of the companion, could just distinguish the bent and shuddering form. Alton laughed shortly and went below again.

"He seemed to prefer being alone," he said, "so I left him."

"May be all right in a few minutes," said Dick, busily collecting sodden garments from the floor. "Takes 'em like that sometimes. He'll get the sea water out of his system anyway."

"Probably that was what did it," said Alton. "I'm just going up to the wheelhouse, I won't be a minute."

"Very good, sir," said Dick professionally. He piled the soaking clothes in a heap and lay down on a bunk to read an Edgar Wallace till it should be time to go on duty.

Alton went out on deck; there were none of the crew about except the man in the wheelhouse for'ard and he had his back turned. His head and shoulders were faintly silhouetted against the binnacle light and he was plainly fighting with the kicking wheel, he would not look round. Muntz was an indistinct heap of misery near the stern, crouched over the rail. Alton took three silent strides towards him, grasped his ankles and with one strong lift heaved him overboard where a rising wave received him before he had time to cry out.

Alton turned almost in the same motion and went forward along the deck, walking heavily; to Dick in the saloon below it seemed as though his captain had but paused at the head of the ladder before going forward. Alton spoke to Johnny at the wheel for a few minutes and then returned to the saloon.

"Passenger all right, sir?" asked Dick, looking up from his book.

"He seemed to be busily occupied," said Alton. "I didn't interrupt."

He lit a cigarette, picked a book out of a rack on the wall and lay down upon the other bunk. Some little time passed before Dick swung his legs to the floor and sat up. Alton looked across at him with raised eyebrows.

"I was wondering, sir, if the old chap was all right. He's been up there some time and it's pretty cold."

"I was beginning to wonder myself," said Alton. "Better bring him down."

The second engineer nodded and went out. Alton waited while the door was shut and steps sounded upon the companion ladder, then he sat up sharply, took Muntz's waterproof packet out of his coat pocket and, pulling up his jersey, stowed it away inside his shirt. Hasty steps sounded overhead; he buttoned up his shirt, pulled down his jersey and was lying at ease once more as the door burst open and Dick rushed in.

"He's not on deck, sir, Johnny hasn't seen him, he's not in the engine room——"

Alton sat up slowly, staring. "Good lord, he must have——"

"Must have gone overboard, sir——"

"I'll come myself."

They searched the cabin cruiser thoroughly but, rather naturally, did not find Muntz anywhere.

"He must have hung too far over the rail and gone in," said Dick. "It's easily done and she has been rolling all ends up."

"I ought to have brought him down myself, when I went up to speak to Johnny," said Alton, sitting down heavily. "I did think of it, but——"

"Bad business, sir," said Dick sympathetically. "Will there be trouble over this?"

"Oh, I expect so," said Alton wearily. "There's one bright spot, we can carry straight on now and come in by daylight; I didn't fancy putting him ashore in the dinghy in this weather. You've lost your clothes, Dick."

"Oh, that," said Dick indifferently.

Eight hours later Stephen Alton landed at Wapping and came up a side street from the stairs he generally used. At the corner where the side street joined the main road he paused, debating whether to travel by tram or walk to the station and go by train.

Twenty yards from Alton's corner a constable upon his beat and a police sergeant upon his rounds were standing together, talking. The sergeant noticed Alton as he paused at the corner and said: "See that man there?"

To reach the station Alton would have to pass them; he decided against it. A tram came clattering along the road; Alton signalled it, swung himself on board as it slowed down, and turned his back to the police as he was borne past them.

"Who is he?" asked the constable.

"Name of Alton, Stephen Alton. You'll know him when you see him again. Notice what he does when you do see him, where he goes and who he's with. We'll get him one of these days."

"What's he been up to?"

"We can't prove it, but the Inspector's pretty sure he's in all or some of these dock robberies we've had lately. Particularly the robberies from lighters; they're done by someone who knows the river well and he does. Someone who even knows which lighter to pick out of a string of 'em."

"There was all those cases of cigarettes went last week," said the constable.

"Ah. And lots of other things too. Been going on a long time, before you came here. He's got away with it so far, but one of these days he'll slip up and we'll get him, my lad, we'll get him. He's got something on his conscience now; he was coming this way and changed his mind when he saw us, you saw that yourself."

"Yes," said the constable.

"Keep on keeping on," said the sergeant.

2

PEPPER AND SPICE

EDWARD JOHN LOGAN, Merchant, had offices in Mincing Lane in the City of London where he dealt in coffee and spices. They were small dark rooms where the electric light burned continuously throughout the working day, and they were not very well ventilated, so that the air was always heavy with a harmony of ginger, nutmeg, cloves, mace, cinnamon and caraway seeds with the smell of coffee as a ground base. Samples of these were kept in a closet called the storeroom; every time the storeroom door was opened a fresh wave of piquancy drifted into Logan's office. His secretary, Nancy Davie, used to say that it was necessary to change down to the skin and have a bath when she reached home at night in order to lose the scent of business and even then it clung to her hair.

Logan was a man in the forties, tall and well set up, dark-haired and with good features, but beginning to show that loss of elasticity which besets men who lead sedentary lives in stuffy offices. His physical reactions were slowing down and his mind was stiffening into grooves. He lived in an expensive flat near Regent's Park with a manservant who was all that bachelors dream of and so seldom find. In a word, Logan was much too comfortable and was beginning to suffer for it.

On a day about two months after the unfortunate Muntz disappeared into the dark North Sea, Logan returned to his office after lunch, put his gloves in his bowler hat, hung it up with his neat umbrella upon their usual peg and rang the bell for his secretary. She came in at once with her hands full of papers.

"Er—Miss Davie—oh, those are my letters, are they? I'll just sign them."

He went through them hastily, signing one after another without reading them, and Miss Davie's eyebrows went up. This was unlike Mr. Logan, but he had been unsettled in manner for several days. There was something in the wind, could he be getting married? Not very likely; this unsettlement was definitely not rapturous. No secret smiles, no song at the lips, no lightness in the tread.

"Mr. Cogsworth rang up; he would like to see you this afternoon if convenient," she said.

Logan looked up at her. No, definitely not happy. His expression was worried, even hunted.

"Oh, I can't see him this afternoon. Ring him up and ask him to come tomorrow, will you?" Logan pushed back his chair, locked the drawers of his desk, put the keys in his pocket and got up. "I have to go out this afternoon," he added, taking down his hat and umbrella. "I shall not be back here today."

"Very good," said Miss Davie dutifully. Then something irresolute in his manner led her beyond the normal limits of office routine and she added impulsively: "I hope there is nothing wrong?"

"What? Oh no, nothing. At least, nothing that a little firmness will not cure," he said with sudden acidity. "Good afternoon, Miss Davie—er—and thank you." He smiled suddenly, put his hat on for the purpose of taking it off to her, hung his umbrella on his arm and walked out into the street.

"Dear me," said Miss Davie thoughtfully.

Edward Logan was going to see his lawyer who inhabited offices so like his own that but for their being on the first floor and not smelling of spices he would hardly have noticed any change in his surroundings.

"Good afternoon, Logan, pleased to see you," said the lawyer, and shook hands warmly.

"Good afternoon, Fenchurch." Logan put down his hat, gloves and umbrella on one chair, sat down slowly on another and looked across the desk at his old friend.

"Well," said Fenchurch, smiling, "what can I do for you?"

"I've been a fool," said Logan abruptly. "What are you laughing at?"

"I thought you were going to say that. There is a faintly sheepish aspect about you this afternoon which is immediately recognizable to any experienced solicitor. It is almost invariably accompanied by the form of words you have just uttered. Or some equivalent synonym."

Logan scowled for a moment and then laughed.

"No doubt you're right. The world is full of people like me. You've got my will, haven't you, Fenchurch?"

"Certainly. You want to look at it? I'll have it brought in." He touched a bell upon his desk, said: "Mr. Logan's will," to the clerk who answered it, and leaned back in his chair.

"I want to tear it up," said Logan energetically. "With my own hands."

"Why not? It's your will," said Fenchurch. "It's also my poor but honest way of making a living." The clerk came back with the will and Fenchurch opened it. "It's very short."

"Give it to me," said Logan, "and may I borrow your wastepaper basket? Thank you. Now," said Logan, tearing the will into small pieces, "I suppose I'd better tell you the rest of the story since I want your advice."

"There are three things," said Fenchurch, taking off his glasses and rubbing them with a corner of his handkerchief, "about which men most commonly make fools of themselves: namely, horses, cards and women. People don't bet on horses as they did, I suppose there isn't the money, and cards have practically gone out compared to the customs of even fifty years ago. But by some dispensation of Providence which I may admire but cannot understand, there seem to be more women about than ever." He put his glasses on and blinked through them at Logan. "Is that your experience also?"

"It isn't the number of women that worries me," said Logan. "It's just one."

"You're lucky," said Fenchurch, "it's generally two. Well now, what about it?"

Logan explained that he had met Elizabeth Alton about three years earlier and was attracted by her calm manner and general air of competence, her clear mind and exact way of speaking. Fenchurch raised his eyebrows but did not interrupt. Logan said that they had seen a good deal of each other and that he had asked her several times, both verbally and in writing, to marry him but she had always put him off. Not a flat refusal, but a postponement; someday, not yet, not just now. They were not even formally engaged. "This has been going on for a long time now," said Logan indignantly, "more than two years, to be exact, and I'm getting very tired of it. Besides, to tell you the truth, I was desperately keen on it at one time but I'm by no means so keen now. It—it takes the edge off one's enthusiasm to be continually held off and disappointed."

Fenchurch nodded. "It does, it does. The lady never tells you what the impediment is, if there is one?"

"No. I asked her bluntly once whether she was married already and she assured me she was not. I believe her, I don't think for a moment that she is. That is, of course, the obvious suggestion, but I don't think it's the right one in this case."

Fenchurch said nothing and Logan went on.

"About nine—no, ten months ago I took her out in my car one Sunday; we went for a run down to Shere in Surrey. Well, as you know, Greene generally drives me—I don't care for driving and I know I'm not good at it—but on this occasion I left him behind and drove the car myself. I was showing off, actually, no doubt," said Logan with an embarrassed laugh. "Well, on the way back there was a misunderstanding at a crossroads and I ran into a lorry. The car was badly damaged but we were not much the worse, physically, that is; it was Betty's nerves which were severely affected."

Fenchurch imagined being driven in Sunday traffic in Surrey by a driver who himself admitted he was not very good. He sympathized with Miss Alton's feelings even before the crash, but did not say so.

"She was under the doctor's care for weeks and weeks," said Logan. "She had to give up her employment—she was private secretary to a Member of Parliament—so, as it was all my fault that she couldn't earn, I thought it only right to make her an allowance until she was quite well again."

"I see," said Fenchurch.

"I mean, it was just that and nothing more; I mean, it was my fault that she was incapacitated, it was merely a temporary arrangement during her illness——"

"I quite understand," said Fenchurch.

"Well, so far as I can see, she is quite fit again and if I ask what the doctor says she says he is quite pleased with her. But she doesn't seem to be making the least effort to get another post and I'm sure she could, she's so extremely competent and well trained. I have a certain delicacy about the matter, but the fact is, Fenchurch, I'm beginning to wonder how long it's going on."

"I don't wonder. I should do the same in your place."

"Then there's another thing. I said that I'm sure she's not married, but I'm beginning to think there's another man hanging about."

"Ah."

"Once when I went there the room smelt of tobacco smoke. Betty smokes, but only mild cigarettes and not many of them. This was quite different, really strong tobacco. Another time when I called unexpectedly she was darning socks. Thick woollen socks, Fenchurch. When I asked her about them she laughed and said I'd surprised her in one of her little charities. Do women darn socks for charity, Fenchurch?"

"I'll ask my wife, she is much occupied with what are called 'good works.' Knit, yes, I've seen her doing it, but darning I doubt."

"So do I," said Logan energetically. "In fact, I doubt a lot of things these days. One evening when I was there her doorbell rang. There are three floors of flats; each tenant has his own doorbell as usual, and Betty's on the first floor. She went down to answer the door and while I was waiting I strolled to the window, quite idly, as one does, you know. A man went away from the door and as he left he turned on the pavement and waved his hand. Like this. Quite carefree and friendly, damn him. He didn't raise his hat, he waved to her. Then she came upstairs again and said it was a man who'd come to the wrong address. I asked if it were anyone she knew and she said, 'Oh no. A total stranger.' He didn't behave like a total stranger, that's all."

"Perhaps he was merely being impertinent," said Fenchurch.

"It's possible, I suppose," said Logan sulkily.

"Tell me," said Fenchurch. "Since you seem to be thoroughly tired of the whole business, is there any reason why you shouldn't simply stay away? You could write her a letter saying that in consequence of her return to health, which delights you beyond measure, you propose to stop the allowance a fortnight from now. That will give her enough time to find another post if she's as good as you say. If she doesn't like it, there doesn't seem to be much she can do about it. Is there?"

There was a short pause.

"I've written a lot of silly letters," said Logan.

"Oh dear. Oh, dear me. How very unfortunate. But does it really matter?"

Logan looked at him. "I was, of course, thinking of a breach-of-promise case and all those letters being read out in court——"

"Of course you were. That's how so many women get away with it. Now let me tell you that, if what you have told me is literally true, she wouldn't have a leg to stand on. There was a time when bringing breach-of-promise actions was a lucrative side line for women; it isn't now. They have to prove that they have lost substantially in either money or reputation. For example, if she'd spent money because she was going to marry you which she wouldn't otherwise have spent—bought a house or furniture or even an expensive trousseau—you might be made to pay up."

"She hasn't," said Logan.

"Or if she had had a child——"

"Great heavens, no. I told you I meant to *marry* her. One doesn't—er——"

"Well, I'm quite sure you didn't, anyway. What makes you afraid she would bring an action? Is she vindictive by nature?"

"Oh, I shouldn't really think so," said poor Logan. "It's just that she is so very competent, I can't imagine any situation with which she couldn't cope and I was wondering how she'd cope with this one. That's all."

"Yes, I see. Get it into your head that an action for breach of promise which was merely vindictive would stand no chance at all of succeeding and no reputable solicitor would handle it. That is, if you have really given me all the relevant information."

"I'm sure I have. She's none the worse for me."

"That's the way to talk," said Fenchurch. "Now all that's worrying you is the letters, eh? Are you sure she has kept them?"

"No. But she did keep them; I mean, I know she used to store them up, she said so."

"Since you really want them—"

"I want to do this with them," said Logan, pointing to the wastepaper basket.

"Why not simply go and ask her for them?"

Logan stood up and said: "Right. I will."

"Just a moment before you rush off. You have just torn up your will; I take it you will want to make another?"

"If I get run over on the way home——"

"These things do happen," said Fenchurch, "unfortunately."

"Then the whole of my estate goes to my next of kin, doesn't it? That's my twin brother Laurence."

"That is so, yes. But the Government claims heavier death duties in the case of an intestacy. Of course it may be that you wish to give the Government a little present—no? No, then don't die intestate. Also, there were other legacies, weren't there?"

"To my secretary Miss Davie and my manservant Greene and one or two others. Yes, I see, I don't want them to be washed out. Can I come and see you one day next week and in the meantime I'll think it over?"

Fenchurch consulted an engagement calendar and said: "Will ten-thirty next Tuesday suit you?"

"Very well," said Logan, backing towards the door. "I'll be here at ten-thirty next Tuesday. Good-bye, Fenchurch."

Elizabeth Alton's flat was in a converted house in West Kensington; other tenants lived on the ground floor and the second storey, the caretaker and his wife in the basement. Logan walked up the two wide steps to the front door and rang the bell.

Nothing happened, so he rang again and yet again. Having screwed up his courage to face an interview he dreaded, exasperation seized him at being balked of it. If she was out he would wait. He opened the door—the main door of the house was only locked at night—and walked upstairs to Elizabeth Alton's own private door. It had a small brass knocker which was a model of the Imp of Lincoln. Logan knocked repeatedly, received no reply, and lost his temper. He grasped the door handle and turned it; to his surprise the door opened. She must be at home.

He put his head in and called: "Betty! Betty, are you there?" There was no answer; he went in and closed the door behind him. There was no entrance lobby; in these converted houses the doors opened straight into the sitting room and the other rooms had been made to open off that.

On the table in the middle there was a sheet of white paper, very conspicuous on the dark wood, and on it a message in Betty's neat writing: "Wait for me, I shan't be more than half an hour."

Logan's first surprised thought was to wonder how on earth she knew he was coming since he had not warned her and at this hour he was normally still at his office. Then it dawned on him that of course the message was not for him but for someone else whom she was expecting. If it were some woman friend it would be awkward being found there, and he almost turned and fled. On the other hand, if it were a man——

He laid his hat, umbrella and gloves down upon the table, walked to the window and stood looking out through the thin net curtains.

Five minutes later a man came walking fast along the street, almost running. Logan, looking down, was nearly certain that this was the same man who, on a previous occasion, had waved to Betty as he turned away.

"If he comes here——" whispered Logan.

The man came up to the front door and turned in. Logan heard the door open and shut and the sound of steps running up the stairs.

Logan picked up his hat, gloves and umbrella from the table and bolted like a rabbit into an inner room which was obviously Betty's bedroom. He looked wildly round for cover; there was a narrow built-in cupboard beside the fireplace with the door ajar. He sprang inside, crushing back dresses which hung there, and tried to pull the door shut; it would not quite close and there was no knob on the inside.

The second visitor knocked with the Lincoln Imp, waited a moment and then walked in, calling Betty's name as he did so. Then the calling stopped—he had evidently seen the note —and Logan distinctly heard him say: "Damn and blast!" in an angry voice.

After that there was silence broken only by the scrape of a match and, a little later, the smell reached him of the same strong tobacco he had smelt there before.

By this time Logan was furious with himself as well as with Betty and the man out there. What had possessed him to panic like that and hide in a dress cupboard? What a fool he would look if he were found. Logan was not the first to find that it is much easier to get into a cupboard than to emerge from it. Also his bowler hat was in his way; there was not much room and it persisted in pushing the door open, so he put it on his head. If only the man would get tired of waiting and go away.

3

HEIRONS

The outer door of the flat opened and shut and Logan heard Betty's voice. "Hello, Steve! How did the business—— What's the matter?"

The man's voice answered her, a deep voice with yet something light and reckless in its tones. "Don't get into a flap, please. There's nothing wrong that a cool head and a little ready money won't cure. I must get away, that's all."

"Steve! Is it the police again?"

Steve laughed. "Well, it's two lots actually, though it's true the police force is one of 'em. Funny thing, that, the police chasing me for something I didn't do."

"If you can prove you didn't do it, why run?"

"Oh, they know I didn't do it."

"Then why are they chasing you?"

"All these questions! Now I'll ask you one. How much money have you got?"

"None for you," said Elizabeth Alton in tones so incisive that Logan could almost see their shape cut in the air. "I've given you money and lent you money—it's the same thing, since you never pay back—and I'm sick of it." The man said something which Logan did not catch but which seemed to infuriate Betty.

"Don't you dare to quote Mother to me again! Yes, I know she left you in my charge, don't I know it! As soon as I'd left school I was working to educate you, then working to help keep you when you got your first job——"

"You got the job, I didn't," interrupted Steve. "You made me into a grubby little office boy ordered about by every——"

"You could have worked up," she said. "I had to. Then you ran away to sea and I had to pay for those binoculars you stole in Cardiff. I wouldn't pay that time you got mixed up with that forged money——"

"Nobody asked you to—Borstal and no option——"

"Then the war broke out and I did think you'd go straight. You couldn't go straight if you were walking down a passage three feet wide. You've ruined my life; I can't have any decent friends, I can't save, I can't marry the man I want to marry, I won't connect a decent man with a jailbird, and if our mother could see you she'd haunt you and serve you right!"

There was a momentary pause during which the implications of "our mother" dawned upon Logan, but before he had time to begin to rejoice Stephen Alton gave him something else to think about.

"So you're going to brush off your little brother for good and all, are you? Not just yet, you're not. It would be so unrefined, would it not"—he mimicked Betty's precise enunciation—"to have a brother tried for murder?"

Silence fell like a dropped curtain; it seemed to Logan that even his heart had stopped beating.

"Don't sit there opening and shutting your mouth like that," said Stephen Alton, "you look like a goldfish with the gapes. Who? Oh, nobody we know, only three policemen."

"*Three policemen?*"

"Yes, and I didn't shoot them, but I might be accused of complicity. You see, they'd just arrested me."

"Stop, stop!" cried Betty. "Listen. You will begin at the beginning and tell me the story plainly and truthfully, or I will ring up the police and give you in charge. I mean it. Now then,"

"Oh, very well. I told you some time ago I'd got a scheme on which would net us pots of money and we could go to America and start a new life. I got hold of some drawings of something frightfully hush-hush which the German scientists in Russia had invented for the Russians. The fellow mainly responsible got out of Russia somehow, I don't know how—nor care—bringing them with him. I got hold of them— I'll tell you how some other time—and I'm selling them to the Russians. They are anxious to buy them back, naturally, and the figure, my dear Betty, is half a million sterling. So I arranged to meet a man this afternoon but I was a bit early, he wasn't in, so I said I'd come back later. On my way down the stairs from his office I met a couple of C.I.D. men. They were waiting for me, actually, wanted to pin some dock robberies onto me, or some such nonsense. So we all came downstairs together, me in the middle and the two dicks one on each side. There was a sort of entrance hall inside the front door. As we started down the last flight three men came into the hall; it was open to the public, you see, the place was a block of offices actually——"

"Get on!"

"I am getting on. I recognized one of the three, he'd been tailing me around, he was a Russian, I knew that. They were the men I was going to meet. He and the other two pulled out revolvers and loosed off with 'em, a regular fusillade, and hit both the dicks with me; why I didn't stop one too I can't think. We all fell down the stairs together amid screams from adjoining offices and one hell of an uproar, and a policeman in uniform came dashing in from the street, so my noble and gallant allies shot him too. Very violent, these Mongols. I picked myself up while the cop was falling, if you get the picture, and made one jump for the door. Outside there was a police car with the door hanging open— that was where the cop came from, he was the driver—so I hopped in and drove rapidly away. I thought it best. When I'd put quite a distance between me and the scene of slaughter I left the car in a quiet street and came on here. That's all. Oh dear——"

"Steve! What—is it your heart again?"

"Only bumping a bit," gasped Steve. "Don't fuss, for goodness' sake."

"I wish you'd see a doctor," said Betty in an anxious voice.

"Doctor nothing! Got any brandy?"

"No, but I'll get some in a——"

"Sit still!"

There was a short silence during which Logan could hear nothing, then Stephen Alton's voice came again, a little less resonant than before but still determined and incisive.

"There you are. Better already. Smoking too much, must cut it down. Funny, I never get an attack when things are really exciting, it's only after it's all over—what were we saying?"

"Hadn't you better lie down for a bit? Lie down on my bed, perhaps you'll sleep for——"

Logan was so horrified by this suggestion that he nearly had a heart attack himself. If they were to come in and find him in the cupboard, having overheard everything, that man would certainly assault him with violence and possibly kill him. But Alton's next words relieved him.

"Don't be so soppy! I'm all right now. About those Russians, wasn't it?"

Betty evidently pulled herself together. "Yes," she said. "Why did the Russians, or whoever they were, shoot the policemen? Surely they must know they will be hunted down for it?"

"Either they meant to shoot me too and take the doings off my dead body or they thought I was going willingly to hand over the doings to the British Government and they didn't approve, or they may even have grasped the fact that I was being arrested and proposed to arrest me themselves. You can believe whichever you like, I didn't wait to ask them."

"I still think you'd be much safer in the hands of the police. You didn't shoot them."

"Safer! My good, worthy elder sister, when has safety ever appealed to me? Can't you get it into your head that I've still got those designs and I'm going to get the money for them? All I want to do is to lie low till the police have caught the Russians—no one ever murders police in this country and gets away with it—and then I'll bob up again and do the deal. These damn' Russkis are an infernal nuisance, they've been trailing me everywhere I go for the past fortnight, in case I double-cross them, I suppose. You know, they're such twisters themselves they can't trust anybody else. It's very difficult to deal with people like that."

There was a prolonged pause; evidently Betty was thinking over the story and Stephen thought it wiser to let her do so undisturbed. Logan, still in the dress cupboard, felt his mind spinning. He had done Betty a series of injustices in his thoughts, that was plain, but if marrying her meant being connected with this appalling Steve he felt less inclined to it than ever.

"What I don't understand," said Betty slowly, "is how those detectives knew you were going to that office this afternoon. You said they were waiting for you."

When Alton came ashore that afternoon in Wapping he went straight to the boardinghouse at the back of Liverpool Street Station where he had a room. It was not at all a nice boardinghouse but it suited Alton since all the boarders were men, and not the sort of men to ask awkward questions. They themselves would not have liked to be asked questions. Do as you would be done by.

He called down the basement stairs to his landlady to tell her that he had come back, and ran upstairs to his own bedroom on the first floor where he shut his door and locked it. He then undressed sufficiently to get poor Muntz's packet out from where it had lain hidden between his shirt and vest and been quite remarkably uncomfortable. Alton opened the packet, spread the sheets out upon the floor and looked at them while he changed into his shore clothes.

There were seven sheets altogether, of large size, about three feet by two feet six inches. They were very beautifully drawn in jet-black Indian ink by a man who knew his work; there were copious annotations in German which conveyed nothing to Alton and they were plainly originals. Alton postponed tying his tie to examine them closely; he could see in places the original pencilling under the ink lines. He was neither a trained engineer nor an explosives expert and frankly admitted to himself that the drawings were completely incomprehensible to him. He did grasp, however, that one of them was a General Arrangement and the others details of the parts shown in outline.

He finished dressing and sat down on his bed to smoke a cigarette, still looking doubtfully at the plans on the floor They were doubtless very beautiful to anyone who liked that kind of thing and, he hoped, immensely valuable, but how horribly large and bulky. Fancy trying to conceal those things where nobody could find them; you might as well try to conceal the Sailing Directions. Well, nearly.

He stubbed out that cigarette, lit another, and lay back on his bed staring at the ceiling and thinking. A quarter of an hour later he got up, packed up the sheets again and went out with them to see a friend of his.

He returned later so pleased with himself that he rang up his sister and took her out to dinner. It was then that he told her that he was on to something which would make both their fortunes, though he did not tell her then what it was. He was not consciously fond of his sister and he alternately raged and sneered when she tried to reform him, but whenever anything either good or bad happened to him some quite irresistible power compelled him to go and tell her about it. The compulsion infuriated him but he went all the same, and what is more, he always told her the truth if not the whole truth. She was twelve years older than he was and all the mother he had ever known.

The next move was to get in touch with the Russians. It was safe to assume that Russia had already found out that their precious design for death was no longer within their borders, or if they hadn't they soon would. When they came to enquire they would probably discover which way their truant expert had fled and where he was making for. After all, where would a truant expert escaping from Russia make for? England, of course, if only en route to the United States. In due course, therefore, pursuant Russians might be expected in London.

Alton let a few days pass and then went to see Ernie Heirons, with whom he had done business before. Heirons was not exactly what is meant by a "fence," although he did not mind receiving stolen goods. He had a quite remarkable gift for finding someone who wanted to buy whatever somebody else wanted to sell. He never handled the goods himself; all he did was to find a buyer for any seller, arrange the terms and take his percentage. He would sell anything from a diamond necklace to a live wart hog with measles, but he never handled either the diamonds or the hog. He had helped Alton to dispose of a lot of miscellaneous items which were listed missing from the London Docks. He was a short fat man with a squint and he never uttered one word more than was necessary.

"I've got a little job for you," said Atlon, "though I don't know when it will come off. Perhaps not for weeks."

Heirons looked at him and away again and Alton said that Russia had lost some plans and might be expected to make enquiry for them in London. Could Heirons get to know if and when any such enquiry were made? They—the Russians —would probably start asking questions in the underworld of London and no doubt Heirons could hear of it through his contacts.

Heirons continued to stare fixedly at his inkpot for some moments after Alton had finished speaking and eventually said: "Don't like it."

"Don't like what?"

"Russians."

"Oh, nonsense," said Alton. "Why not? They want to buy, we want to sell. What's the matter? They're men like anybody else, aren't they?"

"No," said Heirons.

"Look here, Ernie," said Alton, and reasoned with him at some length until eventually Heirons nodded his head unwillingly. It was the mention of half a million sterling which did it. Even a small percentage of half a million is what anybody would call money, and Heiron's percentage was not small.

"I want the money in dollars," said Alton, "paid into an

account in my name in a bank in New York. I'm leaving this country. I'm tired of a place where the police——"

"Go away," said Heirons, and Alton went.

It was nearly seven weeks before Alton had any news about Russians and then Heirons sent for him to tell him that there were three citizens of the Soviet Union, living on a small Polish ship lying near Tower Bridge, who were asking about missing plans in a manner so excessively guarded that it was very difficult to know what, if anything, they were talking about. However, if one guessed what they were trying to say, it was possible to perceive that they were trying to say it. If Alton was still interested Heirons would get into contact with them.

"Still interested?" said Alton. "What, in half a million? What d'you take me for?"

"A fool," said Heirons.

"Don't take that tone with me," snapped Alton. "Why d'you say it, anyway?"

"Won't pay."

"Then they won't get them and I'll go to the British Government instead."

Heirons merely looked at him and then, pointedly, at the door. Alton went, fuming, but he could not afford to quarrel with Heirons, there was nobody like him.

On the same afternoon as that on which Edward Logan went to see his solicitor, Alton had an appointment in Heirons' office at half-past three to meet the Russians and discuss terms. He went at a quarter past, he wanted to see Heirons before the Russians arrived, but the "mercantile agent," as he called himself, was out and his clerk did not know when he would come back. "There is plenty of time, Mr. Alton. It is you who are too early."

"I know," said Alton. "I wanted to see him."

He fidgeted about the office for some five minutes and then said that he would go for a stroll and come back later.

Alton had not spent in idleness his seven weeks of waiting for the Russians. Robberies from the London Docks had continued, culminating in a particularly daring raid upon a bonded warehouse stored with whisky for export to happier lands. This time Alton had done what the Wapping police sergeant had foretold: he had slipped up and somebody had been induced to talk about it. On the morning of the meeting at Heirons' office word had gone out that Alton, if seen, was to be reported at once; photographs and a description accompanied the word. When, therefore, a constable on his beat had seen Alton turn into Heirons' office building he hurried to the nearest police telephone box and rang up Scotland Yard who, in their turn, wirelessed the nearest patrol car. By the time the constable had returned to the interesting spot, the patrol car swept up to the door and two plain-clothes men got out.

"Is he still there?"

"So far as I know. He's only just gone in. He went upstairs."

The plain-clothes men nodded and went inside and the constable continued upon his beat. Those two men could deal with Alton.

Heirons' office was upon the second floor; Alton came out and walked down as far as the first floor. Here, upon the narrow landing, he met two men whom he hardly noticed, being lost in thought upon his own affairs. They stood back politely to let him pass, one upon either side of the way; as he came between them each of them shot out a hand and held him by either arm.

"What the devil——"

"You are Stephen Alton," said one of them. "We are taking you to the police station for questioning in connection with a robbery at the Docks."

Alton forced a laugh. "You're all wrong," he said. "I'm not Stephen whatever-you-said, and I don't know anything about the Docks."

"You can tell them all that at the station. We think you can help us."

There was nothing to be done, especially as they continued to hold his arms. They came down the lower flight of stairs abreast like close friends; as soon as Alton came within sight of the hall below he saw three men standing there as though uncertain where to go. He recognized them at once, for he had had them pointed out to him as the Russians he wanted, and he had seen them several times since. In fact, he seemed to keep on seeing them; there was no doubt but that the interest was mutual nor, also, that someone had pointed him out to them, though they had never made the slightest attempt to speak to him.

Alton, still on the stairs, hung back momentarily and it became obvious that he was being officially escorted. The Russians' eyes widened, one said something to the others and the next moment their guns were out and they were firing up the stairs.

The detective on Alton's left coughed suddenly, let go of

his prisoner's arm and pitched headfirst down the stairs; the one on his right clutched at Alton with both hands as though determined not to lose him, and they rolled down the last half-dozen steps together. Before they had come to rest at the bottom pandemonium had broken out in the offices, doors opened on all sides and heads poked out of them or appeared over the banisters above accompanied by feminine screams and masculine curses. The Russians seemed to be a little disconcerted by this violent reaction to what no doubt appeared to them a simple and even laudable action; they drew together and lowered their guns while Alton shook himself free of the clinging detective and scrambled to his feet. From the two office doors nearest the street bold men dashed out to call in the constable who was usually thereabouts; in the outer doorway they collided with the uniformed driver of the police car who was rushing in. Alton seized the moment of confusion to bolt out at the door; as he leapt for it the fusillade broke out again and one bullet which missed the policeman whistled past Alton's ear into the doorpost.

Just across the narrow pavement the police car was standing with the door open; Alton threw himself into the driver's seat and attempted to drive away. The make of car—a Vauxhall—was unfamiliar to him and he was not a motorist of much experience. He started the engine, put the car into the wrong gear and let in the clutch; the engine naturally stopped again. Frantic with haste, he tried again and was more successful this time; the car moved off, gathered speed and was lost to sight round the next corner.

He did not notice a grey car which came out from a cul-de-sac next to Heirons' office and settled down to follow him. He turned and twisted through the streets, keeping in the general direction of West Kensington; when he was within easy walking distance of Betty's flat he abandoned the car and finished his journey on foot.

The grey car pulled up behind the police car. Its passengers appeared to be holding a conference.

4   HALF A MILLION DOLLARS

"I DON'T KNOW how the police knew I was going to Heirons' office this afternoon," said Stephen Alton slowly. "I haven't had time to think it out. Now you mention it, Betty, it is a bit odd. I wonder if——"

Logan, still hidden in the clothes closet, heard the outer door of the flat open; there was a loud exclamation from Alton and a short scream from Betty. Then a new voice with a tone of command: "Put up your hands!"

"Oh dear," said Logan half aloud, "oh dear, I hope this is the police; oh dear, what the hell possessed me to come here——"

"Madam," said the same voice, doubtless addressing Betty, "be so good as to go and sit in that chair against the wall, be quiet and keep still. *Quieta non movere*, if you have had the benefit of a classical education." The voice was smooth, almost pleasant, and with only a hint of a foreign accent under the correct English.

"Not the police," whispered Logan.

"Now, Mr. Stephen Alton, where are those designs which I understand you have for sale?"

"Where you won't find them," said Alton, and Logan noticed with unwilling admiration that his voice had not changed in the least, it was still careless and confident. "So it's no use your looking for them. When you have paid half a million sterling, in dollars, into a New York bank in my name, I will give them to you without any of this silly gun play."

"Half a million pounds is a lot of money," said the Russian.

"They're worth more than that to you."

"Let us not haggle. You will hand over the designs to me now and we will reward you richly."

"What's your offer?"

"You are a young man, Mr. Alton. Shall we say forty or fifty years of life? A rich reward indeed; what money could buy it? A paltry half million?"

"What are you getting at?"

"Your life, Mr. Alton, your life," said the Russian, and his smooth voice became rasping. "Hand over those drawings and you shall live. If not——"

"If I die you'll never see them," said Alton calmly, "for I'm the only person who knows where they are."

"To die is not so simple, nor so quick. I was not thinking of a bullet through the head. You shall pray for a bullet through the head."

Betty cried out suddenly, "Oh, this is dreadful, dreadful," and burst into loud sobbing.

"There, you see," said the Russian, "you upset your wife, your poor wife who loves you. Consider your poor wife."

"—my 'poor wife,'" said Alton.

"I am tired of this," said the Russian suddenly. "Search him, Piotr. If the papers are not on him we will look further. They are not so small, these plans, it is not easy to hide so large a packet."

Alton's expression did not change; one of the Russians held a gun close to his ear while another ran his hands over his body. It was plain at once that Alton was not carrying on his person any packet of anything like the size of Muntz's original parcel, and the search of the flat began. Logan could hear cupboard doors being opened and the contents pulled out, sometimes with the crash of breaking glass and china. Betty began a loud protest but was snarled into silence. Drawers were pulled right out and overturned on the floor, her two padded armchairs were slashed and the carpet dragged up. The sitting room having yielded nothing, two of the Russians came into the bedroom while the third still stood guard over Alton.

When they flung open the door of the clothes closet Logan drew himself up and stepped out: tall, stern and stately with his bowler hat still upon his head because he had forgotten it was there, his neat umbrella hanging by its crook handle upon his arm and his dark grey suède gloves held firmly in his hand. The Russians uttered loud exclamations of surprise and all three turned to watch Alton's face as Logan stalked past them into the sitting room; their eyebrows went up when they saw that his only reaction was definitely amusement. As Logan came through the doorway Betty looked round and saw him, gave a faint shriek and fainted.

Two of the Russians looked on unmoved but the third doubled up with laughter. He clung to the doorpost, indicated Betty, Alton and Logan with a significant triangular gesture and laughed till the tears rolled down his face. Logan reddened to the hair with anger and embarrassment and dropped into the nearest chair; indeed, his knees were giving way.

The Russians finished searching the bedroom and left it in the same state of chaos as the sitting room; the small kitchen and the bathroom did not detain them long.

"They are not here," said the spokesman. "This is your last chance. Where are they?"

"I told you you wouldn't find them," said Alton contemptuously. "Now will you talk sense? Pay up, and you shall have them."

The Russians consulted together in their own language; Logan, irritated and frightened, craved for a smoke. Lying on the table beside him was a cigarette case; actually it was Stephen Alton's and not his own, but Logan was too preoccupied to notice. He took out a cigarette, lit it at Betty's table lighter which he himself had given her, and unconsciously dropped the case into his own pocket. Betty began to regain consciousness, moving her head and moaning quietly, but no one took any notice of her.

One of the Russians indicated Logan and said something, another seized Logan by the arm, jerked him to his feet and ran quick hands over him as they had done with Alton.

"I protest——" began Logan indignantly, but the Russian who had done all the talking interrupted him.

"Our heartfelt apologies," he said blandly. "We do of course realize—we are men of the world—your interest in this household is not so prosaic as——"

"Damn you, sir," roared Logan, losing his temper completely, "keep your filthy insinuations to yourself!"

"Your interest in this household," said the Russian, tapping him on the chest, "had better be romantic. Exclusively romantic, do you understand? You will find it safer. Much safer. It—is—not—at—all—safe to play with us," emphasizing each word with a jab from a hard finger; "as you say in England, 'If you can't be good, be careful!'" He turned sharply upon Alton, and his tone changed. "You will come with us. One unguarded move, the slightest attempt to escape or attract attention, and I will empty this gun into your body. Remember those policemen? Now, out of the door."

Alton went; he had no choice with a gun in his ribs. They went down the stairs to the front door, Logan staggered to the window and saw them all get into the grey saloon car, which was immediately driven away.

Betty Alton came out of her faint and sat up, shivering miserably, with tears running down her face. Logan was touched with pity; if he had had an ugly hour, what must it have been for her?

"It's all right now," he said gently, "they've all gone away now. I'll lock the outer door," and he did so.

"Steve—my brother—they took him away? Oh, what will they do to him?"

"So far as I can see, that rests with him, m'dear. I gather that he has something they want. Very well. He has only to give it to them and all will be well. Besides, it appears that these are the men who shot three policemen earlier this afternoon in broad daylight in a busy office. Their descriptions will have been circulated all over London by now; they cannot long escape arrest if they haven't been stopped already. I think you should ring up the police and tell them that these Russians have just left here——"

"I can't do that."

"Why not?"

"Because—I don't know how much you heard—the police are after Steve too."

Logan shrugged his shoulders. All this was emphatically no business of his and he was quite determined that it should never become his business. Those dreadful men; suppose Alton would not give them whatever it was, suppose they evaded arrest, they might come back and look for him instead—— He would go away, he would go abroad now, at once, tonight, he would go to Laurence in Paris, Laurence was the man to deal with this kind of thing. He liked excitement and doubtful company and battles of wits in several languages. Odd, thought Edward Logan as he usually did when he thought of his brother, odd that identical twins, born within twenty minutes, and with the same upbringing, should be so alike in outward appearance and so totally different in every other respect. He pulled himself together; this was a moment for action, not meditation.

Betty was moving feebly round the r— picking up things from the floor and putting them aimlessly somewhere else. There was one unbroken out of a set of four Crown Derby cups which she cherished; the Russians had merely swept them off the cupboard shelf. She picked up the unbroken one; it slipped from uncertain fingers to the boards and smashed into a dozen pieces. Elizabeth Alton, that calm competent woman, burst into floods of tears, rushed into her bedroom, slammed the door and locked it.

Logan hardly noticed her going; the first thing to do was to ring up Laurence in Paris, and there was no knowing how long the call would take. Better telephone from here at once.

He sat down by the telephone and gave the operator a Paris number. "Will it be long coming through?" The operator said he couldn't promise, the lines were pretty clear this side but there was no telling what they were like once you got abroad. Logan gave him Betty's number and told him to ring back when the connection was made. "In the meantime I've got one or two local calls to make."

Logan rang up his office and told Miss Davie that he had to go to Paris unexpectedly on urgent business and might be away three or four days. He would write to her from Paris. In the meantime she could carry on. Anything requiring his personal attention must stand over till his return. Nancy Davie made all the correct answers until Logan hung up the receiver; if she hummed "Sous les toits de Paris" after that it did not matter since he could not hear her.

Logan rang up his own flat and his manservant answered the call.

"Greene, this is Mr. Logan. I have to go unexpectedly to Paris tonight by the night ferry service to Dunkirk. Will you pack two bags with all I shall need for four or five days and meet me with the luggage at Victoria just after nine o'clock? I shall want my passport too; it is in the second drawer of the mahogany bureau, on the left-hand side. In the same drawer on the right-hand side there is a bank envelope with fifteen one-pound notes in it. Bring me five of them, please, only five. Buy a second-class return to Paris and a sleeping-car reservation. Is that clear? Luggage, passport, five pounds and my ticket and reservation at Victoria just after nine tonight."

He hung up again and looked anxiously at the telephone. If the call were too slow those horrible men might come back, they might be on their way even now, they might arrive at any moment. All this waiting—he was not really nervous, of course not, but waiting for something unpleasant was a thing to unman the brav——

The telephone bell rang; he started violently and snatched up the receiver, relieved beyond measure to hear his brother's voice at the other end.

"That you, Laurence, thank goodness. Listen, I'm coming over tonight by the Dunkirk ferry; will you meet me at the Gare du Nord in the morning?"

Laurence's voice, cool and faintly mocking: "This is very sudden, brother Edward, you generally give me about six weeks' notice of your rare visits. Still, glad to see you; certainly I'll meet the train. Twenty past nine tomorrow morning."

"Oh, Laurence. Would you please book a room for me. Usual hotel, the D'Amboise."

"Certainly. Oh no, by the way, the D'Amboise is closed for redecoration, I passed it yesterday. I'll get you a room at the St. Pétersbourg in the Rue Caumartin. Lots of English go there, you'll like it."

Edward Logan repeated the name and address. "But are you sure they'll have a room? I must leave my address with Greene."

"I'm not sure, of course, but I expect so. I'll ring up and ask them and ring you back; where are you, at your flat?"

"No—no, I'm not. And I can't wait, Laurence. I—I don't want to stay in this place a minute longer than I can help."

"Edward, Edward, what haunt of vice have you strayed into and——"

"I'm not joking and it isn't funny. I am in great danger, my life is threatened. If I can but catch that train I'll tell you all about it—I want your advice."

"You shall have it. As for catching the train, you have— let me see—something over four hours in which to get to Victoria. You ought to manage it quite easily."

"Laurence, I tell you——"

"All right, all right. Sorry I can't help pulling your leg."

"Where can I go to be safe in the meantime? I don't want to go home, they may know where I live."

"Go and have a Turkish bath. No one, so far as I know, has ever been murdered in a Turkish bath. Well, keep your tail up, old horse. See you tomorrow."

There was a click at the far end of the line; Laurence had hung up. Edward put the receiver back on its rest, stood up and looked anxiously about him. Hat, gloves, umbrella. He listened for a moment at Betty's door; there was no sound from within. Perhaps she had gone to sleep. Best thing possible, sleep. Soothing, refreshing, restorative. It would be cruel to disturb her.

Edward Logan tiptoed to the outer door, let himself out quietly and ran down the stairs. A taxi was in the act of decanting a customer at the house next door. Logan hailed it and was driven to a Turkish bath establishment in Westminster, conveniently near Victoria Station.

"Logan's got them," gasped Alton, and fell back in his chair; a thin trickle of blood was running down his left cheek. The three men who were standing over him looked at each other.

"Logan! Who's Logan?"

"The man you saw at the flat."

"You mean your wife's lover?"

"She's not my wife, she's my sister."

"I believe that," said the first Russian, speaking in that language which Alton did not understand. "That is why he looked amused when we found the man in the cupboard." He reverted to English. "This Logan, who is he?"

"A businessman—Londoner."

"His address?"

Alton thought for a moment and gave it, a block of flats near Regent's Park, Caroline Mansions. "I can't remember the number, but you'll find it in the telephone directory."

"His first names?"

"She called him Edward. E. J. Logan, that's it."

The three men consulted together while Alton lay back in his chair with his eyes closed.

"It could be true, Brachko," said one. "The sister's fiancé, he could have been in the business."

"I don't believe it," said Brachko. "They did not know each other, they neither looked at each other nor spoke. I was there all the time, you remember, Yudin, watching them."

"An act," said Yudin. "They put on an act. These English are above all things deceitful."

"We searched him," objected Brachko. "He had not got them on him."

"That is not to say they are not in his possession. He may have had them for weeks. We can ask this man when he gave Logan the designs. He is in a mood to answer and he had better!"

The third man, who had been questioning Alton, objected to this. "I am a doctor, as you know," he said. "I examined him when we brought him here. I advise you for your own sakes to let him rest for at least two hours. His heart is in a really bad state and you have not improved matters. Any sudden shock might be fatal. I am surprised that he survived the excitement of the attack on the police this afternoon."

Yudin looked annoyed. "Can't you give him something to keep him going, Chadai?"

"What, with a heart in that state? You cannot help being ignorant," said the doctor loftily, "but you need not be foolish, Yudin."

"I will just ask him that one question," said Brachko, and turned towards Alton, who started and shrank back.

"I want a cigarette," he said. "Can I have a cigarette?"

"You may," said Dr. Chadai. "Have one of ours." He turned towards a cigarette box on a shelf screwed to the cabin bulkhead, but Alton said he would rather have one of his own. Moving carefully, he slipped his right hand inside his coat as though to take out a cigarette case, but suddenly a look of incredulous horror crossed his face, he flushed scarlet, the colour ebbed away as quickly, and with one gasping breath he fell sideways in his chair.

The doctor, who had been watching him closely, sprang towards him and bent over the chair. He straightened up a moment later and turned to the others, hands in his pockets and cigarette sticking upwards from the corner of his mouth.

"It's to be hoped that you catch your Logan and that he is willing to talk. This one won't talk any more."

"Why not?"

"Because he's dead. He put his hand across his chest like this. I thought he was feeling for cigarettes but he may have been clutching his heart. Anyway, he's died as I warned you he would."

"It is as well we are on a ship on the river," said Yudin. "It is only to wait till it is dark and drop him over the side. Now we had better go and see the dignified Logan. Brachko, go ashore and ring up Cutler, tell him we want the car again at once."

Brachko nodded and went out. When he came back he said that Cutler would come as soon as possible. "He has driven the grey car away somewhere and left it. He says he will borrow another car and come as quickly as he can; he'll get one from a theatre car-park, it won't be missed till the show's over."

"He will probably be able to put it back before the owner misses it," agreed Yudin. "But why has he abandoned the grey car? I know it was stolen, but he said he had altered it so much that no one would recognize it."

"He is not afraid of its being recognized as stolen. He is afraid it will be recognized as the car which was parked near Heirons' office this afternoon and driven away after the shooting. Our chauffeur, my dear Yudin, violently disapproves of shooting policemen. He says policemen are not shot in England because, if they are, the shooter is always hung."

"Rubbish," said Yudin.

"Always, he says. When I told him that it was police who

had been shot I thought he was going to faint. He says if we shoot any more police we can find another driver."

"An English custom, doubtless," said Dr. Chadai drily. "Like not shooting foxes, you know."

"I daresay," said Brachko, "but they don't hang you for shooting foxes, do they?"

5   *TRAIN FERRY*

THE CAR PASSED the entrance to Caroline Mansions and Chadai got out. "I'll go and find out which floor Logan's flat is on and have a general look round. I wonder whether there is a concierge, for example: commissionaires, they call them here, don't they? Turn the car round, Cutler, and if I signal to you come up to the door."

Chadai had been the spokesman at Elizabeth Alton's flat because his English accent was the best in the party; he always took the lead for this reason whenever it was necessary to talk to the English. He walked back unhurriedly towards the entrance of Caroline Mansions, but just before he reached it a stout middle-aged man came out of the doorway carrying two suitcases which he set down upon the edge of the pavement. They were expensive-looking leather suitcases and bore their owner's name neatly stamped upon the lid: E. J. Logan. The time was a quarter to nine and Logan's manservant Greene was carrying out his instructions. Chadai passed the entrance and paused to tie up his shoelace as the commissionaire came out.

"Shall I ring for a taxi?" he asked, but Greene said he need not bother, there would be one along in a minute. "There's plenty of time," he added. "I've only got to buy his ticket; the train don't go for an hour yet."

"Sudden trip this time, isn't it?"

"In business," said Greene a little stiffly, "we never know."

"No, I don't suppose so," said the commissionaire, and went indoors again. Chadai straightened himself and went back to the waiting car.

"He's going off somewhere," he said. "Cutler, when a taxi

picks up that man, follow and don't lose it on any account."

"I'll do me best," said Cutler surlily, "but you don't get me running down no policemen, not just to chase a blinking taxi."

"My good Cutler," said Chadai, "you have policemen on the brain."

"Ah, I 'ave," agreed Cutler, "and for why? 'Cause I'd rather 'ave cops on the brain than a noose round me neck. You're foreigners, you don't understand."

"You will do what you are ordered to do," said Yudin peremptorily.

"I'll do what I see fit to do," said Cutler angrily. "I'm not your slave. An' I tells you point blank, if those cops this afternoon 'ad been dead, you wouldn't 'ave seen me tonight. No, nor ever again."

"Aren't they dead, then?" asked Yudin indifferently.

"No. Two's in 'ospital, t'other weren't much 'urt; it's in the evenin' paper what I——"

"There's a taxi," interrupted Chadai. "Now."

A taxi drew up at Caroline Mansions, received Greene and the luggage, turned in the road and went off; Cutler followed it. There were some anxious moments at traffic lights and road junctions but they managed to keep the taxi in sight until it turned into the station yard at Victoria and the car followed closely. In the yard the three Russians, Yudin, Brachko and Dr. Chadai, got out; almost before they were clear of the car Cutler slammed the door and drove hastily away.

Logan's manservant was within a few yards of them, paying off his taxi. Chadai indicated him with a glance and the Russians strolled past him towards the station entrance. A moment later he overtook them and they fell in behind.

Greene led the way to the Continental booking office and asked for a second-class return to Paris. "Where do I book a sleeper?"

"Along there and round to the right."

Again the Russians followed. "Paris," said Yudin in a low tone. "Have you got your passport on you, Brachko?"

"Of course."

"Good, so have I. We may have to go to Paris."

Brachko nodded. "It will be pleasant, I like Paris."

The place where sleepers are booked is a brightly lighted room with a long counter, in general arrangement exactly like a bar only with clerks instead of bartenders and not a bottle in sight.

"It would be helpful," said the Russian doctor, "if you knew whereabouts in the train he is travelling."

"You are right, Chadai," said Yudin.

Chadai went in through the glass-panelled doors; there was only one clerk on duty at that time and the Russian waited while he gave Greene the sleeping-car reservation for which he asked.

"There you are," said the clerk. "B 14. You'll have a compartment all to yourself tonight, there aren't many people travelling."

"Thank you, that will be very nice," said Greene. He paid for the reservation and walked out; the clerk turned to the Russian. Chadai asked what time the night-ferry train left, and was told it was twenty-two hours, 10 P.M. English time. He thanked the clerk and went outside.

"The train is half empty," said Chadai to Yudin. "He has a compartment to himself, number B 14. That will be a two-berth compartment numbered thirteen and fourteen; if you could get the one next door, eleven and twelve, it would be a help."

Yudin nodded. "It is necessary to get the tickets first."

"Should we not get them now?" asked Brachko.

"Not yet," said Chadai. "We'll make sure first that he is really going."

"But, even if he does go, how do you know that he will have the stuff on him? If I were in his place I would put it in a bank and——"

"I don't know, of course. But banks close at fifteen hours in this country; we know Alton didn't go to a bank between Heirons' office and his sister's place, and it was too late after that."

"They hadn't got it on them at the flat," objected Brachko.

"We didn't search the woman," said Chadai.

"Why didn't we?"

"Because she'd have screamed the place down, and all the windows were open, didn't you notice?"

"Oh well," said Brachko. "But I still don't understand why you expect to find it on him."

"Fool," said Yudin wearily, "he may have it or he may not, but we have got to make sure. Even you must see that. If he hasn't got it we come back to London, that's all."

They were standing back in the angle of a bookstall, holding unlit cigarettes in their fingers for which Chadai had his lighter ready; Logan might pass them at any moment now. "Be very careful," said Chadai, "not to let him see your face. If he recognizes us he'll yell for the police."

The time dragged on to the half-hour when, just as Brachko

was saying that Logan was not coming, he came in haste and passed close by them. Greene saw him coming and raised his hand; Logan hurried to meet him, looking neither to right nor left. They met, Greene signalled a porter to take the luggage and could be seen giving Logan the tickets. It was enough.

"You wait here," said Yudin, "and watch. He will pass that barrier on the left if he's going. I'll go and get the tickets."

Logan had loitered in his Turkish bath until almost the half-hour and then made a rush for the station. Once inside, among throngs of people and under bright lights, he felt more confident; convinced that danger threatened him only in London, his spirits rose as he saw the familiar barricades, the long slippery Customs bench and the end coaches of the Paris train. Once aboard the train he would be quite safe, once in France safer still, and then in Paris Laurence could take over. He took the tickets from Greene and approved the arrangements.

"Thank you, Greene, thank you. I'll let you know when I'm coming back. Three or four days, probably."

"This way, sir," said the porter, taking his suitcases. "Customs first and then Currency Control. This way."

"Good-bye, Greene."

"Good-bye, sir. I hope you have a good crossing."

Logan smiled, nodded and hurried after the porter. He was out of sight before Yudin came back with the tickets.

"Now for the reservations. Brachko, you'd better come in with me. Chadai, you'll wait?"

The doctor nodded and the other two went into the office.

"Two sleeping-car reservations, please, on tonight's train. Is it going to be very full?"

"No, sir, very empty. Would you—are you two gentlemen travelling together?—would you like separate compartments?"

"No, thanks," said Yudin, "I don't think so. We're used to travelling together."

The clerk nodded and began turning over some small sheets clipped together. "B," he murmured, "C."

"Ah, B," said Yudin with a laugh. "Since you say the train is so empty, you have not by chance got B 11 and 12 available?"

The clerk smiled politely; he spent his days listening to travellers' odd fancies. "We have, sir, as it happens. Would you like that one?"

"Please. It is an odd coincidence, but the last twice I went to Paris on this train I had that compartment and I did very well on arrival—my business, you know. It is perhaps lucky."

"Possibly, sir," said the clerk, filling up the flimsy blue tickets. "At least it is not thirteen."

"Ah," said Yudin gravely, "the unlucky number. No, I should not want that."

Brachko uttered a strangled snort, Yudin trod on his foot and apologized. They went outside and found Chadai waiting; Brachko was spluttering with laughter which ran on into one of his long infectious peals as soon as they were beyond the clerk's hearing.

"What's amusing you?" asked the doctor.

"He's—he's got thirteen——" gurgled Brachko.

"Thirteen what?"

"Thirteen dead tomcats," snarled Yudin.

"No, no, Logan's seat num——"

"Fool," said Chadai savagely. "Now, how much English money have you got? You can only take five pounds. Give me the rest. You have plenty of francs."

They did so quickly and hurried off towards the barrier. Chadai turned on his heel and went out of the station.

"I suppose," said Brachko anxiously, "that that is quite safe? Giving Dr. Chadai all that money?"

"Are you suggesting that Dr. Chadai will make off with it?"

"No—oh no, no. What a dreadful thing to suggest. No, I only thought he might get run over and killed, or be arrested These things do happen, Yudin."

"Tickets, please," said the collector at the gate. "To the left, please, for Customs and Currency Control. Tickets, please."

Brachko hung back behind Yudin.

"What's the matter?"

"Only making sure Logan has gone on out of sight."

"Of course, he's out of sight ten minutes ago. Yes, messieurs," to the Customs men—"we have no luggage. We are but going to Paris for tomorrow and back tomorrow night. A hurried trip, as you say, a hurried trip. This business, what it gives us of trouble. Yes, here are our passports."

Yudin produced two perfectly good French passports which resembled their holders sufficiently nearly except that the names upon them were not Yudin and Brachko. "We are French, as you see, messieurs. We are going home."

They were passed on to Currency Control, one man sitting at a folding table; behind him stands a member of the Security Police whose duty it is to look people over and make sure that they are not wanted for home consumption in the maw of Justice. If the Russians had realized that such a man would be standing just there they might have abandoned their journey though actually they had nothing to fear. The police, desiring at Heirons' office descriptions of the gunmen, had been offered word pictures which would have fitted anyone from Boris Karloff to the Hunchback of Notre Dame. In point of fact Dr. Chadai was dignified and composed and Brachko was small, furtive and inconspicuous; only the tall Yudin looked coldly dangerous.

Yudin and Brachko brazened it out since there was no help for it. The Currency Control officer held out his hand for their passports. "You are travelling to France? You know that you are not allowed to take more than five pounds each in British Treasury notes? How much English money have you, please?"

"Five pounds," said Yudin, showing it, "and some odd silver." He took a handful of small change out of his pocket. "Seven and six—oh, less than ten shillings."

"That is quite in order, thank you. Have you any foreign currency?"

Yudin took out a wallet and opened it. "Five—nearly six thousand French francs. That is all, m'sieu."

"Thank you. You know, do you, that you are not allowed to spend your English money abroad? It is for use on British ships only or for travelling expenses and Customs duties on your return."

"I understand," said Yudin, and made way for Brachko, who also satisfied the Control officer. They passed on together and emerged on the platform where the Paris train stood waiting.

"I have only just realized what a frightful risk we are now running," said Brachko. "He is in that train before us, or perhaps he is standing on the platform talking to a friend. He has only to glance round, or look out of his window, or come into the corridor just as we have entered it and we are lost. He will call the police and we shall be arrested——"

"If you're not careful," said Yudin, turning sharply upon him, "you'll find yourself being sent back to Russia, proved incompetent. You know what that means, don't you? What's the matter with you?"

"I don't like this country," said Brachko. "I know the people are all stupid bourgeoisie, but—I shall be all right when we are again in France.'

"You'd better be. As for his seeing us, he won't. He is not on the platform; look, there is carriage B. That tall man, is he there? No. He is in his compartment, unpacking. I shall take one small precaution only." He pulled down his hatbrim, turned up his collar and put on a pair of smoked glasses. "That will do. You can make what arrangements you please."

Brachko decided to have a bad cold. He retired behind a large coloured handkerchief, blowing his nose and coughing hollowly. They walked along the platform and up the steps into the coach marked B, where they were met by the conductor in charge of it. He led them along the corridor to their compartment, showed them in and said he hoped that they would be comfortable. He would take their passports and tickets now, please, as they had to be shown at Dover and Dunkirk. It would save disturbing the gentlemen again that night. He would bring them back again in the morning in good time before reaching Paris.

"Then," said Brachko, "are we not visited for any purpose at all during the night?" They were speaking French, since the train staff on the Dunkirk ferry are all Frenchmen. Brachko was much more fluent in French than in English.

"Not at all; m'sieu can sleep undisturbed all the way to Paris. If you wish me to come you have only to press that bell."

In the compartment next door Logan had unpacked what he wanted for the night and was getting into his pyjamas before the journey started. It is easier to undress before the train starts rocking. Since he was alone in the compartment he had the spare bunk on which to spread out his things; when he emptied the pockets of the suit he was wearing he found the cigarette case he picked up in Betty's flat.

It puzzled him for a moment, he could not imagine from whence it had come; he opened it and saw engraved inside the two words: "From Betty." With that, recollection returned of taking it from the table and smoking one of the cigarettes it contained; a nasty cigarette, he had not enjoyed it, but at the time everything had been so supremely horrible that it had seemed only natural that even cigarettes should have caught the general contagion. He looked at the cigarettes left in it; he himself always smoked a good Virginian if any, he was not a heavy smoker. This case no doubt belonged to Betty's brother; she should have it back when he returned to London. He dropped the cigarette case into his open suitcase.

The train started smoothly and Logan hung up his suit in the blue enamelled wardrobe. All the fittings and cupboards were enamelled blue in the second-class coaches and Logan admired it. He washed his hands in the little handbasin, drew the blind aside for a moment to watch the lights of Bromley sliding past, and then climbed into his bunk, tucked himself in, and settled down with a book. The light was in his eyes but, after a careful study of an embarrassing array of knobs and switches, he managed to turn on the bed light and turn off the others. He would read for a little and then go to sleep, he could always sleep in a train. It would be agreeable to sleep throughout the Channel crossing; he had always crossed by day before, by the Golden Arrow, and never quite enjoyed the Channel.

He was tired, overexcited and fidgety, sleep would not come. He fell asleep just before they reached Dover and was awakened again by the train stopping, being shunted, stopping again. There was a slight sensation of floating; they must be on the ship and he was wide awake. He drew up his blind and looked out; there were men attaching strong chains between the side of the coach and a sort of little platform. Then there were screwing noises and the coach lifted and steadied. Large jacks are placed under the sleeping cars and screwed up to put the springs out of action, otherwise the motion of the sea would be greatly accentuated. "If I hadn't undressed," he thought, "I could go out and see just what they are doing." He yawned suddenly, lost interest, and climbed back into bed.

He was awakened again by the train being shunted once more; he sat up, pulled aside the blind, and looked out. There was no moon but the scene was illuminated by arc lamps high and lonely on tall standards; there were many railway lines and beyond them the sterile unevenness which marks the site of bombed houses. There was a road with men cycling along it to work—what an hour to start, five in the morning—and, somewhere in the background, a ship.

"Dunkirk," he said. "So I slept soundly all the way across. Good."

He went to sleep again at once and had no idea what the time was when he was once more awakened by a steady persistent tapping at his locked door. He sat up dazedly, switched on the light and said irritably: "Well? What is it?"

A deprecating voice outside said that it was desolated to disturb monsieur but they had now cleared Dunkirk and, his passport being no longer required, it was now being returned, please.

"Go away," said Logan, and amended it to "*Allez-en. Je ne le*—I don't want it now. Keep it till we get to Paris. *Retenez-le enfin*——" He forgot the word for "until" and started again. "*Retournez-le à moi au temps que nous venons à Paris.*"

"*Pardon, m'sieu?*"

"*A Paris, seulement.*"

The voice outside said certainly, monsieur, the train only went to Paris and would monsieur have the infinite goodness to unlock his door and receive his passport?

"*Je ne veux que sommelier,*" roared Logan, intending to say that he only wanted to sleep, but the French language is full of pitfalls for the inexperienced and he was further enraged when the voice said that it wasn't the butler, it was the conductor, and m'sieu's passport——

Logan switched out the light, threw himself back in the bed and covered his head with the bedclothes, but the quiet persistent tapping went on. He sprang up in a rage, switched on the light, flung open the door and was beginning: "I shall make a serious complaint——" when it dawned upon him that he was not looking at the homely features of the *chef de train* but the cold eyes and grim mouth of Yudin with the rat-face of Brachko peering round his shoulder. Logan recognized them at once and opened his mouth to yell for help, but Yudin gripped his throat and choked him into silence while Brachko held down the flailing arms. Logan left off struggling; Yudin let the limp body slip to the floor and Brachko shut the door and locked it.

"That's good," he said contentedly. "Now if we go through his things quickly we can be out again before he recovers."

"Recovers?" said Yudin.

6

MONSIEUR LOGAN

YUDIN BEGAN BY TURNING out the contents of one of Logan's suitcases upon the lower bunk, feeling all round the lining and even slitting it carefully in one or two places. "I don't think this lining has been disturbed," he said; "it takes an expert workman to put it in as neatly as this, I am just making sure. We will examine everything and pack it again. Wake up!" he added sharply. "What are you pawing him about for? He won't interfere."

"I was trying to feel his heart," said Brachko.

"You won't unless you cut him open. He's dead, you fool. Come and help me look through these things."

Brachko stood up and began to unfold Logan's things, examine them carefully and fold them up again. "Why are we taking all this trouble? I understood it was a large packet."

"It was, but he may have opened it and hidden each sheet separately." Yudin glanced at his watch. "Well, that one's done and they are not there. I suppose he hasn't got them on him, strapped to his body with sticking plaster? Lend a hand, Brachko. What's the matter? Moonstruck?"

"Are you sure he is really dead?"

"Of course he's dead. Look at him. Feel his pulse if you know how. Do you want Chadai here to give a death certificate? The man hasn't breathed for more than ten minutes." Yudin glanced at his watch again and Brachko noticed it.

"Why do you keep on doing that?"

"Because in about five minutes or a little more this train will slow down to cross the marshalling yards at Hazebrouck. Trains don't run fast over numerous rail crossings and points, you know. Something might happen and railwaymen don't like that. It reflects upon their professional honour, you know. Besides, there's a row about it." Yudin was busily transferring odds and ends from the pockets of the long loose overcoat he wore into the pockets of the suit underneath; he then took off the overcoat. "It's a pity to sacrifice this coat but it's all in a good cause. I can buy another in Paris."

"What are you going to do?"

"Put this coat on him to cover his pyjamas, just in case someone looks into the corridor at the wrong moment. Then, when the train slows down, we walk him along the corridor between us, open the door and push him out."

"But," objected Brachko, "suppose somebody comes along the corridor just then?"

"Then we are all looking out of the window. He will be held up between us and we shall flatten ourselves to let whoever it is go by. But it's not likely."

"And why wait till the train slows down?"

"Help me lift him, he's heavy. I want his arm through this sleeve. We wait, my good Brachko, because it is quite easy to fall out of an open door on a swiftly moving train, especially if you are trying to push someone else out, and I have no ambition—hurry up, she's slowing down—to accompany him on to the metals. You can do as you like. Now the other arm."

"Are you really quite sure," said Brachko earnestly, "that he is dead?"

"Are you really quite idiotic?" asked Yudin. "For the fourth time, yes. Why?"

"He is still warm; he is quite limp too."

"Haven't you ever seen a corpse before?"

"Of course I have," said Brachko indignantly, "hundreds of them; that's why I ask. Haven't you? Corpses are quite cold, cold as stones and stiff; if you lift them they come up all in one piece. Not like this," he said, shaking Logan's arm; "look at his hand. It waggles."

"Now lift him up. Hold him under the arm and lift, that's right. Higher yet, you're letting him droop your side."

"He is too tall for me," complained Brachko.

"Well, do your best; we must go now or we shall be right in the station. Open the door."

Since Logan's compartment was at the end of the coach it was only a couple of yards to the outer door at the end. The conductor was not on his little seat at the end of the corridor—he does not sit there all night—no one came along or even looked out from any compartment. Yudin opened the outer door; there was an awkward shuffle for a moment and then Logan's body pitched forward down the steps and disappeared. Yudin shut the door again just in time as a goods engine, drawing a long string of clanking trucks, hissed past within a yard of them.

"There," said Yudin, pushing Brachko before him, "now are you satisfied he's dead?"

The Paris train, which had slowed to almost walking pace, now began to pick up speed. The two Russians continued their search of Logan's possessions and found nothing to interest them, not even in the suit hanging in the wardrobe, though they examined it with scrupulous care. Nor was there anything hidden in the compartment, though they searched both bunks, all the cupboards and under the carpet. At last even Yudin stopped hunting.

"They are not here," he said, "those designs."

"So he need not have been killed."

"Of course he had to die, why can't you think? He had recognized us, hadn't he? Now we tidy up thoroughly. Fold up that suit. Wait a minute, put these things in the pockets. Keys, handkerchief and so on off that little shelf. They were in those pockets, weren't they? You took them out. Sponge off the washstand——"

"What's the idea?" asked Brachko.

"To give the impression that he finished the journey, of course. They can hunt for him in Paris."

"They will find the body on the line."

"I never met your equal," said Yudin energetically, "for

making difficulties and suggesting obstacles. Of course they'll find the body on the line, but even if it's recognizable, which would surprise me, they won't connect it with a passenger who has apparently disappeared on arrival. At least, not till long after we're back in London. Put both cases on the bottom bunk, that's right. Now let's go and have a couple of hours' sleep, we've earned it."

"What shall we do when we get to Paris?"

"Go and report, of course. Probably they'll send us straight back to London, or we may be here a few days."

"I wouldn't mind if we did," said Brachko. "I don't care so much for London."

At twenty minutes past nine Laurence Logan strode into the Nord station in Paris just in time to see the foremost passengers coming along the platform from the Dunkirk ferry train. He paused, murmured that he supposed he'd better go right along to the train or Edward would be getting fussed, and went to buy himself a platform ticket. He turned away from the platform entrance just as the first passengers came streaming out, among them two Russians who seemed to be in haste. They almost ran out of the station, leapt into a taxi and were whirled away.

Laurence Logan returned to the barrier and had to push his way through the crowd outside it waiting to greet arriving friends; once through the barrier he had to struggle against the passengers themselves. He looked over people's heads, for he was as tall as his brother, but could not see anything of that other tall figure with the face so like his own. He walked along beside the sleeping-car coaches, looking up at the windows as he passed. He was already a little uneasy, since Edward was not a man to conjure up imaginary dangers, he had far too little imagination. Laurence, in spite of his casual manner on the telephone, had been unpleasantly impressed by Edward's words. Why wasn't Edward hopping on the steps of his coach impatiently awaiting him as usual?

He reached the last of the sleeping cars and turned back; at the doorway of the next one he was stopped by a man calling his name.

"M'sieu Logan! M'sieu Logan!"

He turned and ran up the steps into the coach, where the conductor seized upon him. "M'sieu, I have been seeking you in vain, there is your Customs declaration form not completed, I have here your passport, the Customs officers are waiting, did you not know it is strictly forbidden to leave the train until you have passed the Customs, I have been looking for m'sieu this half hour——"

Evidently there was something very wrong here; where was Edward? In the meantime the conductor had obviously taken him for the missing man; there was nothing new in that, they had been mistaken for each other all their lives. Laurence, who was extremely fluent in French, remembered that his brother was not. All the better; if he could pretend not to understand it would give him more time to think.

"I am sorry," he began in slow, awkward French. "I only got out to buy a paper." He indicated the *Daily Telegraph* under his arm which it was his habit to buy every morning. "I was coming back——"

He was hustled into his brother's compartment, all neat and tidy except for the rumpled bedclothes on the upper bunk. Two suitcases on the lower bunk were packed, but had their lids thrown back ready for the Customs examination; Laurence noticed them. "I am sorry," he repeated. "I left the cases open like that for the officers; I thought that would"—he hesitated for a French equivalent for "do" and selected *"faire"*—*"Je crois que ça sera faire*—and if that doesn't convince them," he added to himself, "nothing will."

"But m'sieu is English," said the Customs men, a phrase which excuses any idiocy and produces immediate assistance.

"Yes," said Laurence apologetically and maintained that character by heavily overtipping the conductor, who thanked him in the warmest terms. The three Frenchmen then went into committee to help him fill up his Customs declaration, leaving Laurence nothing to do but sign E. J. Logan along the bottom. He then handed out cigarettes all round and when one of the Customs men remarked that they were French, Laurence said that of course they were, he liked them, and they were in fact one of his motives for leaping out of the train as soon as it stopped.

"M'sieu has been in France before," said the other Customs officer kindly. Laurence said he had, on several occasions, but the last was some years ago. "I am horrified," he added, "to find my French so rusty——"

"It will come back," said the conductor, patting him on the arm, "m'sieu will find that it will all come back when he hears it spoken all around him."

"Do you not wish to go through my luggage?"

The Customs men said that nothing was further from their thoughts and took their leave with great friendliness while the conductor called up a porter. Laurence, left alone for a moment, looked rapidly and efficiently round the compartment. If something unpleasant had happened to Edward there might be bloodstains or some other sign of struggle. He was examining the bedclothes when the conductor came back.

"M'sieu has lost something?"

"No, no. I was only making sure I had not left a handkerchief under the pillow."

"Already m'sieu's French returns," said the conductor approvingly. "He hardly hesitated that time."

"I shall be quite fluent tomorrow," laughed monsieur, and closed the suitcases for the porter to take. Laurence did not, as a rule, wear a hat even in Paris; he picked up Edward's bowler, gloves and umbrella and asked the porter what the taxi situation was like in Paris these days, was there any chance of getting one?

He was driven to the St. Pétersbourg Hotel in the Rue Caumartin, conducted to the office and given a white form to fill up. This was simple, though Laurence hesitated for a moment over: "Reason for the journey: Business—Health—Pleasure (cross out whichever is inapplicable)" and decided upon Business, though Health was, he felt, more strictly accurate. It was natural to copy the particulars required out of Edward's passport, for who remembers the date and number of his own? He signed it Edw. J. Logan, having refreshed his memory of Edward's formal signature in the passport, and handed the white paper to those whose duty it was to copy the particulars (a) on a green form to be sent to the police within twenty-four hours and (b) into the hotel register. It is not known what becomes of the original white paper completed and signed by the traveller.

Logan was then taken upstairs to his room, number twelve on the mezzanine floor; it had the advantage of being at the top of one flight only, so that there was no need at any time to await an absent lift. Number twelve was a pleasant room, though its window looked out into a light well instead of upon the street; just below the window was the skylight of the dining room below, and round the edge of this a narrow path for the use of men cleaning the skylight. Laurence looked thoughtfully at it; it offered a possible escape route in case of emergency and he had no idea at all in what sort of an emergency Edward had become entangled. Selling peppers and spices appeared such a harmless and peaceful trade unless, as a result of the pepper shortage, someone had produced a recipe for synthetic pepper which was worth a fortune to its possessor and Edward had got it. There was a gang of ruffians, mused Laurence, waiting for the luggage to come up; ruffians subsidized by rival pepper firms in the City who were prepared to stop at nothing to wrest the Sneezo formula from poor Edward. Or perhaps Edward had stolen the formula and was fleeing before its justly indignant owner. Or possibly——

There was a tap at the door and Laurence abandoned his thriller plots to receive the luggage. He looked it over; there were the same two cases Edward always used, one slightly larger than the other but otherwise similar, with his name stamped upon the lids. Laurence opened the cases, thinking as he did so of how often he had met Edward upon arrival and come up to some hotel bedroom with him to wait while he tidied himself up after the journey before they went out to have dinner together. Edward used to turn the lids back carefully in order not to damage the hinges, and there on the top of the smaller case would be his sponge bag, shaving kit and hairbrushes, with his pyjamas next below that, all ready for——

They were not there. That is, they were not on the top, ready to be taken out and used first. Laurence stood back and looked at the case. Well, perhaps the faithful Greene had not packed them this time, perhaps he was away or ill and some hireling had taken his place. These things were not on the top of the larger case, either.

Laurence unpacked the smaller case first. Shirts, ties, collars, change of underwear all present and correct. He ran his finger along the side of the lining of the case and almost at once it caught upon something; he bent over and looked closely. The lining had been very carefully slit here and there, no more than was absolutely necessary to ensure that there was nothing hidden behind it. Judging by the space between the slits, the object sought was not so very small, say about the size of a half sheet of note paper.

He turned to the larger case which contained suits; it appeared to be rather tightly packed. A light raincoat on the top, a lounge suit, a dinner-jacket outfit complete, a second lounge suit. As he took this out something rattled in one of the pockets, some small change in English money. Laurence snatched up the coat and felt through all the pockets, laying the contents on the dressing table. Wallet containing five pounds in one-pound notes, two keys on a ring—the keys of the suitcases—a silver pencil, a packet of twenty Churchman's No. 1 with two cigarettes missing, a silver lighter with Edward's initials on it and a used handkerchief.

Laurence dropped the coat on the floor, sat down on a chair and lit a cigarette. It was one of Edward's most fixed habits—he had many—always to take everything out of his pockets when he took off his suit; even when they were little boys together Edward had done this in spite of being laughed at for a sissy. He was just as naturally methodical and tidy as Laurence was the reverse, and he had kept it up. Only the last time they were together when Edward was changing he had done this and Laurence had commented. "Why spoil the shape of your pockets?" said Edward reasonably. "It doesn't take a moment to empty them."

So this was the suit he had been wearing. Laurence sprang up suddenly and hunted through the piles of clothes on the bed. Pyjamas, where were they? There were none. So wherever Edward was and whatever he was doing, he was dressed simply in a pair of pyjamas, probably with brown stripes. Edward liked brown stripes. The dressing gown was there, also bedroom slippers and two pairs of shoes. In pyjamas and with bare feet . . .

There was something loose in the bottom of the second case and Laurence took it out, a silver engine-turned cigarette case without initials but with an inscription on the inside in facsimile of a neat feminine handwriting: "From Betty." The case contained half a dozen Russian cigarettes.

"Who the devil," said Logan aloud, "is Betty? A girl friend, I suppose, but why Russian cigarettes? Edward hated them. Or does this case belong to the fellow who searched the cases? He might have dropped it in when he was repacking—is this lining cut too? Yes."

Another thought occurred to him and he examined the suits. In each case the lining had been slit to uncover the padding in the shoulders.

Laurence abandoned his examination to go and stare unseeingly out of the window. Something had happened, and it had happened on that train. Not even in Paris does one walk out of a main-line terminus at half-past nine in the morning in pyjamas and with bare feet, not without attracting attention. Least of all a man like Edward, who was acutely unhappy if he were wearing the wrong sort of tie.

Would it be any good questioning the conductor of Edward's coach? Of course not; the man had accepted Laurence without hesitation as the Mr. Logan who had travelled that night. Nor had he appeared in the least surprised or embarrassed, as he certainly would have been if he had had a hand in whatever had been done.

As for the man's readiness to mistake him for his brother, there was nothing remarkable in that. They had always been ludicrously alike and still were, except for the odd marks and scars that a man acquires as time goes on and the difference in manner and bearing born of their very different modes of life. No casual acquaintance had ever known them apart.

Poor old Edward, honest, conscientious, kindly, a slave to habit and the world's most crashing bore. They had next to nothing in common, but the deep unreasoning tie of blood remained, even that closer tie which unites twins. Laurence's jaw came forward. Go to the police? No. He would see this through himself.

7

FEET IN THE FENDER

THOMAS ELPHINSTONE HAMBLEDON looked up from his desk as the door opened and Superintendent Bagshott came in.

"Hullo, Bagshott. Come in and sit down. What can we do for you today? A nice line in broken bottles from Glasgow or a fresh issue of subversive activities at Plymouth?"

Bagshott sat down, helped himself to one of Hambledon's cigars and said it was about that fellow Muntz.

"Muntz. Oh yes, the Herr Doctor of Physics Ignatius Muntz, originally of Heidelberg, and his ultra-sonic beam."

"Ultra——"

"Sonic. Beyond the range of audible sound, though the vibrations are such as would produce a sound if there were anyone capable of hearing it, if you see what I mean."

"Don't I remember hearing something about this in Germany,' 'said Bagshott, "towards the end of the war? One of Hitler's secret weapons? I thought it was all just yap."

"Oh no, it wasn't," said Tommy. "I mean, it was quite true that they were trying to produce a beam which, when turned upon people—or, more likely, when they walked into it— would disintegrate them or send them gaga. They got so far as producing the desired—er—influence, but they couldn't control it. Instead of getting a beam localized like a searchlight, the contraption radiated in all directions like a burning haystack, so that all the scientists concerned went gaga and it was understandably difficult to finish the job. I understand that dogs, when they meet an ultra-sonic—er—emanation, leap into the air and rush yelping away; presumably it is hoped that an opposing army will do the same. A scene of wild enchantment, don't you agree?"

"And Muntz is supposed to have found a means of controlling it?"

"That's the idea, though whether he really did is quite another thing. Why, has he turned up at last?"

"No. You remember you traced him as far as a ship from Rotterdam bound for Spain. He was taken off her in the Channel by some people in a cabin cruiser. We've traced the cabin cruiser."

"Receive my full-throated roar of approval and tell me all about it."

"The cabin cruiser," said Bagshott, lighting the cigar, "belonged to a man named Stephen Alton, ex-Navy hostilities-only; he kept her at Wapping. The river, dock and riverside police have had their eye on him for some time in connection with robberies from the dock area but they couldn't pin anything on him. Two days ago they got a line on him for a whisky robbery from a bonded warehouse, so when he was seen entering a block of offices behind City Road a couple of policemen went in to pick him up. They met him on the stairs and were bringing him down when three men who were standing in the entrance hall opened fire on them."

"I saw that in the paper," said Hambledon. "Three policemen, weren't there?"

Bagshott nodded. "The third was the police driver. One of them is still pretty bad but he won't die; the other two will be all right in a matter of days. Alton escaped in the police car and the three men in the hall ran out and disappeared for the time. Now Alton's body has been picked out of the river by the River Police, who recognized it. He had been tortured, Hambledon."

"Died under it?"

"According to the p.m., he died of heart failure; his injuries were not severe enough in themselves to kill him. Well, the Wapping police went to pick up his crew, but they have all scattered except the second engineer, who was living peacefully at home with his mother. He is a new hand and it seems quite likely that he didn't know what Alton was actually doing. He identified Alton without hesitation and was quite willing to talk, especially when he had been shown the —er—evidence. Asked if he knew any possible reason, however vague, why anyone should torture Alton, he told a long and detailed story about taking a chap off a ship in mid-Channel one stormy night. The dates and description match, I've no doubt myself that it was Muntz, but I daresay you'll want to interview this man yourself. Muntz—let's call him that—was carrying a brief case containing papers which he said were worth vast sums to the Russians and when the British Government saw them they would dance ring-o'-roses round Nelson's Column. So said the second engineer."

"Muntz, all right," said Hambledon.

"Very well, then. This fellow says it was one of the roughest nights he was ever out in and the boat was doing everything but turn somersaults. Muntz was overcome by seasickness and went up on deck to get the fresh air and hang over the rail. A little later, when this young chap went up to look for him, he'd disappeared. Fallen overboard, apparently; it seems that it would have been more than possible."

"What became of the brief case and the papers?"

"The second engineer said he wondered that, but Alton was not a man one questioned about what wasn't one's business. He said it was his first trip and the papers were the skipper's responsibility anyway——"

"He's right there, of course. I'll see him sometime," said Hambledon, "when you've done with him."

"There's something else," said Bagshott. "When Alton drove off after the police were shot, the three men who did it also ran out, as I said. We have now found somebody who saw them jump into a grey saloon car, parked round the corner, and drive away. Our informant, a woman, didn't know the make or number of the car but she did know the driver, one Mick Cutler. We know Mr. Cutler; we think he is, or was, the driver for a gang of car thieves. What is more, for a short time before that he had been driving a grey saloon car for private hire. Later in the evening of the day the shooting took place—two days ago; that was Tuesday, then—a grey saloon car was found abandoned on a bombed site in Pimlico, having had the number plates removed and the engine number filed off."

"And where is Cutler?"

"We're looking for him and I imagine we shall find him. He was in Bermondsey early this morning. He lives there."

It was quite true that Mick Cutler lived in Bermondsey; he rented a room in a house belonging to a widow. He was also courting the widow; she was older than he but she owned a house; besides, if one is courting the householder one is not confined to one's bed-sitting-room. One sits in the kitchen with one's feet in the fender, which is so much pleasanter.

He also had a place of business tucked away in the bombed area near Jamaica Road. It consisted of one large corrugated-iron shed on a levelled space behind a row of uninhabitable houses; the way in to the shed was down an alley between two of the houses, an alley so narrow that one would not think a car could pass along it. At the end there was a sharp left-hand turn so acute that even Cutler could not get a car round without backing; after that there came a right-hand turn into the shed doors and here the space was so constricted that the only way to get a car in was to jack up the back wheels and then push it sideways till the jack fell over and the back wheels had been moved a foot or so to the left. In short, it was so nearly impossible to get a car in there at all that the police never bothered to look, which was as well for Cutler, since it was here that stolen cars were resprayed a different colour and fitted with different number plates. There was an air compressor complete with paint sprayer in one corner of the shed, another corner at the far end was partitioned off into a small office with a fixed desk, a chair and a couple of shelves holding some dusty files, a pile of road maps and one each of the A.A. and R.A.C. handbooks.

Cutler spent the morning clearing up after the last job, cleaning out the paint sprayer and tidying up generally. There was no car in at that moment but Cutler had good reason to think that if all went well there would be one tomorrow night. He had told the widow he would be home to dinner at midday; he washed his hands in a pail of paraffin and went out, locking both the office door and the postern in the big outer doors.

He walked home, since it was no great distance, and was just about to turn the last corner into the street where he lived when a small and dirty boy dashed up to him.

"Look out—cops!"

"What?"

"Cops arstin' for you—comin' this way—come in 'ere."

They rushed in at the open door of the house they were passing at the moment and the door was shut and locked. A cautious voice called down the stairs:

"That you, Ernie?"

"Yes, mum, an' I got 'im!"

"Good boy." The woman came down the stairs. "Mrs. Lake's Annie come round sayin' the cops was at your 'ouse arstin' for you, so I guess you'd best stop 'ere for a bit."

He stayed there till well after dark, since the police continued to obstruct the passage of free men by hanging about all day and inconveniently looking round corners. Bulletins from the front were brought in at intervals by the children of the district, artfully careful not to be seen entering the house. Between ten and eleven at night Cutler watched his opportunity and slipped away, leaving a message for the widow that he would sleep elsewhere till things settled down. He went back by devious routes to his workshop; there were some sacks there, he could sleep on the office floor for tonight and go further away tomorrow.

The workshop was all in darkness as expected. He locked the postern door after himself and, by the light of matches, closed the lightproof shutters which he had fitted over the windows. He made his way to the office door, unlocked it and switched on the light——

Chadai was sitting on the chair inside, Chadai as unruffled, composed and well-groomed as ever with his gold-rimmed spectacles upon his face.

Cutler gasped for breath, clutched the doorpost and gasped again.

"You seem surprised," said Chadai calmly. "I have been waiting here for you for"—he glanced at his watch—"nearly three hours."

"Sittin' there in the dark—with your spectacles on——"

"Why not? Do you know the police are after you?"

"Course I do. I been 'iding from 'em all day."

"I have come," said Chadai, "to help you in your predicament. There is a ship coming into the docks tonight; I will tell you where to find her, the *Kalisz*. You will make your way to her tomorrow; you need not fear a search, they will hide you. You will be better out of this country for a time, you agree with me, I am sure."

"Th-thank you for the kind thought——"

"Here is some money." Chaidai stood up, took a thick wad of notes out of an inner pocket and gave them to Cutler. "You see, if you stay here the police will catch you and then you will talk. I cannot have talk, that is why I am giving you money."

Cutler was examining the notes. "What are these, they ain't English."

"They are Polish."

"Besides, I don't want money, thanks a lot all the same. I've got some, see? That's what I come 'ere for, mainly."

Cutler crouched down and levered up one of the floorboards with his knife. Underneath was a tin box almost full of pound and ten-shilling notes held together by rubber bands. "Plenty of money," he said, straightening up with the notes in his hand. "As I say, thanks a lot, but—"

"Those will be of no use to you in Poland," said Chadai patiently.

"I'm not going to Poland. What's the use of me going there; I can't speak their lingo, I don't know their ways and if I put a foot wrong it'll be me for a concentration camp to be starved and worked to death. No, mister, I ain't going."

Chadai sighed, picked up the Polish money and put it in his pocket. "You will not go abroad, you will stay here, then, your mind is made up?"

"That's right, mister. As I say—"

"Stay here, then!" snapped Chadai, and shot him through the head. The Russian looked round to make sure he had left no traces of his presence, stepped over Cutler's body and switched out the light. He had a small electric torch which guided him to the postern door; he unlocked it, locked it again after him, and walked quietly away in the darkness.

Three days after Edward Logan's flight to Paris the police station at West Kensington received a telephone call from a lady who complained that her flat had been broken into during her absence at business and would somebody please do something. The desk sergeant reassured her and the Inspector detailed a young detective sergeant to go round and see what had happened. "Name of Allen," he said, and added the address. "First-floor flat."

When the detective sergeant arrived at the front door and looked at the cards over the different bells he found that the first-floor tenant's name was Alton, not Allen. He paused for a moment, remembering a general order that any stray gleam of light which might fall upon one Stephen Alton, recently deceased, was to be reported at once direct to Superintendent Bagshott at Scotland Yard. This was a Miss Elizabeth Alton, not a common surname. He rang the bell, and Betty Alton, who had been watching him from the window, ran downstairs to let him in.

"Miss Alton? I am Detective Sergeant Waller of the Metropolitan Police. I understand you have had some sort of trouble here?"

"Please come up," said Betty Alton. "I am so glad to see you; this sort of thing is rather frightening when one lives alone. This is my flat, see for yourself."

There was certainly plenty to see, for the flat had been thoroughly and systematically ransacked. When the Russians had searched it at the time they took Stephen Alton, they had merely turned out cupboards and drawers, assuming that Alton had brought the packet with him a quarter of an hour earlier and that therefore it would be only superficially concealed. Betty had tidied up after them, swept up broken glass and china and sewn up slits in the chair covers. This time the search had been much more thorough and damaging. In addition to throwing on the floor everything which cupboards and drawers contained, heavy furniture had been pulled away from the walls, the pictures had been taken down and ejected from their frames and every piece of padding in the flat from Betty's mattress to the stuffed seats on her two dining-table chairs had been slashed open and the insides dragged out. The carpets had been pulled up and thrown in a heap over the table.

"Oh dear, oh dear," said Waller sympathetically, "this is a horrid sight, it is really."

The sympathy was a mistake, for Betty sat down heavily on the nearest chair and burst into tears. Waller left her to it and walked round the flat looking at the devastation; he paused in the kitchen long enough to put the kettle on and came back.

"Could you tell me, madam, whether there is anything missing?" The deliberately official tone had its effect; Betty wiped her eyes and sat up. "If you have any jewellery or other valuables—money——"

"In my bedroom, a few things—I'll go and see."

"I hope you'll forgive me, madam, when I was in the kitchen I took the liberty of putting the kettle on. I thought a nice cup of tea——"

"You are very kind," said Betty.

"You live here alone, you said? Have you any relations anywhere handy?"

"My brother is the only relation I have and he's away at the moment."

"That's a pity. Can you get in touch with him?"

"I—I don't think so, I don't know his address at the moment. You see, he travels a lot and he's just gone away again. I shall hear from him—oh, any time now."

"Well, now, if I might have a few particulars," said Waller, and brought out his notebook. "The usual tiresome formalities, you know."

The usual tiresome formalities include her brother's name and the address of the boardinghouse near Liverpool Street where he lived when he was at home. When these were completed Waller asked if she had touched anything in the room since she came in.

"Oh, I don't know, why? Oh, fingerprints, I suppose. I used the telephone to ring you up."

"Naturally. Of course you did. Still, I don't think we'll use it again just yet. I saw a telephone box just at the corner; I'll go and ring up my superiors from there and perhaps while I'm doing so you'll just make sure if your valuables are safe, and then perhaps that kettle will be boiling, what? I won't be more than a few minutes."

"You are very kind," she said again, and he went out of the flat to report to Bagshott. "Her brother's name is Stephen, the address is the same and she doesn't know where he is at the moment but she evidently has no idea he is dead—if it is the same man," said Waller.

"I'll bring the fingerprint experts along with me and examine the place thoroughly," said Bagshott. "Don't say anything more to the woman; I am coming along myself at once." He put down the receiver and immediately lifted it again to ring up Hambledon. "The late Stephen Alton apparently had a sister whose flat has been ransacked this afternoon."

"Oh, really," said Hambledon. "Looks rather as though he didn't talk in spite of the treatment, doesn't it? Are you going there, wherever it is? West Kensington. Call for me on your way, won't you?"

"Stephen Alton is her brother," said Bagshott when Hambledon got into the car. "The address she gave as his is the place where he lived—I mean where the dead man lived."

"When he was alive, yes."

"And she doesn't know he's dead."

"Oh," said Hambledon. "In that case, if you'll drop me at a tobacconist's near the flat I'll walk on and join you in a few minutes. I want some cigarettes."

"Don't worry, I've got plenty," said Bagshott and added: "Coward," as an afterthought.

"I don't like weeps," explained Hambledon.

"Think of all the weeping you've occasioned and haven't seen," said Bagshott callously, "that'll level things up."

8 *THE MARBLE GENTLEMAN*

WHEN THEY went upstairs to the flat they found Waller standing about near the door and Betty Alton, red-eyed but calm, drinking tea. The finger-print expert and his attendant photographer got to work at once and Bagshott introduced himself.

"I am Superintendent Bagshott and this is Mr. Hambledon. Miss Alton, is there anywhere where we could have a quiet talk for a few minutes?"

"There's the kitchen," she said; "it's very small but it isn't such a mess as this room. There's only one chair in it but there's another in the bathroom and——"

"We'll manage," said Bagshott, shepherding her along, "we'll manage. I'm sure the kitchen will do perfectly. Do you smoke?" he added as they settled round the kitchen table with Hambledon perched on the bathroom stool. "Let me offer you a cigarette, that's right. I've got a lighter. There. Now, Miss Alton, I am very sorry to have to say that I'm afraid we've got some bad news for you. I'm quite sure that you will be brave and help us in every——"

"Stephen?" she whispered.

"He had a cabin cruiser at Wapping——"

"For pity's sake tell me."

"He is dead, Miss Alton. His body was taken out of the river early this morning."

"Then those horrible men killed him. Oh, I knew they would, I warned him, I begged him to go to the police but—— Oh, this is too much! To have my flat wrecked twice inside a week and now you tell me they've killed poor Steve, oh, Steve—Mother, I did my best—Steve——"

Hambledon looked reproachfully at Bagshott and edged his stool as far as possible into the corner. Bagshott waited until the storm of sobbing had slowed down and then spoke in an authoritative voice.

"Miss Alton. I can't tell you how sorry I am to be the bearer of such bad news. But it is quite evident that you know a great deal which would help us in finding the criminals. If you could manage to answer a few questions I should be so very grateful."

Betty Alton looked at him for a moment. "Very well. I'll tell you all I know. There's no point in keeping secrets any longer. Can I have a drink?"

"Anything you like——"

"Just water, thanks, I'm thirsty. Where do you want me to start? When the Russians came in?"

"What Russians?"

"The ones who shot the policemen the other day."

"Is that really the beginning of the story?" asked Bagshott.

Betty Alton took a long drink of water from the glass Hambledon had filled for her, took a clean handkerchief from a pile of ironing on the dresser to dry her eyes, and began.

"I think it all started when he got hold of some drawings belonging to the Russians, somebody had brought them out of Russia. I don't know how Steve got hold of them——"

She had had a sound secretarial training and could give a clear account of events in their order. Bagshott took notes and did not interrupt more than was absolutely necessary; at the mention of "half a million" he raised his eyebrows but made no comment. She went unhesitatingly through everything that Stephen had told her that evening before the Russians entered the flat; it was only when she went on to describe their search of the flat for "a packet, not so small" that the account faltered and Bagshott's long years of experience told him that she was suppressing something.

"You are sure they didn't find anything?"

"Quite sure. That's why they took Steve away. They said they would make him tell them where it was. Besides, if they'd got it they wouldn't have come back today, would they?"

"No. Do you know where it is—the packet, I mean?"

"I haven't the faintest idea. Believe me, if I'd known I would have told them myself."

Bagshott nodded.

"Now, are you quite sure you've told us everything that happened?"

She nodded, but the policeman's sixth sense told him she was lying.

"And there were—how many people in the flat?"

He was on the right track, she didn't like that question. It wasn't a thing she was keeping quiet about, it was a person.

"There was my brother, and me, and the three Russians——"

"Nobody else?"

"Only a friend of mine who had called to see me," she said unwillingly, "but he had nothing whatever to do with it. Even the Russians saw that and they let him alone."

Bagshott tried to conjure up a picture of some man so patently innocent in every respect that even the Russians didn't suspect him, and failed completely.

"What is his name?"

"I don't want to tell you," she said desperately. "He is a City merchant of good standing and greatly respected. I don't want him dragged into this sordid case. Can't we leave him out of it? He has been endlessly kind to me and wants to marry me, but I wouldn't while Steve was—while I'd still got Steve. You never knew what Steve was going to do next; I was ashamed, I never even told him I'd got a brother. You know what Steve was," she ended lamely, "don't you?"

"I think you have had more than your share of trouble, Miss Alton, and believe me, I do sympathize. But don't you see——"

"I did my best to keep Steve straight, but nobody could," she said tearfully. "I promised Mother, but I suppose he was made like that."

"Some of them are," said Bagshott, "some of them are. Born with a kink. I am sure you did all you could."

"Oh, I did! Even when he was a little boy——"

"Yes, I'm sure of it. Reverting to the other gentleman, don't you see that if the Russians don't find what they want they may attack him?"

"They don't know who he is."

"But your brother might have told them after he left here, you know. Your brother knew who he was, of course?"

"He may have guessed——"

"But if they were both here at once, didn't you introduce them to each other?"

"No, I didn't. I didn't have an opportunity, actually. But I'm sure Steve wouldn't tell them, he wouldn't do a thing like that, ever. He wasn't honest, I know, but not like that. Why, when he was at school there was a boy who——"

"Let's get this straight, shall we?" said Bagshott. "When you say you had no chance to introduce them, do you mean the gentleman came in after the Russians were in the room?"

"I think he must have done," she said vaguely. "They were searching the place, one of them was holding Steve up with a gun, I was terrified and upset and suddenly I looked up and there he was, right in front of me. I—it was very silly, but it seemed the last straw after keeping quiet about Steve all this time and there he was right in the middle of the worst of it—I fainted."

"I see. And when you came round?"

"They had all gone. The Russians, I mean, and Steve. I think they'd only just gone; I seem to remember hearing them go, and the door shutting. Edw—the gentleman said it was all right, they'd gone."

"So you don't know what the Russians said to him, really, do you? If you were unconscious from the moment he came in until after they left?"

She stared at him. "Well, no. But I'm sure they didn't suspect him. No one would."

"He must have been a very impressive figure," said Hambledon, speaking for the first time.

"Oh, he is," she said simply. "Besides, you could see they hadn't touched him at all; he was still perfectly tidy as always, not a hair out of place, as they say." She giggled nervously.

"I'm sorry to be so persistent," said Bagshott, "but you must see that he is the only one who can tell us what happened during the time you were unconscious, and something might have been said which would unlock the whole thing if only we knew it. I cannot see what you are afraid of. He knows about your brother now; presumably you told him when you came round? Yes; well, as you say, he knows the worst of it and the most that can possibly happen so far as we are concerned is that he might possibly be called to give very brief evidence about what happened during that five or ten minutes; I don't suppose it was more from what you say. He must give evidence if required; it's his duty as a citizen, you know that. If he's done nothing to be ashamed of, it won't hurt him. If I were in your place I should be much more afraid of what those Russians will do if we can't catch them."

She sat in silence for a moment and then said: "Very well. Mr. Edward Logan. He is a spice importer with an office in Mincing Lane. His private address is Caroline Mansions near Regent's Park; you'll find both in the telephone directory."

"Thank you very much indeed," said Bagshott. "I'm sure you have acted wisely. He went away, did he, soon after the Russians went? Yes, I see. Have you seen him since?"

"No. No, I haven't. He was very kind that evening, but I'm afraid he—he may be disgusted. In any case, I've been busy. I've not been working for some time, owing to ill-health, but I have got a new post now, I started there today."

Bagshott asked for a description of the three Russians. The one who talked English—and very good English with only a slight foreign accent—was a man of about fifty with a smooth, rather plump face, smooth fair hair retiring from his temples and a short fair beard. He was about five feet seven inches in height, solid rather than stout in body and wearing gold-rimmed spectacles. "If he'd been English," said Betty, "I would have said he was a professional man rather than in business, a schoolmaster or a dentist or a bank manager, perhaps. Oh, he quoted Latin, or what I thought was Latin, and said something about a classical education."

Betty Alton was much less definite about the other two. The one who had held up Steve with a gun while the others searched the flat was a weaselly little rat of a man, dark-haired, with dark eyes too near to a long thin nose. Not very tall, no, definitely short. The third man was taller than either, nearly as tall as Mr. Logan, with a horrid face. Pressed to say what she meant by "horrid," Betty said he looked cruel. Not ugly, no, just dangerous. Colourless hair and pale eyes and a wide thin mouth. High cheekbones and his jawbones prominent.

Asked about their dress, Betty said that the spokesman was wearing a very nice lounge suit which fitted him exactly. An English suit, undoubtedly, and not a cheap one, either. The others' clothes were not so good and looked foreign. "Oh, by the way, they called the little one Peter. I don't really remember the other two very clearly, only the one who talked. He was the leader, I expect that's why."

Bagshott asked a few more questions to clear up minor points, told Betty that if—with a glance round the wrecked flat—she changed her address she must notify the police, and went away with Hambledon, leaving the fingerprint expert and the photographer to finish their monotonous task.

"Well, you got quite a lot out of that, didn't you?" said Hambledon. "Where do we go from here?"

"To Logan's flat," said Bagshott, giving the police driver the Caroline Mansions address.

"To see the marble gentleman."

"The marble gentleman?"

"Didn't you get that impression? One whom even the Russians could not suspect suggests to me the statue of Palmerston or Canning or whoever it is in a white marble frock coat on a pedestal in Parliament Square. With ponderous but stupendous dignity he descends from his rostrum and his marble footsteps shake the ground like the statue of the Comandante in *Don Giovanni*, striking sparks from the pavement and awe into the hearts of all beholders, even a trio of Russian thugs who don't even respect the police."

"I should be happier in my mind," said Bagshott, "if I were quite sure they did respect Logan. She doesn't know what happened after she fainted, if she did faint."

"But, you forget, he was quite unruffled afterwards in every way. Even his whiskers were not tousled."

"Whiskers?"

"Sorry, I'm still thinking of Canning, or is it Palmerston? She did say that he hadn't a hair out of place. Have we arrived?"

"This is Caroline Mansions, sir," said the police driver.

Hambledon got out, followed by Bagshott, who asked the commissionaire which flat was Mr. Logan's.

"On the third floor, sir."

"Do you happen to know if he is at home?"

"I understand as Mr. Logan's abroad, sir, in Paris, I believe, but 'is manservant will tell you. Here's the lift, sir, if you'll kindly shut both doors and press the button marked third——"

Hambledon and Bagshott rose like Elijah out of sight, reached the third floor and knocked at Logan's door. No one came to it and they knocked again.

"Must be out," said Bagshott.

"Listen," said Hambledon, who had remarkably quick hearing. Bagshott laid his ear against the panel.

"Sounds like a dog whining," he said, "only there's a bumping noise too."

Hambledon applied his ear also to the door panel. "Sounds like a bee in a bottle to me. Also, such noises do men produce when they have been gagged."

The lift was still waiting behind them; Bagshott dived into it and took it down to ground level. The commissionaire came forward and Bagshott said: "Does Mr. Logan keep a dog?"

"No, sir. No dogs allowed 'ere, sir."

"Oh. Are you sure the manservant is in?"

"Well, fairly sure, sir. He went up, oh, 'bout four o'clock and said as he was going to 'ave a nice quiet evening."

"You have passkeys to all these flats, have you? Well, bring them along and we'll go up."

"I beg your pardon, sir, you are——"

Bagshott showed his card, the commissionaire sprang to

attention and the lift practically simultaneously, and they went up to the third floor again. Logan's door opened without difficulty and the commissionaire threw it wide.

"Good Lord alive and watchin', look at that!"

9 MUCH-PUBLICIZED NUMBER

THE PICTURE presented was very like that which they had looked upon earlier in Betty Logan's flat with one addition. There was a central-heating radiator against the opposite wall and a wooden chair was tethered to this. Upon the chair a figure was sitting; it was impossible to recognize it because it was covered by the hearthrug, which had been thrown right over it so that the only part visible was the lower eighteen inches or so of two naked human legs. These were kicking and winding round each other; from beneath the rug came also the whining noise which had been audible through the door. Bagshott and Hambledon carefully lifted the rug away and disclosed a man, naked as the day he was born, lashed to the chair and having his mouth closed up with adhesive tape.

They cut the cords and released him; he himself pulled the tape away from his mouth and only then did the commissionaire, standing thunderstruck in the doorway, recognize the man.

"Greene!" he cried. "Good lor', man, who done that?"

Greene snatched up his clothes which were lying in a heap on the floor and began in frantic haste to dress himself. Bagshott turned to the commissionaire.

"You know who I am, Superintendent Bagshott of Scotland Yard. Go downstairs now to your usual post in the hall and stay there till I call you up again. In the meantime you will not say one word to anyone of what you have seen here. Understand?"

"Yes, sir," said the commissionaire, saluting, "certainly, sir." He turned smartly about and marched out of the flat, shutting the door behind him.

Bagshott turned to Greene, who had, by then, at least covered his skin, and said: "Are you hurt?"

"Not to say hurt. That is, not in body, sir, if I may so express it, but my mind, sir, is in a turmoil." He indued himself, as the old chroniclers would say, in his trousers and seemed to feel all the better for it.

"Your name is Greene, is that right?"

"Yes, sir."

"And you are Mr. Logan's manservant?"

"That is so, sir." He hopped about, trying to put his socks on, and Bagshott told him to sit down, man, and put them on in comfort.

"Thank you, sir. Very humiliating, all this has been."

"I don't doubt it. Well now, never mind your collar and tie, they'll do presently. I want you to try to give me a clear account of what has happened. In the first place, where is Mr. Logan?"

"In Paris, sir."

Greene picked up his coat, slid one hand into the armhole, snatched the coat off again and looked at the inside. Where the lining covered the shoulder padding it had been cut through and the padding torn about.

"My coat, sir! Look at it!"

"Yes," said Bagshott, "yes. Your visitor was looking for something and did not miss any possible hiding place. Never mind your coat for the moment, we will excuse your shirt sleeves. When did your master go to Paris?"

"Three days ago, sir, in the evening, by the Dunkirk train ferry."

"Do you know his address?"

"The St. Pétersbourg Hotel, Rue Caumartin, sir."

"And he left you to look after the flat? All alone, are you—Mr. Logan lived alone here with you, did he, or are there more than one in the family?"

"Oh no, sir. Mr. Logan was a bachelor and he always left the flat in my care if he went away anywhere."

"I see. Now about what happened this evening."

Greene said that he had been out in the afternoon and had come in just after four o'clock, promising himself a nice quiet evening with the wireless and some writing he had to do. Bagshott surmised football pools but did not say so. At about half-past four there came a ring at the front door of the flat and he went to answer it; there was a gentleman outside who asked if this was Mr. Logan's flat.

"I said it was, sir, and he said: 'Are you Mr. Logan's manservant?' I said I was and he said in a very quiet mournful sort of voice that he was very sorry but he had some bad news for me.

"Well, with that, sir, my thoughts flew to the master and I wondered whether he had met with an accident or even if he was dead; it was the solemn way he spoke, sir. I was struck dumb, like, for the moment, remembering he had gone on a foreign journey, and this gentleman—as he seemed then—being a foreigner, I wondered if he was the French police or some messenger from them."

"How did you know he was a foreigner?"

"By his speech, sir. He spoke very good English but there was that little something these foreigners can't lose; the words are all right but their voices go up and down in the wrong places, if you know what I mean."

Bagshott nodded and the man went on.

"I didn't say a word; I opened the door wide and stood back while he walked in and then shut it. I turned round to him and why I didn't drop dead, sir, I'll never know, for I was looking straight down the barrel of a revolver levelled at me!"

Greene paused for sympathy and Hambledon said that it was difficult to conceive of anything more overwhelmingly disconcerting.

"But there was worse to follow. He said I'd better do what I was told because he'd made dogs' meat of better men than me many a time, and, sirs, I believed him. He made me undress and tied me to that chair and said if I moved he'd blow my head off. Then he started on the room, as you see. He'd been hunting about ten minutes or so, taking no notice of me, when all of a sudden he looks across and says I'm taking too much interest in what doesn't concern me and with that he picks up the rug and throws it right over me. I suppose after a time he'd finished in here and he comes across and drags the rug off. 'I can't have you roaming about,' he says and with that he drags my chair back against the radiator and ties it there, else I could have shuffled along on my feet. 'We won't have no yells either,' he says, and he whips a spool of that sticky tape doctors use out of his pocket, cuts off three short lengths with his pocket nail scissors and puts them down careful on the table, sticky side up, while he puts the scissors and that back in his pocket. I just sat there like a mesmerized rabbit, as they say, sir; it just put me in mind of going to the doctor to have a boil lanced and dressed when I was a lad. Then he says, 'Shut your mouth,' he says, 'you do look a fool with it hanging open,' and he pushed my mouth shut and taped it up, and then put the rug back over me.

"Well, after that I don't know what happened except what I could hear going on, though he didn't make a lot of noise, considering. I don't know how long it was when I heard him walk through this room and the front door open and shut and he was gone. He never said a word in going but just went, and I might have sat there till I starved but for you gentlemen coming and that's all I know."

"Now, will you describe him for me?"

Greene did so and there could be no doubt that this was the same man whom Elizabeth Alton had described as the leader of the party who took away her brother. "A very smooth-looking man, if you get me, not a ruffian at all to look at, with a short fair beard, quite the gentleman. Oh dear, oh dear," said Greene, showing signs of the onset of reaction, "what times we do live in, gentlemen. All my life I've lived quiet and respectable except for the First War and never had so much as burglars in the house and now two shocks in one week. It's enough to make a man give up service and take a——"

"What did you say?" said Bagshott sharply.

"I said, sir, that it's enough to make a respectable man give up service and take——"

"No, no. You said you'd had two shocks this week; what was the earlier one?"

"Why, Mr. Logan going off abroad like that all in a rush with no proper preparation. When Mr. Logan goes abroad, sir, which he does occasionally, not every year but sometimes, we arrange for it weeks beforehand. We book a room at the hotel, we get traveller's cheques and fill up forms for the Treasury, we book a seat in the train and so on all well in advance. Why, I even pack his suitcases the day before so as to be sure nothing is forgotten, all but his shaving kit which goes in on the top. A very methodical gentleman, sir, Mr. Logan."

"And this time?"

"He rang me up just after six, sir; 'Pack two cases, I'm going to Paris tonight.' Sir, believe me, I almost said: 'What on earth's happened?' only I hope I know my place better. Never even come home before he started; I had to meet him at Victoria with the cases and buy his ticket and all before he got there. Didn't leave himself a lot of time, either, only half an hour to pass Customs and catch the train and, believe me, sir, as a rule he gets there that early the Customs aren't open. He seemed all right, though, when I saw him. A bit

excited, like, that was all. But how a gentleman so set in his
ways come to change like that——"

"Some emergency, no doubt. Some business matter," said
Bagshott soothingly, but Greene looked as though sudden
emergencies were unthinkable in connection with Edward
Logan. "I think," said Bagshott, "that we ought to telephone
your master in Paris to tell him what has happened. Do you
know the number?"

"No, sir, he hasn't stayed there before. He only gave me
the address."

"Never mind, I'll find out what it is."

Greene asked if he could begin tidying up.

"Not yet, I'm afraid. I must get my men on to this. Don't
touch anything, just go and sit down. Fingerprints, you know.
They'll be back at the Yard by now," he added to Hambledon
and rang up the much-publicized number to ask Superintendent Sherry and assistants to come along as soon as
possible. He also asked for the St. Pétersbourg's telephone
number in Paris, put a call through and was so fortunate as
to get his connection almost at once; moreover, Mr. Logan was
in the hotel and would be summoned.

Presently a voice at the other end said that Logan was
speaking and who was that, please?

Bagshott announced himself and described what had happened. "Your man Greene let in the visitor because he said
he had brought bad news. Greene was afraid something might
have happened to you."

There was a little gasp at the other end, as though the
speaker were startled or amused. "No, I'm all right," he said
after the most momentary hesitation, "but poor Greene, was
he hurt? Is he all right?"

"Suffering from shock and fright, naturally, but not hurt.
I'm afraid the place is badly wrecked, though," said Bagshott.

"Sounds bad," said the voice from Paris. "Never mind, it
can't be helped. At least we're spared arson and murder. You
have a description of the man responsible, haven't you,
Superintendent?"

Bagshott naturally assumed that Logan wanted to know
whether the despoiled of his home were one of the three men
he had seen at Betty Alton's flat. The Superintendent therefore gave a detailed description of the smooth professional
type who had so alarmed Greene, and added: "There is no
doubt in my mind, sir, that this is one of the three men you
saw at Miss Alton's flat and probably——"

"I beg your pardon," said Laurence Logan, realizing at

once that this was part of the puzzle, "whose flat did you say? I missed it, there is a certain amount of noise this end."

"Sorry, sir," said Bagshott, raising his voice and speaking more slowly, "Miss Alton. Miss Elizabeth Alton, Stephen Alton's sister. She gave me a description of the three Russians who entered her flat last Tuesday and were searching the place when you came in. Can you hear me better now?"

"Yes, thank you," said Laurence slowly. "No wonder Edward fled," he added to himself. "Please go on."

"Greene's account tallies exactly with Miss Alton's description of the man who did all the talking, you remember."

"Poisonous blighter," said Logan. "No doubt it was the same man, to my mind."

"And the same man again ransacked Miss Alton's flat this afternoon."

"What, again?"

"Yes, sir."

Laurence considered that a little interest in Miss Alton's welfare was not only seemly but loudly called for.

"Miss Alton," he said anxiously, "is she all right? This man, he didn't molest her in any way?"

"She was out——"

"Thank goodness!"

"She came home, and finding the place in complete disorder, rang up the police. I went there myself and then came on here—to your flat—to ask you if you could tell me what happened last Tuesday after Miss Alton fainted and before they took her brother away."

Laurence Logan was a quick thinker, but on this occassion he felt his mind extended to full stretch. What was the brother's name? Stephen, yes, and the Russians had taken him away.

"Stephen," he said hurriedly, "have you any news of Stephen?"

Bagshott said that he was sorry to have to tell him that Stephen Alton's body had been taken out of the Thames. He had been tortured.

Logan remembered the cigarette case with "From Betty" inside it.

"Great heavens, how awful. Has Betty—does Betty know?"

"I told her myself that he was dead, no more than that, no gruesome details——"

"Thank you," said Logan in a deeply moved voice, "thank you. I cannot express—— Never mind that. You don't need my thanks."

Superintendent Sherry, with assistants, came to the door of the flat and Hambledon let them in. Bagshott indicated with a gesture the scope for their activities and turned back to the telephone.

"Mr. Logan, I must ask you very seriously. Have you got it?"

Laurence felt that this was really beyond him.

"Got what?"

"What they were looking for."

"Oh, ah, of course. Excuse my stupidity; your news has rather overcome me, you know. No, I haven't got it."

"Have you any idea where it is?"

"Upon my honour," said Logan with perfect truth, "I have not the faintest idea. Why? Am I supposed to have it?"

"Apparently the Russians think you have."

"Oh dear. By the way—apropos of that—do you know what has become of the other two Russians?"

"No, sir. They are, of course, being sought for."

"And I hope you find them. I am a quiet businessman, Superintendent, I have no wish to spend my days dodging assassins."

"Who would?" said Bagshott. "When were you thinking of returning to London?"

"Not for a few days; I have some business appointments here which are keeping me busy. Could I speak to Greene a moment?" He had no hesitation in talking to Greene, since the likeness between the brothers extended to their voices.

"Certainly," said Bagshott. "Greene! Mr. Logan wishes to speak to you. Don't ring off when you've finished; I want to say something else." Logan heard him quite plainly and remarked to himself: "Not if I know it."

"Greene?" he said. "Sorry you've had this nasty experience. A shock for you."

"Oh, sir! It's dreadful here. Everything tore up and thrown about and your Satsuma bowl broken, I don't hardly know where to begin——"

"Don't worry, Greene. Take it easy. Send the furniture to be repaired and get someone in to do what's necessary. What?"

"Your suits, sir, linings all cut open——"

"Send them to the tailor's. Now don't worry over it, it wasn't your fault. Take it easy and carry on till I come back."

"You are very good, sir," began Greene, but was interrupted by a click at the other end. "Hello! Hello! You there, Mr. Logan? We've been cut off," he added to Bagshott.

Logan leaned against the wall of the telephone cabinet and said: "Poor Edward. Poor old Edward. No wonder he bolted—I'd better bolt too, before that fellow rings up again to ask me what happened after the lovely Betty fainted." He came out of the cabinet and walked straight through the hall and out into the street.

Greene put the telephone on its cradle and Bagshott said: "Well, now you know he's all right. That's the main thing, isn't it?"

"Yes," said Greene rather doubtfully, "I suppose so."

"Why? What's the matter?"

"Taking it like that," muttered Greene. " 'Tisn't like him. Anybody'd think all this"—he gestured round the devastated flat—"didn't matter. Mr. Logan, sir, if I may say so with perfect respect for a kind and considerate master, is a fusser. Even little things upset him, especially if they interfere in any way with routine. When the bathroom pipe burst in the night three winters ago and we was woke up in the morning by the commissionaire because the water was running through the ceilings next below and up here it was all over the floors and the carpet soaked, really, sir, you'd think the world had come to an end. The damage—the damp—we'd all get rheumatism——"

"Yes, I see," said Bagshott. "Look, Greene, my men will be here for some little time, I'm afraid. They will tell you when they have finished with any part of the flat and you will be able to follow on behind them clearing up. Come on, Hambledon, we'll have a word with the commissionaire." While they were on the landing waiting for the lift, he added: "What did you think of all that?"

"The important question, as yet unanswered," said Hambledon, "is whether the Russian found what he was looking for."

"And if not, where he will look next."

"Exactly. Would it, do you think, be at Edward Logan in Paris?"

Bagshott looked at his watch. "It is now past ten and the train ferry has left Victoria. I'll have it looked through at Dover for the smooth gentleman——"

"Only to find that he's gone by the seven-something airliner from London Airport."

The lift took them down and Bagshott turned the commissionaire out of his own office to telephone in privacy to Scotland Yard for instructions to be sent to the Security Police at Dover. He was about to hang up when evidently someone at the other end started a topic of their own and Bagshott listened with interest. He hung up the receiver and turned to Hambledon.

"Well, that's that. Mick Cutler, the man who drove the grey saloon, has just been found, shot dead."

"Oh, really," said Hambledon, "how tiresome just when we wanted him to talk. That, of course, is why. It was yesterday morning you started to look for him, wasn't it? When did he die, do they know?"

"About twenty-four hours ago, they think," said Bagshott, and told him where Cutler had been found. "He was lying half in and half out of his little office; there was a hole in the floor where a short length of flooring had been taken up, and in his hand was a packet of Treasury notes totalling two hundred and thirty-seven pounds ten shillings."

"The hole in the floor was his safe, no doubt."

"I expect so. We were right in supposing that he faked up stolen cars, we thought he did. Not that that matters now. Our people are trying to induce his friends to talk; perhaps they will now he's dead, if they know anything to talk about. Now where's the commissionaire?"

The commissionaire was asked whether he had seen anything of Greene's assailant either coming or going. He had not; he explained that he was not continuously at the entrance as his duties took him all over the building wherever his services might be required. He was very sorry.

"Can't be helped," said Bagshott. "I expect he dodged you deliberately."

"Do you know what I think?" said the commissionaire. "I think Greene's lucky to be alive."

"I agree," said Bagshott, and signalled to his car.

"Probably an oversight," said Hambledon. "The rug, you know."

10   METRO TO MONTPARNASSE

IT WILL BE REMEMBERED that on the morning when Edward Logan failed to arrive in Paris his brother Laurence collected his suitcases from the Nord station, took them to the room in the Hotel St. Pétersbourg which had been booked overnight by telephone, and went through them carefully. He sat down, smoked a cigarette right through and then went down to one of the hotel's telephone cabinets to ring up a number in the Montparnasse district.

"Is Monsieur Alphonse Papert in the house, please? Oh, thank you so much. Yes, I will. . . . Hullo, Alphonse, Logan here. I say, I want to talk to you. Could you come to the St. Pétersbourg Hotel in the Rue Caumartin? . . . Well, right away if you're not doing anything. . . . Right. Tell them to show you up to my room. Room twelve. Good."

He occupied the next half hour in putting away the clothes which were strewn all over the room, so that when the porter came up with his visitor the place was commendably tidy. Alphonse Papert was a small man with a round body on short legs, a round face with bright black eyes and a smooth head of shining black hair. Logan asked what he would like to drink and gave the order. Alphonse sat down very upright on a chair with his hands on his knees and looked round the room with his head a little on one side like an intelligent sparrow.

"We have nice quarters here," he remarked. "You have a change from your flat for a few days? Or perhaps you have the painters in? It is bad for the stomach, the smell of paint."

"Something rather serious has happened, Alphonse; I'll tell you about it when the drinks have come and we are alone again. Also, I think I am a fool."

Alphonse nodded, took a cigarette from a blue packet of Gauloises and lit it. "He will not be long, he has the energetic manner. As for your being a fool, it will not be the first time, and generally it turns out very well. For us, if not for other people. I hope it is amusing." He glanced up quickly at Logan and down again. "No. I see by your face it is not amusing, I am sorry. Are we, then, about to make someone else sorry also?"

"That's the general idea," said Logan. The waiter came in with two glasses and a bottle of Beaujolais and went away again. "Now listen."

Laurence told his friend the whole story so far as he knew it, starting with Edward telephoning from London in a state of agitation and ending by displaying the slit linings of suitcases and suits.

"I remember your brother," said Alphonse. "I saw you together once walking in the Rue Royale. If you had been dressed alike it would have been like one man walking with a mirror, a thing to reform Bacchus. It is not to be wondered at if the *chef de train* thought you were he. What do you suspect?"

"Somebody was looking for something which they thought Edward had got," said Laurence slowly. "So much is obvious. Beyond that I haven't the faintest idea what this is all about, I wish I had."

"Your brother—I did not know him—it would not be drugs or stolen jewels——"

Laurence laughed aloud. "My brother was everything which I am not: painfully honest, conventional, quite incapable of anything even faintly near the knuckle. He was a businessman of high reputation and impeccable behaviour. No, it isn't that."

"And what do you think has happened to him?"

"I think that he was killed and thrown out of the train by those who searched his baggage, but that may have been merely to prevent his giving evidence against them."

"There may be a little paragraph in the papers," said Alphonse, sipping his red wine. "A body in pyjamas, you think he was wearing only pyjamas. Tomorrow's papers; it is too soon today. My friend, if his killers were on that train, it follows that they are now in Paris."

"Unless they've gone on somewhere else. Or back to London."

"You are right, we don't know enough about it. Let us arrange the ideas," said Alphonse. "First, either your brother had it, whatever it was——"

"Then I should think they found it; they searched thoroughly enough."

"In which case they have probably gone away happy."

"Yes," said Logan. "Where to?"

Papert lifted his shoulders. "Secondly, your brother did not have it, so they did not find it. What will they do next? Did they, perhaps, know that he was coming to you?"

"I think that's very unlikely. Edward disapproved of me so entirely that he never mentioned my name to anyone, I know that. Only a few very old friends who knew us as boys would know he had a brother at all and they probably think I'm dead. I've been out of England ever since I was seventeen. That's what comes of being the black sheep of the flock."

Alphonse emptied his glass and poured out another. "It must have been something very important for them to commit murder to get it, especially on that train."

"Why on that train?"

"It is of the utmost respectability. It is a famous train, all the great distinguished travellers come by it. It is not a train upon which one murders. I was about to say that if your brother was carrying anything so important as that, surely somebody must know he had it. He got it from somewhere or someone; was he perhaps just conveying it to somebody here?"

"In that case somebody will turn up and ask for it, presumably. Or someone will ring up from London to ask how he got on."

"Then," said Alphonse, "you have only to wait here until the mystery is explained and that will—let us hope—give you a line on who did it."

"I think that's very probable," said Laurence slowly. "On the other hand, if no one knew he had it except his killers, nothing more will happen until Edward himself is sought for. It will then emerge that I have been posing as my brother, signing papers in his name and living here as Edward Logan. A pretty fool I shall look; it's enough to make anyone think I murdered him myself." He paused a moment and went on. "If only I were quite sure they had not found it. No, that won't help. They have searched his things, they will have written him off. They——"

"They may say to themselves that it is not in his baggage so perhaps he sent it to himself here in Paris. Registered air mail. The suitcases, are they labelled to this hotel?"

Laurence got up and looked. "No. No labels."

"I wonder whether they saw you at the Gare du Nord."

"I haven't the faintest idea. Nobody registered excitement upon seeing me, so far as I noticed, but I wasn't looking about much. I was looking for Edward, you know."

"In a crowd, yes," nodded Alphonse. "One looks for one figure and sees no others. But nobody uttered cries or fainted or even ran away? I do not think they could have seen you. One murders a man, it happens sometimes; one kills let us say, for it is not always murder. But one does not expect to meet him next morning taking the air with a flower in his buttonhole and a cigar between his lips. It is not reasonable, it is disconcerting. One would at least poke him to see if he is real."

"Nobody poked me," said Laurence, "or even sprinkled me with holy water, so far as I noticed. Listen, Alphonse. It seems to me an even chance whether or not anyone enquires further about this thing, whatever it is. I must decide now whether to wait here and see what happens or to leave the hotel, drop this pretence and inform the police both here and in London."

"You do not know yet for certain that a crime has been committed," said Alphonse Papert. "Your brother may have gone elsewhere for some purpose."

"In his pyjamas and barefoot?"

"A lady, perhaps, a sudden impulse—no? Well, you knew him."

"One does not leap after even the loveliest lady from an express train," said Laurence gloomily.

"No. You are probably right. Now, my friend, imagine yourself transported five years forward in time and looking back upon this episode. Will you say to yourself: 'I did all I could, I informed the police,' or will you be saying——"

"'I hunted them down and twisted their filthy necks'? That's what you want me to say, isn't it, Alphonse?"

"It is for you to decide," said Papert with the indescribable gesture with which the Frenchman transfers responsibility. "Nevertheless, with due respect to your brother's revered memory, I think the hunt may be amusing. Life has been dull lately, has it not, and we are not getting younger with the passing days, you and I. Alas, we are not. Perhaps, after all, it will be better to leave it alone. The police are paid out of——"

"No, I'm damned if I will," said Logan.

"Will which?"

"Inform the police. Ring up——"

"Aha!" cried Papert. "*Vogue la galère!* We are off again on the old road; we wait, we walk by night, we listen and at last we strike! Let your brother's offended spirit sleep, we two will attend to his affairs. We who——"

"I thought I was quite mad," said Laurence Logan, re-filling both their glasses, "to take his place like that on the instant, on impulse. The thing offered itself and I took it. But there is one thing which is quite certain: if I am mad you are a whole lot madder."

Papert laughed. "It is all there in what you say, 'The thing offered itself and I took it,' that is you, always. When France fell and the dogs of Vichy licked the boots of the Boche, we were with the Legion, you remember, with the Bat' d'Af' at Boghar with a hundred miles of desert and mountain between us and Algiers. Do you remember? We of the Legion were to be handed over to take orders from some bull-necked Boche and fight for Germany. Had we a chance of escape? Had we a plan? Not till that pale fragile general came to review us—he could not look us in the eyes—and you and I and Vladimir were told off to wash his car and fill her up with oil and petrol ready for the morning—aha! They should not have left us the ignition keys and the petrol stores open and the little flag on the bonnet, ah, the little flag on the bonnet!"

"How you do run on," said Logan.

"So we drove through the night, you in your driver's uniform and Vladimir and me in the back in those so-beautiful staff overcoats they left in the car, and the troops presenting arms at the roadside as we went by, three children of the Legion making the promenade—aha!"

"Ah, but it was you who sold the car to an Arab in Algiers to alter into a bus——"

"Well, my friend, the money was useful just then, was it not? How otherwise should we have reached France to become the backbone of the Resistance?"

"The Resistance had as many backbones as a gross of Victorian corsets——"

"So now we are on the offensive again," said Alphonse, relapsing comfortably into his chair. "It is well."

"For me," said Logan, "being on the offensive means sitting tight in this hotel waiting for something to happen."

"Something always happens," encouraged Papert. "Remember the widow at Amiens."

So Laurence Logan settled down in the Hotel St. Pétersbourg to spend three of the most boring days of his life waiting for someone else to make a move. On the second day Papert came to him with a copy of *Le Matin*, pointing out a small paragraph at the bottom of a page. It said that there was something of a mystery about the body of a man found on the lines of the railway marshalling yards at Hazebrouck. It was greatly mutilated, having been run over by several trains, but it had been established that the body was dressed only in pyjamas covered by an overcoat still bearing a label which showed that it had been bought in Paris. The French police were of the opinion that the unfortunate man was a sleepwalker who had strayed on to the lines and been cut down by a train, of which there were many in that busy sector. The most exhaustive enquiries had, however, failed to establish the identity of the victim, nor had anyone in the district been reported missing.

"French overcoat?" said Logan when he read this. "A French overcoat? Surely not. It can't be Edward."

"Why not?" said Alphonse reasonably. "If your brother at

any time bought an overcoat in Paris it would be natural to bring it with him when he came again."

"Edward wouldn't wear clothes made in France or anywhere else abroad. London, to him, was the only place. I could as soon imagine you in a kilt."

"Ah, the national dress of Scotland, I have seen it once. I admired it very much. I think," said Alphonse, glancing down at his substantial legs, "that I myself would look most distinguished in a kilt. But let us be serious. This matter of the body at Hazebrouck, I wonder whether——"

"Whether it is in any way recognizable?"

"I was thinking that. Out of respect for your natural feelings, my old friend, would you like me to go and make enquiry?"

"Not only my personal feelings," said Logan. "I can't leave here at the moment to chase odd corpses all over France. I don't believe it is Edward, but perhaps one ought to make sure. If there was anything in the pockets, for example."

Papert went off to Hazebrouck, leaving Logan to another interminable day of loitering about the hotel; as it happened, the weather was uninterruptedly wet and it was natural to stay indoors. Logan had another motive, which he had not mentioned to Papert, for dealing with this case himself instead of telling the police; it was that his brother, scrupulously honest himself, might have been inveigled into some piece of very crooked dealing without realizing it until he was deeply committed. If it came out now Edward's name might be blackened and the credit of the firm seriously impaired. The fact was that Laurence always regarded Edward as being just a trifle simple, merely because he had not had so wide an experience of the world as his twin brother. Laurence spent quite a lot of time picturing different ways in which his brother might have been entrapped and working out appropriate schemes for dealing with each case.

Papert went to the police at Hazebrouck with the cutting from *Le Matin* in his wallet. He brought it out to show them and said that he was more than grieved to give them any trouble in what was, he was convinced, a quite unnecessary enquiry, but his wife's sister (Papert had no wife) had a husband who had gone to Lille for two days on business and had been away for five. "Messieurs, I ask not only for your indulgence but also for your sympathy. My sister-in-law's husband is, I am convinced, not only well but happy. She, however, is not happy. She and my wife sit side by side in my only sitting room and inflame each other with macabre imaginings. When they saw this paragraph nothing would serve but that I should come and identify the lost one."

The police said that certainly Monsieur Papert's unhappy position was fully realized and as for identifying the corpse there was no difficulty about that. The head, by some chance, had remained practically intact; having been cleanly severed from the trunk, it had rolled between the lines. This way, please.

Papert had seen in his time many such sights as are rightly called unpleasant and he was naturally tough, but he had to control himself severely when a cloth was lifted from a white enamelled tray to disclose a head which was to all appearances that of the friend he had left that morning at the Hotel St. Pétersbourg. He crossed himself and stepped back hastily; if he turned a little green the police quite understood it.

"Thank you, thank you," said Papert, and went outside into the fresh air. "It is not he, the husband of my sister-in-law. I shall be able to reassure her, that is my recompense. But as for myself, it reminds me of some of those great pictures by the masters of classical painting. Salome with the head of John the Baptist? Ugh. I shall do my best to forget it as soon as possible. Thank you again."

The police said that, as for his missing relation, they would be happy to make any necessary enquiry if it was desired. Papert said that he was quite sure that any such enquiry would be not only unnecessary but tactless, and returned to Paris with his news.

"When we were little boys," said Laurence after a short silence, "our nurse used to say that one of us would come to a bad end and it wouldn't be Edward. I've often remembered the remark in various tight corners, but she was wrong after all. Did you see the French overcoat?"

"No. After disclaiming any knowledge——"

"Exactly. You were quite right, but it still seems to me one of the oddest bits of the puzzle. However, at last we know something definite. My brother was killed on the Dunkirk night ferry train and thrown out on the line at Hazebrouck. We make progress."

The following day, the third Laurence had spent in the hotel, dragged even more unbearably than the previous two. Laurence, idling at the hotel bar in the evening, was just saying to himself that one more day would see the end of his patience, when the porter came hastily to find him, a call from London for Monsieur Logan—the second cabinet—thank you.

Logan picked up the receiver and said: "Logan speaking. Who is that, please?"

"Chief Inspector Bagshott of Scotland Yard. I am speaking from your flat in Caroline Mansions, Regent's Park. I'm sorry to have to tell you, Mr. Logan, that your flat has been ransacked and considerable damage done."

Logan's reaction of: "At last, thank goodness!" was so extreme that he all but said it aloud. He listened, enthralled, to Bagshott's account of the search and drank in every hint he could gather from the various references to Betty Alton's flat; to her brother Stephen who had apparently been murdered; and to three Russians, two of whom had disappeared. Bagshott supplied an excellent description of the third. Finally, the guarded allusion to "it." "I must ask you very seriously, have you got it?"

Logan almost danced out of the hotel feeling like a prisoner let out of jail and went by Métro to Montparnasse to find Papert. Alphonse had regular habits, if he were not in one place he would be in another, and Laurence did not mind how long it took him to find Alphonse. The days of stagnation were over, the time for action had begun.

He ran Papert to earth at last at the Rotonde and poured out his story.

"We've got something now," he said. "The London police have missed two of the Russkis, but there's no doubt what they did. They came over on the same train as my brother and killed him soon after leaving Dunkirk, so we're looking for two Russians, Alphonse. Moreover, whatever 'it' is, they didn't find it on Edward, since it was still being hunted for in London today."

"Also," said Papert eagerly, "the two who came here did not go straight back to London, since you say today's jobs were done by one man working alone."

"That's right, but that's not to say they stayed in Paris. I got a good description of the man who stayed in London, but I couldn't ask for a description of the other two because I am supposed to have seen them at Betty's flat. I wonder what she's like."

"I have a thought; it is this. If they see you here in Paris they will recognize you—or think they do—but you don't know them from any other son of Adam."

Laurence looked round the café, crowded, smoke-filled, noisy and cheerful. "Are they here, Alphonse, do you think? Are they here; will they look round in a moment and spring to their feet?"

"I sincerely hope so. Then we shall have them."

"It might perhaps be a good plan to stop being a Parisian and become the English tourist that my brother was. We don't know how much they knew of his habits."

Papert laughed. "I shall enjoy seeing 'Monsieur Laurent' conducted to the Bal Tabarin and the Caveau de la Terreur in a party of English with a guide to protect his morals. 'Not that way, m'sieu! Please keep with the party, m'sieu! Oh, m'sieu, it is strictly unseemly to throw pennies onto the stage!' "

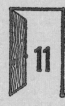

11   PRIVATE ENQUIRY AGENT

THE MAN CALLED VLADIMIR who had been in the French Foreign Legion with Logan and Papert was a Russian by birth. When the Bolshevik revolution began he was an enthusiastic Comrade who saw a chance of making something for himself out of it, as did so many others. This lasted long enough for him to have accumulated quite a nice nest egg when his local Soviet Committee began to think that he was misleading them in financial matters. They were quite right, he was. He left Russia abruptly without notice and came to Paris in 1935.

Here he discovered that if one was a Russian it paid to be a prince; he became one. He told a beautifully detailed story about how his faithful valet had warned him that the Bolsheviki were coming to sack his ancestral palace in such a hurry that he had only time to pour the ancestral jewels into an ironbound chest and bury it under an apple tree in the park. "I love that tree—when we were children we had a swing on one of its branches, I and my sister Natasha. Poor Natasha," said Vladimir, wiping away a tear, or several tears if it had been a wet evening. "I will not speak of Natasha, forgive me. The apple tree——"

The apple tree became the objective of a small private company formed of innocent people who thought that by organizing an expedition to dig round the roots of the apple tree they would make at least a hundred per cent upon their investments and probably more. The money was coming in well when one fatal evening one of the investors brought along another Russian whom he had met. The idea was that the two Russians, fellow victims of the brutal Soviet, should fall on each other's necks and live together happily ever after. The mutual friend began the introductions: "Prince Vladimir, have I your leave to introduce——" but a look of horror spread upon the face of Vladimir and he backed away. The other Russian dragged him back, examined his shrinking form under the light and burst into roars of laughter.

"Prince Vladimir my foot! This is the son of my old uncle Vassily's coachman. My friends, you are being had for mugs; I am sorry, but that is the case. Here, you, fellow——"

But Vladimir tore himself loose, slipped through the crowd and out by a back door into the night, for the other Russian really was a prince and everybody knew it. Vladimir, with generations of slavery behind him, fled terrified from the district, went into hiding for the night and joined the Foreign Legion early next morning. He travelled from Paris to Marseilles with an Englishman, one Laurence Logan, and a Frenchman named Alphonse Papert who said he was a Belgian in order to qualify, for the Foreign Legion does not, if it knows it, include the French. Papert had had a serious disagreement with a friend and had left him for dead in an alley in the Bastille area; he and Vladimir bemoaned their hard luck all the way to Marseilles while the Englishman, who had merely joined because he wanted to, sat and laughed at them.

After escaping from the Legion in 1940 all three crossed to France; Logan and Papert went into Occupied France and joined the Resistance but Vladimir did not. He explained that he was by nature a man of peace and desired no more danger, terror and discomfort, he had had enough of that in the Legion. He lived through the war somehow and after it was all over they met accidentally in Paris, but the relations between them were not what they had been. Those who have served the Resistance hold their heads high, and rightly; Vladimir felt his inferior status and tended to avoid them. Logan almost forgot the man but Papert saw him sometimes and was sorry for him, for Alphonse had a kind heart. "Poor little so-and-so," he said. "If the good God has denied a man the gift of courage it is no reason why he should starve to death on the streets." Alphonse, in one of his wealthier moments, even lent Vladimir two thousand francs—about two pounds.

Vladimir was a good-looking man with the manners of a gentleman, however acquired. He was always well turned out, preferring to go short of food rather than be shabbily dressed. He haunted the cafés where tourists gather, placing his knowledge of Paris at their disposal, having meals at their expense and getting a rake-off from the restaurants, places of amusement, and small shops to which he introduced them. He confided to Alphonse that one day he hoped to meet a rich widow, well, rich enough and preferably American, who would marry him and keep him from want for the rest of his life. "Why not? I will make her a good husband, faithful, devoted. Gratitude will demand it, my honour will ensure it. How wonderful," sighed Vladimir, "to be able to be strictly honest and have no fear of any police. I have always wanted to be honest, always."

Two days after Logan had his telephone conversation with Chief Inspector Bagshott, Vladimir rang up the concierge of the house where Papert lived. He was not in, that was sad. Could a message be given to Monsieur Papert, please, that his old friend Vladimir had something to tell him and would like him to come to the Scott Bar as soon as possible? A thousand thanks.

As luck would have it, Papert came in ten minutes later, received the message, raised his eyebrows and strolled round to the Scott Bar. Vladimir was there talking to the bartender; when Papert came in the Russian seized upon him with joyful cries and dragged him off to a table in a corner.

"Champagne for my friend and me," said Vladimir. "At once, please. My dear Papert, I have had a stroke of luck. Also I have found a new profession—I think. Before we go any further, allow me the personal satisfaction of returning your two thousand francs which you so kindly lent me when I was temporarily embarrassed. None shall say that Vladimir does not pay his debts."

Alphonse, who had never expected to see his money again, though hope, we are told, is a Christian virtue, was naturally pleased to see it again, and said so. "You have, it seems, entered at last upon good days. Here's to their long continuance."

"I thank you. Yesterday my good fortune began to rise. I was in the Dôme having a small glass before lunch when three foreigners came in together. They were not speaking French but I understood their language. There was one with a beard who was the master and two underlings; these two had been entrusted with some mission and had failed in it and the leader was rating them severely. They were, I gathered, to meet someone at the Gare du Nord and they had missed him. 'Now,' said the master, 'I have to bestir myself to redeem your mistakes. I must find a private enquiry agent and put the matter in his hands, but first we will lunch.' They were having the little apéritifs, you understand.

"It was then, my friend, that the great idea came to me. I went across to the waiter, the thin one, and said: 'Look, Xavier, at those three men by the window. They are just going to have lunch. They are foreigners, you would not understand their language, but I do. They have just said that they want to employ a private detective on a small matter. Xavier, I am a private detective. You will ask, by way of being civil, whether you can help them to enjoy Paris. It is more than probable that they may ask you where to find a private enquiry agent, and you will say that I am one. I am going away now for an hour or so,' I said; 'when I come back they will be at the coffee stage and you will indicate me to them.' Xavier is an obliging fellow, he agreed at once."

(In point of fact Vladimir said: "If you pull this off, Xavier, there's five per cent for you of whatever I make."

"Ten," said Xavier.

"Seven and a half."

"Done.")

"So I went away for an hour and a quarter and when I got back it was all arranged. Xavier called to me to come to their table and I found the master very civil. He said he wanted a private enquiry agent and understood that I was one. I said that that was so but that perhaps I was not quite the type he wanted for some simple enquiry since I was at the head of my profession and my charges were, they would understand, commensurate. My experienced staff, I said, were also highly paid."

"You champion humbug," said Alphonse, laughing.

"Let me refill your glass. I knew you would congratulate me. This man said that money was no object provided results could be obtained by someone who could be relied upon to hold his tongue. I said that if I chose to speak of what I knew, some in high places would be begging in the gutter. Secrets, I said, these hands are full of secrets. So he said I was to go to the Gare du Nord, get on the track of a traveller who arrived on a certain train and find out where in Paris he is staying. I said: 'Messieurs, you will be lunching here tomorrow? After lunch tomorrow, then, I shall have the honour of presenting you with the information you require.' I bowed and went out. Oh, I forgot to say, I gave them a card, a nice card; engraved, not merely printed. It had a name on it and the words 'private enquiry agent' at the bottom."

"Where did you get that from?" asked Papert, beginning to be a little bored.

"Oh, I had it by me," said Vladimir offhandedly. It had, actually, been presented to him on an occasion he preferred not to remember by the owner who had unkindly squashed flat one of Vladimir's most promising schemes. "I went outside and walked away, thinking. How do I know how these men work? I went to the Gare du Nord and asked the porters about this traveller, giving the description my employer had given me. The porters knew nothing, so I went down the rank of taxi drivers asking them whether they had driven such a man on such a day. None of them knew anything."

"Tiresome," said Papert, stifling a yawn.

"I tried the café opposite which these taxi drivers frequent. My enquiries cost me much money for *blanc sec* but still no one could tell me——"

Papert's attention wandered while Vladimir talked on and on. "An old taxi driver who came on duty later—he drank only *fine* but he had driven my traveller—I got the record typed out together with my account—my friend, I thought my employer was about to embrace me. 'Not only the hotel but even the room number,' he said; 'it is well seen that you are at the top of your profession.' I asked ten thousand francs; I was a fool, he would have paid double and all for an address. I shall take this up as a profession, this is the garden where the money grows."

"Splendid," said Papert. "Magnificent." He yawned again.

"As soon as I got the money my first thought was that now at last I can repay my old friend what I owe him, and with that I remembered why the name sounded familiar."

"Whose name?"

"The traveller's, whom I was paid to trace."

"Oh yes. And why was it familiar?"

"Because it was the same name as our mutual friend of old days. Logan."

"*What?*"

"Logan. That was the name. An English traveller. No doubt there are many of that name in England."

"And the hotel?"

"The St. Pétersbourg, room twelve."

Papert sprang to his feet muttering something Vladimir did not catch, and then: "Your employers, what nationality were they?"

"Russians. That is why I understood their speech, though naturally I did not tell them I was a Russian. I never wish to——"

Papert sat down again oppoiste Vladimir, took firm hold of both his wrists across the small table and said urgently: "Now listen, this is important. These Russians were talking together in their own tongue when they first came into the café. You heard and understood what they said?"

"Every word, my dear Papert. But——"

"No buts. Throw your mind back to when they first came in and try to tell me every single word they said. I remember of old, you have a wonderful memory when you like. Now, then. They are coming in at the door——"

"There are three of them," said Valdimir. "The one who talked to me, the professional type wearing English clothes, I will call him the master. Then a big man and a small one——"

"Describe them all," said Papert softly.

Vladimir gave a description of "the master" which tallied in all respects with the description Bagshott had telephoned to Laurence Logan, and Papert nodded. "Now the tall one."

"A dangerous man, he has the cold eyes of the killer and a wide thin mouth, cheekbones like a Slav and his jawbones showed, pale hair and light blue eyes. He had bought his clothes in France, I think, or possibly Belgium. The third man was a little creature like a rat, dark hair and eyes and a long pointed nose, shabbily dressed. He moves his shoulders when he walks as though he were all the time passing through gaps not quite wide enough to admit him."

"Good," said Papert, "good. Now for what they said."

"They came in in silence and sat at a small table in the window; the master ordered drinks, using excellent French. The other two just sat looking down, not speaking. After the drinks were brought the master broke out again, for you could tell that this was a conversation renewed. He said: 'Do you now begin to understand what you have done, muttonheads——' A lot of rude names, Papert——"

"Omit them."

" 'He fooled you completely, mugs that you are. He had no weapon, you took him by surprise, he did the only possible thing. He is clever and quick-witted, that one. He shammed dead, hoping you would go away and leave him. You carried him to the carriage door and pushed him out, he let himself roll down the steps, picked himself up again and—you said the train stopped, or almost stopped, dead slow then—he let one or two coaches go by and then swung himself up the steps near the end of the train. He—he——' I forget what came next. One moment," said Vladimir, releasing his hands from Papert's to cover his eyes. "I have it. 'He waited long enough for you to go back to your compartment; he probably went to a lavatory and washed his dirty hands. Then he walked along the corridors through the coaches, passing your door, you—you——' More bad names——"

"Omit them again."

" '—and went back to bed, locking his door that time. In the morning he got up and dressed like any other passenger, and if you hadn't bolted away from the train the moment it stopped you would have seen him.' Then the big one said: 'No. I tell you he was dead. I handled him, I know. I put my own coat on him to make him less conspicuous——' "

"Ah," said Papert, "the French overcoat."

"What French overcoat?"

"Never mind, go on. The tall one said Logan was dead."

"But the little one said: 'No. I said he was not dead. I said so, Yudin, at the time.' The tall one—he would be Yudin, yes—he said: 'This fool thinks that when people die they go cold and stiff all at once, phut! like that.' The master said: 'For the first time, I agree with Piotr.' So the little one is called Piotr, it comes back to me as I talk. The master said: 'I knew you were no good but, by God, you are worse than I thought. When I went to the Gare du Nord this morning to get his luggage I thought no more than that you had failed to find the drawings and, after all, some men can hide things so that the devil himself wouldn't find them. But I saw his signature on the baggage declaration and the Customs man recollected the traveller easily, yes, and agreed with my description of him—so now he is loose in Paris and has been so for three days, and where are the designs now? Moreover, when he sees you he will call the police because you committed an assault upon him in France. Oh, if I had a couple of deaf-mutes from a home for the mentally deficient to take your place, I would show you what it means to be assaulted until there is not enough left of you for anyone to put the pieces together and say that this was a man.' Then they all sat there saying nothing until the master said they would have lunch and then he would engage an enquiry agent, and you know the rest."

"Vladimir. When did you give this man your report?"

"This afternoon. Two—no, three hours ago. Tell me, Papert, have I——"

"I must go," said Papert, getting up hastily. "I have an important appointment. Thank you for your champagne. Till we meet again."

"Papert, stop, tell me, was it then——"

But Papert tore himself free, rushed out of the café, stopped a passing taxi and, leaping into it, was borne from sight.

12 PRAYERS FOR THE SERGEANT MAJOR

PAPERT'S TAXI, driven as taxis are driven only in Paris, pulled up at the door of the St. Péters-bourg, and Alphonse, telling the man to wait, rushed into the hotel. Logan was in his room; Papert took the stairs two at a time and knocked at the door.

"Come in!"

"He does not even lock his door," said Papert, bolting into the room, turning the key and setting a chair under the door handle. "Are we, then, still in the Legion and compassed about with trigger-happy sentries?"

Logan, with half his face covered with lather, turned with his razor in his hand. "In the name of heaven, what bug has bitten you?"

"Pack your things and leave here instantly," said Papert, putting the suitcases on the bed and flinging the lids open; "those three Russians know where you are and have known for the past three hours. I have a taxi waiting."

"It can wait until I have finished shaving. Besides, now I come to think of it, I don't know that I want to leave this hotel. I am very comfortable here."

Papert abandoned the shirt he was folding to shake both fists in the air.

"Doubtless the good God had something in His mind when He made the English as they are, but——"

"Let there be no flap," said Logan. "Three Russians, so the third has arrived. Interesting, very. Where are they, have you seen them?"

Papert gave him a brief outline of what Vladimir had told him.

"I see," said Logan, lifting a dripping face from his hand-basin. "They think I'm still alive and will hand them over to the police on sight. It's a pity I wouldn't know them from Shadrach, Meshach and Abednego if I met them face to face."

"You need not leave this hotel for good," argued Papert, resuming the packing. "It is only to go away for a day or two, then after they have asked here for you and been told you have left, you can return."

"Umf," said Logan from the folds of a towel. "Perhaps you are right." He dropped the towel on the floor and packed the other case; in five minutes they were strapped and ready. Logan finished dressing and looked round the room for strays. "We don't seem to have left anything. Let's go.

They ran down the stairs and Papert took the luggage out to the waiting taxi while Logan dashed into the office. "My bill, please. I have been unexpectedly called away, urgent business; I'll let you know my address later in case there are any letters for me——"

"As for not knowing them," said Papert as they drove away with Logan sitting well back in the taxi, "I have good descriptions of them." He gave them.

"One unhurried glance is worth six pages of descriptions," said Laurence sententiously. "By the way, where are we going?"

"I told the driver the Ambassador. If they are full we will go on somewhere else."

"I wonder where Yudin—you said Yudin?—and supporting company are staying. If we picked on their hotel I suppose it would be their turn to pack up and leave, eh? I should laugh for a week."

Papert looked at his friend.

"I know what you're thinking," went on Logan, "only you're too polite to say: 'O afflicted of Allah!' Vladimir, now, how far do you think we can trust Vladimir? Does he know it's me they're after?"

"I didn't actually say so, but I think it must have been pretty obvious," said Papert, and gave a detailed account of the conversation.

"They know me; I don't know them, though they think I I do; but Vladimir knows both sides. Quite a strong position for a man who's chronically hard up and likes his comforts."

But Papert would not have this.

"It is a temptation, as you say, and had it been anyone but you or I, I would not say no; but betray an old fellow sufferer of the Legion? Never. He would not do it. Vladimir is not too honest, it is true, but he has a good heart."

"I sincerely hope so. Besides, we can always avoid him."

"Besides also," added Papert, "he knows that if he did that I should cut his throat. Here we are at the hotel. Now, if those three *Russes* are here——"

"I'll say: 'Tickets, please,' and they will all fall down dead."

But they were not there, and Laurence Logan engaged a room without difficulty. Later that evening he said to Papert that he wanted to return to the St. Pétersbourg for a few minutes. "Only to pick up any letters there may be and to ask them to take telephone messages. You hustled me so that I forgot about telephones."

"Ring them up," said Alphonse.

"And if there are any letters, am I to give this address? Then, when the Russians go there, they will be told that m'sieu has removed himself to the Ambassador. I might as well have stayed where I was."

"Let me go for the letters. Give me a note of authorization——"

"Ten thousand devils, no. What, am I to be terrorized off the streets of Paris? You will be suggesting next that I should assault the police in order to get myself locked up."

"We might do just that if necessary," said Alphonse. "You would at least be safe in jail."

Laurence snorted, got to his feet and said he was going then and there. "Why, dammit, it's quite early yet, only half-past ten."

Alphonse sighed and got up. "At least allow me to walk ahead of you along the street, and may I beg that if you go in at the front door you will at least come out at the back?"

"Alphonse," said Logan solemnly, "you are making me nervous."

"I wish I could," said Papert, but he said it to himself.

Alphonse wandered leisurely along the Rue Caumartin, looking in the shopwindows and glancing into the cafés. Logan came along behind until, just before they reached the door of the St. Pétersbourg Hotel, he overtook Papert, passed him with no sign of recognition in case they were watched by unfriendly eyes, and turned into the hotel. There were no letters for him; he asked that any telephone message should be carefully noted, especially if it came from London, and thereafter tipped the porter to show him out by the back door. He joined Alphonse by previous arrangement at a café at the end of the street which had tables set out upon the pavement. Here the two men retired behind a potted palm and ordered drinks, since it was evident that Alphonse had something to say.

"They are sitting at a table in the Athénée," he said. "I think it must be they. I saw them there; one could not pick out one man by a description from among all the crowds of Paris unless one were a *flic*, but three men together, it is different. I went in and had a *blanc sec;* as I passed them, they were watching the door of the hotel and talking to each other; I don't know the language but it was not French."

"If only I'd had the sense to provide myself with a nice bushy false beard, I could go and sit beside them and they wouldn't know me," said Logan plaintively. "At least, that sort of thing always works in books. Where are you going?"

"For a little walk along the street; stay there, I will come back."

Alphonse went off towards the hotel, Logan ordered himself another *brun* and waited. In ten minutes Alphonse came back.

"The one with the beard whom Vladimir called the master has gone into the hotel, the other two are still at the Athénée, waiting."

Papert was quite right in his identification; it was Dr. Chadai who sat with Yudin and Brachko in the Athénée, which is directly opposite the hotel, and watched Logan come up the street and turn into the St. Pétersbourg.

"What did I tell you?" said Chadai. "There he goes. Does he look dead? Is he transparent? Does he float along instead of walking? He is as alive as you are, much more so in every respect that matters. You strangled him, Yudin, didn't you? He has not even got a stiff neck."

Yudin said in awed tones that it was not natural, it was magic. The man was not mortal.

Brachko said that of course the man wasn't dead, he had said so all along.

"We will give him time to get up to his room and into bed and then I will go up and see if he is mortal," said Chadai. "He has not gone into the bar, you can see that from this window."

They waited half an hour.

"Stay here," said Chadai. "I will go now."

He got up and strolled along the pavement opposite the St. Pétersbourg; the porter's desk is in full view from the outside and he was in his place. Chadai crossed the road and strolled back. The porter rummaged under his desk, took something out, got up and went away out of sight somewhere at the back of the hall. Chadai immediately turned in through the open door and walked unhurriedly across the hall, look-

ing for the stairs; they were round to the left and there was
nobody in sight except the lift attendant waiting for custom.
Chadai glanced towards him, said "Good night" in his pleasant voice, and ran lightly up the stairs.

Facing the head of the stairs there was a bathroom and a
passage running off to the left; Chadai went along the passage
and saw that the room numbers were low, so number twelve
would be on this floor. There was nobody about; it was, after
all, nearly midnight. Chadai stopped outside room twelve;
there was no sound from within nor any light visible under
the door. He took a small bottle from one pocket, a pad of
cotton wool from another and poured the contents of the bottle upon the pad. He opened the door very silently and crept
in.

The room was not completely dark, for just below the window was the skylight covering the dining room, where the
lights were still on. Chadai closed the door behind him and
stood for a moment to get his bearings and accustom his eyes
to the dimness. There was the bed, along the wall on the left,
and there was a sleeper in the bed, for he could see a long
mound under the bedclothes and a handful of dark hair on
the pillow. Chadai moved his chloroformed pad to his right
hand and took two silent steps forward.

The figure in the bed moved suddenly, something which
felt like a wooden hook caught Chadai round the back of his
neck, jerking his head forward to receive a most resounding
slap in the face. He dropped the pad to try to free himself——

"That'll teach you," said a furious voice in English, and a
woman's voice at that, "leaving me here all alone hours an'
hours while you go racketing round—where's this damned
switch—spending our money——"

The light went on suddenly and revealed the combatants
to each other, and the lady uttered a piercing scream. She
was a stout middle-aged woman with a red face, and the thing
round Chadai's neck was the crook of a thoroughly sensible
English umbrella of which she was holding the other end.
He freed himself but did not back away quickly enough, for
she struck at him with the umbrella, knocked off his glasses
and caught him on the nose, which began to bleed copiously.

"Get out, you horrible brute, get out, how dare you——"

Chadai asked nothing better than to get out. He snatched
up his spectacles but unfortunately reached the door just as
someone else was trying to come in, and the advantage, as
always with a door which opens inwards, was with the in-

comer. Chadai was pushed violently back as a large red-faced man came in, shut the door and put his back against it.

"What the —— —— ——'s this? Lily, who's this man you've got——"

"I haven't got him! Horrible beast coming in 'ere and I thought it was you——"

"I'll bet you thought it was me——"

"It's your fault, leaving me 'ere all alone. 'Alf an hour you said you'd be and that's four hours back, an' now you're sozzled——"

"Fine thing if a man can't go out with a pal without 'is wife 'avin' men in 'er room——"

"How dare you!" she shrieked and sprang out of bed; the man, who had certainly had enough to drink, staggered away from the door; Chadai saw his chance and leapt for it. He was out of the door and running down the passage before they realized he had gone, and the sounds of conflict followed him, since the bedroom door was wide open. Chadai heard voices below and the sound of steps running up the stairs, no doubt the night porter and the lift attendant coming to hush the riot. Chadai dived into the bathroom at the top of the stairs and locked himself in.

"Behaviour of the most outrageous," said the lift attendant's voice, passing the bathroom door.

"Tomorrow morning they leave," said a second voice ominously, and went on down the passage.

Chadai opened the door cautiously and peered out; there was no one in the passage, because both men had entered the bedroom, but there were sounds of stirring from the other rooms and one door was being unlocked. The uproar from the bedroom, which had ceased for a moment, broke out again and somebody apparently threw something which smashed.

Chadai, holding a handkerchief to his aching nose, ran rapidly down the stairs and out into the street.

Logan, still in his corner behind the potted palm, signalled a waiter and ordered a drink for Alphonse.

"Let's stay here for a little while," he said. "They may come this way and then you can point them out to me. Pass me that paper on the chair there, will you, I can take cover behind it if they come. Thanks. But what that fellow you call 'the master' thinks he can do in a perfectly respectable hotel I can't imagine."

"He knows your room number," said Papert.

"Not my room any longer," said Logan, "it's been let again;

the porter told me so when I went in—he thought I'd changed my mind and wanted it back. A large couple from London, he said. I gathered that he didn't think they quite came up to the St. Pétersbourg standard—— What is it?"

"Here they come," said Alphonse, and Logan snatched up the paper to peep round it at the passers-by. The three Russians came along the pavement within a yard of the potted palm; the tall Yudin on one side, the furtive Brachko on the other and between them the neat figure of Chadai, not so dignified as usual and holding his nose with a stained handkerchief. They were talking earnestly together and not looking about them; Logan had a good view of them.

"Something's happened," he said gleefully; "somebody's clouted him, his nose is bleeding. And they are talking Russian, Alphonse, you're quite right. Not that I know any, but their noises are just like those Vladimir used to make in the Legion when he used to pray for the sergeant major."

Tommy Hambledon went to Paris to look for the missing papers, whatever they were, which the unfortunate Muntz had brought out of Russia only to be parted from them in the cold North Sea, on the threshold of safety. Tommy's only clue was Logan, the slightly stuffy habit-ridden businessman who had left so abruptly for Paris after encountering three Russians in a lady's flat. These Russians had almost certainly committed two murders in London; if the English police could catch them and prove their guilt there would be no need to bother about them any more forever, but Hambledon was not really interested in the Russians or their murders. That was Bagshott's job and he would perform it with his customary efficiency and despatch if he could once get a lead. Tommy's job was simply to find the missing papers and deliver them to the British Government. Logan's Paris address was the Hotel St. Pétersbourg. Very well. He would go to the St. Pétersbourg.

He did, only to be told that Monsieur Logan had left the previous day. No, the management regretted, they had no idea where he had gone. He had said that he would give them a forwarding address for letters as soon as possible; as soon as that came they would be most happy, et cetera, et cetera. Perhaps Monsieur Logan, if still in Paris, would come in for his letters himself. Tommy, who had had the privilege of examining an excellent studio portrait of Edward Logan in a narrow gilt frame in Betty Alton's flat, knew what to look for and was pretty sure he would know it when he saw it. He stayed at the St. Pétersbourg for three days and saw nothing resembling Edward Logan, height six foot two inches, thick dark brown hair, and so on. Men of over six foot are not so common.

Alphonse Papert came up to Logan's room at the Ambassador and found him irritable and fidgety.

"This is all very well," he said. "We gave those Russians the slip very nicely at the Pétersbourg and one of them met with a thump on the nose which is right and proper, but it isn't getting us anywhere, is it? I want to knock them down and run over them with a steam roller, not dodge them. If only we knew where they're staying——"

Papert sat down on the edge of a chair in his favourite attitude, very upright with his hands on his knees and his head a little on one side. "See how long it lasts," he said, "this Legion training. Seek out the enemy *au pas gymnastique*, attack, attack, *mes enfants. L'audace, toujours l'audace.* Forward to glory, scum of the gutters!"

Logan laughed and then said that he was serious.

"I know," said Papert. "I have been giving it my intense consideration. It is first of all necessary to get in touch with them, and I strongly suggest that we enlist Vladimir on our side."

"What, that overdressed little squirt?"

"Listen," said Papert. "I tell you to your face, you are unfair. Because he did not join in the Resistance, you wipe him off like a smear on a plate. I tell you, that sort of thing was not his *métier* and he was right to keep out of it. There is a gift for that sort of thing and there is an absence of gift. Can you imagine Vladimir sliding about in the dark cutting throats or even telephone wires? The idea is absurd, and if he had fallen into the hands of the Gestapo—— I tell you, he was right to refuse to endanger others by taking on more than the good God meant him to carry."

"You may be right, but——"

"No buts, I am right. He was a good comrade in the Legion, was he not? If he had anything, he shared it; if we had anything, he guarded it. I'll tell you something else, he has an intense attachment to you."

"Oh, don't be ridiculous!"

"I never am except when I mean to be. You saved his life that time when he broke his leg in the desert; he's never forgotten that, and we got him out with us when we came away from Boghar in the general's limousine. We could have left him behind, he knows that. He——"

"I've only seen him twice since we parted at Vichy and each time I've handed him off," said Logan.

"I know, but that makes no difference. He feels himself inferior, since we were in the Resistance; he does not resent it from you. I tell you, Logan, he is by nature humble and that is why he dresses up and strolls upon the boulevards with rings on his fingers and a camellia in his buttonhole. It is the psychology, you have not studied it."

Logan laughed at him, but Papert persisted.

"He will not betray you, believe me, and think how useful he will be. Besides, if he does, we can always push him under the steam roller."

"Well, what do you suggest?"

"Let me see him and tell him how these men have murdered your brother and you are set to avenge him. Then we can lay a trap and he will lead them into it."

Logan hesitated a moment while Papert watched him.

"Very well," he said at last. "Go and tell him the story, and then I suppose you'd better bring him to see me."

Papert came next day bringing Vladimir.

"I have told him," said Papert, sitting down on a chair and lighting a Gauloise out of a blue packet.

"You are quite sure, Vladimir, that you want to come in on this? These are not very nice people to mix with."

"Quite sure, thank you. In fact, I am in it already by my own act; Alphonse told you, perhaps. Yes. Well now, already I am holding the tiger by the tail and what happens when I let go? You see, I understand their language, though they don't know that, and last night after they had given me my instructions the leader—his name is Chadai—said to the others that when this business is done they will have to silence me, I know too much. I do not like their methods of silencing people. So I am very glad when Alphonse comes to me and tells me that we are to be together in this. It is reinforcements for me, and I feel I need them; three to one is too much for me. Moreover, it is like the old times come back, when we three were together in Algeria. It is well."

"Good," said Logan. "We'll have drinks on that and then get down to business."

When the drinks were before them Vladimir looked at Logan. "I hope you will believe," he said hesitantly, "that when I traced a Monsieur Logan to the Pétersbourg for those devil's children, the Russians, I had no idea it was you. They said he was an Englishman new come to Paris, a London businessman; true, they said he was tall with brown hair, but what is that? They said he was stiff and prim and proper, he wore the bowler hat and carried a rolled-up umbrella with a crook handle having a gold band round it. It did not remind me in the least of Legionnaire Laurent, indeed it did not——"

Logan laughed and clapped him on the shoulder. "Of course it didn't, how should it? In fact, they were describing my brother, not me; how were you to know that he was my brother and that I had taken his place at the hotel? You didn't even know that he was dead. The name Logan, it is not so common but there are other Logans. Put it out of your mind, Vladimir."

Vladimir looked relieved. "I cannot remember your even having said that you had a brother, still less a twin. Never mind, since you understand. Now, what is it you wish to do?"

"Destroy them."

"I also," said Vladimir, nodding; "if possible, before they destroy me."

"At present," said Logan, "they have lost me."

"I know," said Vladimir, "and last night I received orders to find you. That was late last night, after Alphonse had told me your story. I said to them that it was difficult but I would go into the matter with all my resources. Then I went home and walked up and down my room all night, thinking. Towards dawn I had an idea. Listen. If they were told that you were going away, home to England by a certain train from the Gare du Nord, they would have to act quickly, would they not?"

"I think so," said Logan. "I understand that there is a murder charge against them in London. I think they would prefer not to go back there if it can be avoided."

"I asked them which they really wanted, you or your luggage, and they said both. Definitely both."

"Nice of them."

"Yes. Now, listen to my idea and then between us no doubt we can improve on it."

Vladimir finished his drink, stubbed out his cigarette, leaned across the table and talked.

On the fourth day, when he was beginning to think that Logan must have left Paris for good, Hambledon was standing by the porter's desk looking at leaflets when a small roundabout Frenchman came in and asked the porter whether there were any letters for Monsieur Edouard Logan. The porter turned to the pigeonholes behind him and said there were two, doubtless m'sieu had some authorization to show for collecting them? The small man said he had; while he was producing it from a shabby wallet Hambledon strolled out of the front door. When the messenger came out Hambledon followed him up the Rue Caumartin, to the right across the Rue Auber and along the Rue des Mathurins, across the back of the Opéra and into the Boulevard Haussmann. Here the procession of two, well spaced out, crossed the road and proceeded eastward for a short distance until the leader turned in through the swinging glass doors of the Hotel Ambassador and the follower went in after him.

Alphonse Papert was at the porter's desk; as Hambledon passed he heard Papert ask whether Logan was in the hotel and the porter answer that he was not. Tommy walked through to the bar, where he spent half an hour cultivating the acquaintance of another hotel resident with whom he exchanged names, just in order to have someone else to ask for, and strolled out again well satisfied. He knew where Logan lived; probably the best time to find him in would be early in the morning. Not too early; after breakfast. About ten o'clock.

13 | *QUIET FUNERAL*

HAMBLEDON WENT to the Ambassador Hotel soon after ten the following morning and asked for Logan. The porter said that Monsieur Logan had not yet descended and should he telephone his bedroom to tell him that a visitor awaited him? Hambledon said by no means let the gentleman be urged to descend before he was ready and willing to do so. He himself, said Hambledon, violently disliked being urged to unnecessarily early rising and he would not think of subjecting the gentleman to such an infliction. The porter said that for those who could stay in bed as long as they wished it was indeed well and Hambledon said he would wait awhile and if Monsieur Logan didn't show up it didn't matter, another time would do. He nodded to the porter and passed on, turning right towards the bar, but it was not yet open, so he sat down in one of the Ambassador's comfortable chairs, lit a cigarette and read a newspaper.

Presently a particularly smart and rather too-well-dressed man came into the lounge from the street; he also turned right towards the bar and sat down opposite Hambledon, whose attention was momentarily attracted because the man was carrying two suitcases. Men who dress as well as this one do not as a rule carry suitcases; porters do it for them. He set down the suitcases beside his chair and kept glancing towards them with an expression of marked distaste; every little while he moved them slightly, further from his chair as though he did not want them too close and then nearer again as though to protect them from the foot of the casual passer-by. Tommy, behind his newspaper, observed this with natural interest and wondered what on earth there could be in those cases to arouse at once so much care and so much aversion. It couldn't be a body, however severally dissected; they weren't big enough. Presently one of the rearrangements showed a name painted on the lid of one of the cases and Hambledon's idle interest awoke to full life when he read the name; it was E. J. Logan. One of his associates, presumably. Ha.

Hambledon went on sitting and the nervous gentleman went on fidgeting until the swing doors opened to admit the same man whom Hambledon had followed the day before. He paused at the desk to speak to the porter, who nodded and reached for the house telephone while the newcomer hurried on round the corner by the glass showcases and greeted the nervous gentleman, who was plainly both pleased and relieved to see him.

"It's all right," said the newcomer, "they've bitten."

"Where are they?"

"Waiting just down the street in a car, an old Citroën tourer, open. Look out they don't see you here."

"I sat here out of sight from the door," said the anxious man, "on purpose. They won't come in, will they?"

"Not likely. I got the porter to ring Logan; he'll be down in a minute."

"I shall be glad when this is over," began the nervous man, but at that moment a lift whined down, gates clashed, and Logan came quickly across the hall with a coat over his arm.

"All set?" he asked cheerfully, and the newcomer repeated

the news about the Citroën tourer waiting down the street.
"Good," said Logan. "Splendid. Well done, Vladimir. Alphonse, you'll be coming along?"

"I'll be just behind you."

"Then I'll go," said Logan, and picked up the suitcases,
which were at once taken from him by an attentive porter.
"I want a taxi for the Gare du Nord," added Logan, addressing the porter, who said: "*Bien, m'sieu*," and hurried towards
the doors with Logan following closely. Hambledon noticed
with absorbed interest that the first arrival, the nervous one
whose name was apparently Vladimir, watched the departure
of the suitcases with relief and drew back politely as they
were borne past him.

"Those three are up to some devilment," said Hambledon
to himself. The two who were left, Vladimir and Alphonse,
stood back in the entrance hall and watched through the wide
glass doors as Logan was handed into a taxi and the suitcases
put at his feet. The taxi drove away; Alphonse said: "Now
then," and a shabby grey Citroën touring car with the hood
down drew slowly past the hotel entrance, following the taxi.
Hambledon walked out of the hotel, more or less accompanied by Vladimir, and lit a cigarette on the edge of the
pavement while another taxi was called up. Vladimir said:
"Gare du Nord," sprang into it and was borne away. He was
hardly away before Alphonse did exactly the same thing;
Hambledon, consumed by curiosity, called up yet another
and also said: "Gare du Nord, quick. I'm going to sit next to you
if you don't mind." The taxi started and Hambledon asked if
the man had seen a grey Citroën pull out to follow a taxi
a moment ago.

"I saw it, m'sieu, yes."

"Can you catch it, do you think?"

The man grinned and put on speed, although the grey car
was by then out of sight. He passed Alphonse's taxi and then
Vladimir's; at a place where the road was straight they saw
the Citroën not far ahead.

"Listen," said Hambledon. "At the Gare du Nord, draw
up near that car. When it leaves the station again I want
to follow it, so be ready to go when it does. I am going into
the station but I shall come out again before they leave. I
want to know where it goes to. Understood?"

Logan's taxi pulled up in front of the station and the
grey Citroën also, but some distance behind, Hambledon's
driver put his car in close behind the Citroën. Hambledon
was in a very strong position since he knew all the actors in

the drama and none of them knew him. He saw Logan alight, discourage a porter and carry his suitcases into the station himself. For a man who was ostensibly catching a train, his progress was singularly unhurried and, indeed, vague. He did not seem to know where he wanted to go. The three Russians got out of their car and consulted together; Vladimir's taxi went past towards the far end of the immensely long station frontage; it looked as though Vladimir were keeping out of sight. Not so Alphonse Papert, who sprang out of his taxi the moment it stopped, paid off the man and hurried after Logan, who had already passed out of sight among the crowd in the station hall.

There was a crowd indeed. The Gare du Nord, one of Paris's most important main stations, is not at any time a deserted spot, but on this occasion it was thronged and Hambledon noticed that a large proportion of the throng were police, very much on their toes. He glanced at the Russians; they were still conferring and the smallest one appeared to be jibbing. Actually, Brachko did not like the array of police and was saying so with emphasis. Hambledon turned to his own driver, gave him some notes to go on with, and again told him to wait. "What," he added, "is the reason for all this crowd?"

"Communists, m'sieu, for the funeral."

"Funeral?"

"M'sieu had not heard? A week ago there was a Communist demonstration in the Bastille area which ended in a riot; the police were called out, they fired their little guns and one Communist was killed. So today they are burying him at Père Lachaise and all good little Communists for miles round are come to march in procession with banners. One demonstrates the solidarity, you understand. They assemble here and the police——"

"Excuse me," said Hambledon, seeing the Russians on the move at last, and slipped off after them. Even in such a crowd a man of Logan's height was readily seen; Chadai and Yudin, with Brachko trailing behind, forced their way towards him.

When they overtook him Chadai touched him on the arm and said something Hambledon did not hear, but he was near enough to see Logan put his suitcases down and turn to face Chadai with an expression of polite interest. Instantly Brachko dodged around behind Logan, picked up the suitcases and made off towards the car outside. Hambledon hesitated momentarily; he was more interested in the suitcases than in the men, but the situation looked interesting and he could move faster through the concourse than the encumbered Brachko. Chadai—Tommy did not know his name; he called him Jacob because he was "a smooth man"— Chadai had his right hand in his coat pocket and Tommy said to himself that there was a gun in it too. Chadai said something to Logan, speaking in a low voice but imperatively, and Logan instantly hit him under the jaw and knocked him down. Chadai must have had his finger on the trigger, for there was a loud bang as the gun went off and a Communist in his immediate neighbourhood clutched at his own arm and uttered a loud yell.

Pandemonium broke out at once and Hambledon turned to escape, seeing as he did so the rotund Frenchman called Alphonse hurl himself at the tall Yudin while Chadai scrambled to his feet. Yudin tore himself free and the two men lost themselves in the crowd, not so difficult a matter as it might seem with people milling round, screaming and waving their arms, while others with more experience or discretion threw themselves flat or crouched behind barrowloads of luggage and "those behind cried 'Forward!' while those in front cried 'Back!'" At that point some of the Communists lost their heads and began shooting, the police went into action and a genuine riot began.

Hambledon fought his way out in time to see the grey Citroën disappearing out of the station yard; his own driver was holding the taxi door open for Hambledon and started off in pursuit so abruptly that Tommy fell heavily into the seat and the door swung to upon his foot.

"How many men in the car?" he asked, pulling himself up.

"One only, m'sieu, the small one. He had two suitcases and he paused by the car as though waiting until there came a sound like a shot or a backfire——"

"A shot," said Tommy.

"Indeed? Then he leapt in the car and drove hastily away. One would—— There he is——"

He was interrupted by the two-note horn of a police car— ee-aw! or possibly cuckoo—and drew in to his right to let it overtake. "Best to let such as they have the road if they want it——"

"Do you know," said Tommy excitedly, "I believe they're chasing him too."

The Citroën was showing an amazing turn of speed; whatever else Brachko might bungle, he could certainly drive. He swung round the Place de Valenciennes on two wheels, occasioning yells of protest from other road-users, and shot down the Boulevard de Magenta with the police car screaming on his tail and Tommy's taxi bucketing along behind. At the Boulevard de Strasbourg crossing, where the traffic from the Gare de l'Est emerges upon Paris, Hambledon clung on and shut his eyes, for cars were coming at them from all angles and death seemed imminent. But by some miracle there was no crash and all three cars roared on towards the Place de la République. Here Brachko tried to throw off the pursuit by swinging round the quite terrific Monument of the Republic, but the police car was equally as capable as the Citroën of turning impossible corners and they came out round the end of the gardens so close in front of Hambledon that his taxi nearly rammed the police car.

Going down the Boulevard du Temple, the police tried to crowd the Citroën against the pavement and apparently its driver lost his temper. He turned in his seat, fired a revolver at the police car and smashed the windscreen.

"You know," said Hambledon justly, "that's pretty shooting, going at that speed."

"The m'sieu is a connoisseur of violence, evidently," said his driver, who appeared to be enjoying himself. "Did he, then, know that all this was going to happen?"

"I thought something might, but not—— Now the police are loosing off at him."

"We are better, following, than the pedestrians in advance, are we not? What——"

The Citroën had drawn a little ahead, since a smashed windscreen will embarrass even the demon drivers of the Paris police, and they were hoping to put a bullet through his tyres or, indeed, through Brachko. Quite without warning there was an appalling explosion and the Citroën dissolved into a cloud of debris. One of the fragments having hit the police driver, the car went out of control, bumped the pavement, slewed across the road and rolled over on its side. Hambledon's driver managed by something like a miracle to miss it and slithered past the debris of the Citroën with no more damage than broken glass in one front tyre. He stopped and Hambledon got out.

The police were swarming out of the overturned car to take control of a situation which required controlling. Windows and shop fronts on both sides of the road had been blown in, women were screaming, people were rushing out of houses, and cars were beginning to gather on either side of the traffic block, since the Boulevard du Temple is a busy thoroughfare. Two men dealt with that while a third ran to the nearest telephone, and the police driver crawled out more slowly, holding a handkerchief to his face.

Hambledon went up to him, helped him down to the ground and said: "I hope you are not much hurt."

"Thank you, m'sieu, I think not. It is only that to be struck on the end of the nose fills with tears the eyes one wants to see with. In effect, one cannot see just when it is most urgently necessary."

"Glad it's no worse," said Hambledon and returned to his taxi, which was being told to pass along there, please, or its French equivalent. But the driver said he would do so when he had changed his wheel, he couldn't drive on a flat tyre, what did they take him for, a ruddy tricycle, and what did they mean by pulling up like that, hadn't their mothers ever told them to hold their hands out? The police shrugged and went away upon more urgent errands while Hambledon sat down on the running board and lit a cigarette. He felt as though rather too much incident had been crammed into the last half hour.

Presently the results of the police telephoning began to arrive: mobile police on motorcycles, a salvage squad of the Paris fire brigade to put up barricades at either end of the affected block when the clotted traffic had been moved back, and finally two large cars, the first containing a high official of the Sûreté with detectives and the second one just detectives. They were passed through the barricades and drew up close to the overturned car.

The high official got out and looked round him, gave orders to his men and looked round again. This time he noticed Hambledon, whom he had met some years before, and came across to greet him warmly. "What a day we are having," he added. "A full-scale riot in progress at the Gare du Nord and now this. I wish the devil would fly away with his little children, the Communists. May I, without being indiscreet, ask if my old friend Hambledon has any hand in this game?"

"None at all," said Hambledon. "I happened to be driving along here at the moment when it happened, that's all. Actually, I am on holiday."

The Sûreté man's eyebrows went up but he only said that he was fortunate in having so experienced and observant a witness. "Is there anything you can tell me about all this?"

Hambledon told him that the vanished car was an open tourer containing one man with a couple of suitcases on the seat beside him. "I imagine that one of these cases contained explosives," he added, "and I venture the suggestion that one of your men put a bullet into it."

"Very likely. Excuse me one moment——"

One of the detectives came up with a ragged piece of what had once been a suitcase; it had a handle and part of the lid still attached by the lock.

"You are right," said Hambledon's friend, displaying this relic. "This burst open from within, look. We shall never find the man, I fear, though I would much like to know who he was. This chase started from the Gare du Nord, so I assume he was a Communist." Hambledon hesitated and the Sûreté man saw it. "I know you are on holiday, since you say so yourself, but if by any chance you happen to know anything which would help me——"

"I don't know much," said Hambledon truthfully, "but I can tell you that this man was a Russian, one of a party of three who came here from London. I don't know any of their names but I can give you descriptions of them. They are, actually, wanted in London for murder, so unless you want them particularly——"

"If we catch them you shall have them, my friend, and welcome. *Merde!* We have plenty of that sort here, we do not need to be greedy. Thank you for your immense help; even on holiday you observe more than most men do when they're working. Let my fellow here take down their descriptions, if you will be so kind, and then may I hope the rest of your vacation may be as placid and happy as an infant's dreams? Come and see me before you go—a little dinner somewhere; where are you staying? But it won't be tonight —tonight I am busy, I believe! *Au'voir.*"

He swaggered off and Hambledon looked after him. A charming fellow and genuinely friendly, but that wouldn't stop him from having Tommy kept under observation for the rest of his stay in Paris just in case anything could be learned from his contacts. Tommy bore him no malice, he would have done just the same thing if their positions had been reversed. He dictated descriptions of the three Russians to a waiting detective, adding: "The little one, you need not look for him. Doubtless his spirit is still about us here, suffering from acute astonishment."

Logan, Vladimir and Alphonse Papert met by arrangement at the bar of the Ambassador Hotel for a modest celebration; since it was still only midday the bar was almost empty and they could talk together without being overheard.

"Well," said Logan, "that didn't take long, did it? Half an

hour and we are back here safe and sound. I think it all went off extremely well, and on the part of all three of us I congratulate us warmly. *Salut!*"

"Talking about going off," said Alphonse, "no doubt somebody will notice it and the news will spread and in due course we shall hear about it. *Salut!*"

"Or read it in the papers," said Vladimir. "*Salut!* They did not all go away in the grey Citroën, only Brachko by himself, I saw him. But it does not matter. They will wait till they are all together in some private room ,probably Chadai's bedroom. Then, since the cases are locked and they have not the keys, they will force the locks open. After that the room will require redecoration."

"What did you put in the wretched box?" asked Logan.

"Twenty kilos of blasting powder. I will admit quite frankly that I was very glad to see it go; I did not enjoy having it about and it took years off my life when your porter here banged it against the taxi door."

"What did Chadai say to you at the station?" asked Papert.

"He said: 'Excuse me, m'sieu,' very politely, so I put down my cases for Brachko to take and turned my back on them in order not to embarrass him. I too, Vladimir, was not sorry when I heard a little scraping sound as he picked them up. I looked at Chadai and said: 'Good morning, Monsieur Chadai. What can I do for you today?' He said: 'You are coming with us and it is useless to make a fuss because I have a gun and we are surrounded by friends here.' So I hit him."

"Not hard enough," said Papert disapprovingly. "He got up again at once."

"You called him Chadai?" said Vladimir.

"Certainly. Why not?"

"Only because you didn't know his name till I told you and they will guess that."

"Oh. Oh, that's all right. My brother knew them, you see, and they think I am my brother."

"Of course," said Vladimir, nodding. "Besides, they are about to die, so it doesn't matter what they guess."

At this point the cloistered calm of the Ambassador bar was dispelled completely by the entry of a dozen or more English guests all talking excitedly among themselves.

"We are back again, as you see," said one of them, addressing the bartender, who said that they were, naturally, extremely welcome and he was glad to see that they had changed their minds about leaving.

"We had them changed for us," complained the Englishman. "There is a young civil war raging round the Gare du Nord, Communists with assorted firearms versus the police with riot guns. The dead are being deposited in the left-luggage office."

"And which side, gentlemen, do you think is winning?"

"The Communists were doing quite nicely," said another Englishman, "until the police made a well-timed flank attack from the first-class gents' and shoved the Reds back towards the suburban booking hall. But, just as we were leaving, a strong column of reinforcements arrived, terrible with hammer-and-sickle banners and headed by a coffin. Curiously macabre symbols these people adopt."

"They seemed to me to have the right idea," said another, "except that one coffin won't be enough."

"Oh, that," said the bartender, "that was already occupied. It wasn't a symbol, it was a funeral." He told them about the man who had been killed a week earlier.

"I always understood," said the first Englishman, "that this sort of thing was one of the old-established customs of Paris, but I don't think they ought to allow it just when the Golden Arrow is due to start. Bad for *le tourisme*, ain't it?"

"I expect they will have got it all cleared up by this evening," said the bartender. "These affairs generally settle themselves in a few hours. They are not popular, you understand, if maintained for too long."

"Besides," said one of the English, "the combatants get hungry. Wonderful what an appetite fighting gives you."

"Thirsty, too," said another. "This round is on me."

"We could go across by the night ferry from Dunkirk tonight if it's all quiet on the Nord front by then."

"I was wondering," said an elderly man, "whether I had better hire a taxi to drive to Calais. I must get home, and my wife is nervous."

"Good idea but expensive. I haven't enough of my travel allowance left for that."

Two more men came in and said that really things were a bit hot. Not content with this rumpus at the Nord station, one of those damned Communists had exploded a whole carload of bombs somewhere down near the Place de la République. Nasty business, very. Good many people killed, from what they heard. Houses and shops were wrecked, that sort of thing. They were coming up the Boulevard St. Martin at the time and heard it distinctly. Must say these French police are on the spot; before you could say "knife" the area was cordoned off and nobody allowed in. Police cars, fire engines, ambulances, all that sort of thing simply buzzing round like flies. Dreadful business, actually.

Logan, Alphonse and Vladimir looked at each other with raised eyebrows, finished their drinks and walked quietly out.

"It would appear that our celebration was a little premature," said Vladimir. "Chadai and Yudin are still alive."

"Their father the Devil is looking after them," said Papert angrily. "Why could they not all drive away together like sensible men?"

14

QUAI DES ORFEVRES

HAMBLEDON'S FRIEND at the Sûreté went back to his office and gave orders for a general roundup of, as far as possible, the Russians in Paris. The collection would start at half-past twenty-one hours, which is 9:30 P.M., "for," he said out of his long experience, "the riot at the Nord will be over before that and they will assemble in cafés and places where they drink to tell each other how brave they are. Their homes will be visited at the same time. All vans out at once."

He was quite right, the disturbance at the Nord station died down soon after half-past four, the last of the prisoners was rounded up and removed by five and the station floors were hosed down, clean and tidy by the time the Golden Arrow passengers from London arrived in Paris at eight minutes to six. The door of the left-luggage office was kept locked.

Vladimir was returning to the room where he lived soon after ten that night when, just as he was about to enter the house, he met an acquaintance who asked him if he'd seen the police vans going round.

"No," said Vladimir indifferently. "What for?"

"They are collecting Russians," said the acquaintance, who knew nothing of Vladimir's origin. "An odd taste. Some collect stamps and some door knockers. Our Prefect of Police collects Russians."

"Communists, you mean. On account of that uproar at the Gare du Nord."

"Not only Communists. They roped in poor old Ivan, who

lives over the tobacconist's in the Rue Boissonade yonder, and took him away although everyone knows he is Tsarist to the back teeth. I tell you, the things he said when they pushed him in the van along with the Communist greengrocer from the corner did your heart good to hear. Words you wouldn't think he'd know and him a gentleman once."

"Well, well," said Vladimir, and strolled on. He decided not to return to his room just yet, he had no desire to be herded into a van with a lot of angry supporters of the Soviet. He knew these police raids; it was only necessary to keep on the move till they had finished with that district and then one could quietly go home.

He lit a cigarette and turned into the Boulevard du Montparnasse; he was walking slowly along, thinking of nothing in particular, when a tall man came up from behind and took him firmly by the arm. Vladimir looked round at the cold eyes and hard mouth of Yudin.

"We take a little walk along here," he said, holding the startled Vladimir close to his side. "You will not try to escape, because I have a gun in my pocket. There is a café along here where we shall meet Chadai and he will decide what shall be done with you."

Vladimir pulled his wits together; they were not likely to murder him in a café, and perhaps he could get someone to telephone to Alphonse. Besides, the police were looking for Russians and were sure to visit the cafés; it was only to hold these fellows in talk until they came in. Probably Yudin had not heard about the raid.

"There is no need to be so rudely insistent," said Vladimir with some dignity. "I am happy to met Monsieur Chadai at any time convenient to him." He tried to draw himself away but Yudin's grip tightened on his arm.

"You won't be so happy this time. We have found you out, cheat, imposter, police spy."

"You are evidently drunk," said Vladimir coldly.

"We had our doubts about you," said Yudin confidentially. "You looked just a little too intelligent when we were talking Russian. So we went to the enquiry agency whose address is on that card you gave us and they didn't know you. We even saw the man whose name is on that card and he wasn't you. Not anything like you. Strange, wasn't it? We go in here," said Yudin, propelling him into a café of the poorest sort, "we will sit at a table and wait for Chadai. I will even buy you a drink. It is very good of me, but probably it will be the last you'll ever have, so there's no chance of its becoming a habit. *Garçon! Deux blancs secs.*"

"You are either drunk or mad," said Vladimir. "I shall be glad when Monsieur Chadai comes, I will complain to him about your manners."

Yudin laughed heartily. "Tell me, clever fellow. How did Logan know Chadai's name this morning at the Gare du Nord?"

"Did he? How should I know? Presumably he learnt it in London."

"That's where you're wrong. Nobody knew our names in London, not one single soul. We lived on a ship and had no occasion to give our names to anyone. You told him."

"This is becoming wearisome," said Vladimir disdainfully. "Drink your wine yourself," he added, pushing the second glass towards Yudin, "I do not choose to drink with men of your type." (Were the police never coming?)

"You are also a murderer," said Yudin, drinking the second glass without acknowledgment. "You arranged that explosion which killed Brachko this morning. It is true that Brachko is not much loss but he was my comrade and I will not have my comrades killed by——"

The lights across the street were suddenly obscured by a large vehicle which drew up outside, and the next moment two men in police uniforms came into the room and looked about them. They nodded to several people whom they knew and then spoke to the bartender in low voices which were nevertheless plainly audible, so deep was the hush which had settled upon the company.

"Are any of these people here known Russians?"

"Not to my knowledge, messieurs."

The sergeant nodded; he and his companion went from table to table saying: "Your papers, if you please," to any whom they did not know personally. Vladimir glanced at Yudin for signs of alarm but he looked perfectly confident and even mildly amused. He was not afraid, evidently, of having his papers examined; it followed therefore that he must have French papers, false or stolen.

Vladimir waited patiently till the police reached their table and then said quietly: "This man is a Russian. He is covering me with a gun in his pocket."

The police pounced like cats upon Yudin; there was a gun in his pocket and the safety catch was off. He kicked out, the table went over, and one or two women screamed. But the French police are trained to deal with that kind of thing;

another of them came in and Yudin was scooped up and thrown into the prison van outside.

"Much obliged, m'sieu. How did you know he was a Russian?"

"I have heard him speak that language."

"I see. Your papers, if you please?"

Vladimir handed them over.

"You also, then, are Russian?"

"By birth, yes. I have lived in France this fifteen years and more."

"I am sorry, m'sieu, but I must take you to the station. I have my orders."

"But——" began Vladimir.

"I am sorry," repeated the sergeant with a decisive gesture towards the van. "If you have lived here so long you have nothing to fear; it is only to establish your identity in the morning. A mere formality."

"I object——" began Vladimir, but the police sergeant cut him short.

"It is an order," he said abruptly. Vladimir was hustled out of the café and pushed into the van, an affair like a furniture van of the smaller size with a bench down each side for the captives to sit upon. What Vladimir objected to was not the police interrogation, which he had no reason to fear, but being boxed in with Yudin, doubly savage now at having been denounced to the police. However, the open doors showed that there were already a dozen or more men inside, and even Yudin would not commit a murder before witnesses and in a police van of all places. Besides, he had been disarmed. Vladimir bowed to the inevitable and entered.

The police escort mounted to the front of the van and collected from two or three more cafés, adding another half-dozen passengers to their load. These passengers were not, as Vladimir had been told, all of the same political convictions, and recrimination broke out among them. Voices rose and tempers with them; insults led to blows.

"That's all in this street," said the police sergeant. "I don't know if it's worth while starting on another——"

"They are getting noisy in there," said the police driver, listening to yells and bumping noises which culminated in a crash against the panel just behind him. "If that was somebody's head it was a hard one."

"We'll take them down to the station and get rid of them before we collect any more," said the sergeant. He hammered with his fist upon the side of the van and shouted: "Silence in there! Order!" which had absolutely no effect whatever.

The van drove into the police-station yard in the Quai des Orfèvres, the gates were shut behind it and the van doors were opened. The prisoners got out panting and dishevelled, most of them suffering from minor injuries such as pulled noses or trodden toes. They were urged across the yard into the police station while the sergeant counted his black sheep.

"One short."

"He is at the far end. Come out, you! Is he drunk or asleep?"

"Shake him up, Jean," said the sergeant.

Jean climbed into the van, went along to the far end and gave the unresponsive figure a push, at which it merely rolled off the bench to the floor and was dragged out by the shoulders.

"This one's dead!" said Jean in a scandalized voice. "Dead as a tombstone."

"Throttled," said the sergeant, making an expert examination. "Which one is this, then—where are his papers?" There'll be trouble over this—— Here we are. Name of Vladimir."

On the following morning Hambledon was rung up on the telephone by his friend at the Sûreté.

"I spent a large part of last night," said the French official, "collecting Russians of all shapes, sizes, and shades of political opinion. Would you like to come and look them over? I haven't got more than a percentage of our Russian population, of course, but your bad boys might, with luck, be among them."

Hambledon went and inspected a very large collection of miscellaneous immigrants. Chadai was not among them but Yudin was, and Tommy pointed him out.

"May we have that one if you don't want him? That's one of the remaining two of the trio we were looking for."

"Certainly," said his friend. "We will put him away for you in a separate cupboard. You'll arrange about the application for extradition; won't you? By the way, there's one dead one; you'd better have a look at him just in case."

When the sheet was drawn back from the body on the mortuary slab Hambeldon found himself looking down at the classic features and neatly pointed beard of Logan's friend Vladimir. Death ennobles some faces; it did this one. Hambledon stood, hat in hand, and wondered whether Logan had yet heard this news and what his reaction would be. The last thing Hambledon wished to do was to interest the French police in Logan; the designs, drawings, specifications or whatever they were which the unlucky Muntz had brought out of Russia were a matter for the British Government to investigate and the less said the better.

"No," said Tommy, "no, this isn't the man. I thought for a moment that it was, on account of the beard, but I was wrong." He turned away. "It's a pity; it would have been so very agreeable if it had been the other fellow. Thank you very much."

"We will continue to seek for him. Perhaps he will come to interview his friend whom we have got."

Hambledon laughed. "Not he. If your prisoner was silly enough to get himself captured, his employers will simply write him off. There are plenty more where he comes from. I suppose you've got some charge you can hold him on?"

"Oh, certainly. Several of them. Being in possession of a false passport, for one; we don't know now what his real name is. Being in possession of a loaded firearm. Resisting the police. If those aren't enough we can easily think up a few more."

Alphonse Papert heard of the police collection of Russians while it was happening; in fact, he saw it in progress and wondered idly whether they would also acquire Vladimir. Probably not; Vladimir was perfectly capable of evading police drives, and even if he had not there would be no harm done. He was the last man in Paris to take part in riots or engage personally in violence of any kind; he could arrange to explode Brachko but he would never have hit him on the head. The police could have nothing against Vladimir; a night in the cells while waiting to be interviewed was the worst thing they would be likely to inflict upon him, and what is a night in the cells? A temporary inconvenience, no more.

Vladimir lived in a tall old house in the Montparnasse district of Paris with rooms let off separately all up the dark and grimy stone stair; the concierge was an elderly widow with several daughters who provided such attendance as the tenants were prepared to pay for. She was a hard-bitten old woman with few illusions, she sat in her little hutch by the entrance door and summed up all who came with more accuracy than charity; one would have said that in her the milk of human kindness had dried up these many years. None the less, when Papert came marching along the street on the morning after the raid and turned into the entrance, he found her weeping.

"Good mor— Dear madame, what can be the matter?"

"My only real gentleman! Every time he passed he would sweep off his hat as though I were a duchess——"

"Who—what is all this?" stammered Papert, a horrible conviction creeping upon him as he remembered Vladimir's elaborate manner to all women old or young, poor or rich ugly or beautiful.

"Can it be that you have not heard? *Ces diables de flics,* they have killed him."

"What? Vladimir?"

She sobbed loudly.

"He did not return last night. I was anxious, he might be staying with some friend—possibly you, m'sieu——"

"I wish to heaven he had been!"

"Or even be picked up by the police with all the other Russians. Why not? He did no harm, the poor innocent gentleman; they needed only to hold him till they established the identity and then let him go. But why kill him? I asked the fatherless orphan of a police agent who brought the message, 'Why did you kill him?' I said. He said they did not, it was an accident. I said it was the business of the police to prevent accidents, not cause them. I said it was well seen that we have the Gestapo still with us——"

"Listen, madame. He had, I know, no relations and there will be arrangements to be made. Where is he, did they tell you?"

"At the Quai des Orfèvres, of course. He asked me, this man, this monster of a policeman, who would make the arrangements about the funeral, and I told him to go away. I would let them know. I was going to send Désirée or Madeleine or Justine to find you when they had done their work, but they are paid to do their work. However, you have come, it will save all that."

"I will go," said Papert sternly, "and look into this matter at once, myself. If an evil deed has been done, the miscreant shall suffer if I have to appeal to my Deputy."

"It is well, it is all very well, but who will replace my fine gentleman? He gave a tone to my house, m'sieu, he alone in this district of the collarless and unshaven, only he in his good clothes and clean linen and the flower in his buttonhole. When I had an apartment to let I would arrange for the tenants to see Monsieur Vladimir walk out, swinging his cane and taking off his hat with the most distinguished courtesy imaginable. It was worth another hundred francs on the rent, m'sieu, again and again it was, but who is there now to bring the air of a Court to my poor house?" She wept again.

Papert uttered an expression of profound disgust and walked off angrily to the Quai des Orfèvres. He was still nourishing a very faint hope that it might perhaps be a case of mistaken identity, of *papiers d'identité* muddled together in the rush of so many prisoners, but the hope died when he stood beside the slab in the mortuary where Vladimir lay, looking more like a prince in death than he had ever done in life. Alphonse was so sincerely shocked and grieved that even the busy police found time to be sorry for him and told him all they knew about it. He was found dead in one of the police vans on arrival at the station, that was all they knew. Yes, he had been murdered, no doubt about that, but which of the twenty or so abominables shut up with him in the dark van had done it, ah, m'sieu——

"Can you tell me the names of those others who were with him?"

After a prolonged wait the list was produced but, since Yudin was using an alias, none of them conveyed anything to Papert, who shook his head.

"One moment, m'sieu. I see over there the constable who was on duty with that van, I will bring him here."

The man called Jean came at once, he who had taken from the van the body of Vladimir; he told Papert all that he knew. "He complained, your friend, that this Russian was holding him up with a gun, and it is true that when we searched the man we found a gun on him. But as to whether it was he who killed your friend or some other person, possibly in mistake for someone else in that dark van, who can tell? We have not even interrogated those others yet; they may be doing so now, we are a little busy this morning, as you see. But they are all being held for questioning, you may be sure of that."

Alphonse nodded and looked vaguely about him, for they were standing in the courtyard. It was a miserable overcast morning; as they talked it began to rain a thin drizzle and Papert turned up his coat collar. They walked across towards the entrance gates together.

"You picked them up at a café in the Boulevard du Montparnasse, did you not?"

"We did," said the constable, and told him which one. "You know," he added, "that you may remove the body whenever you please? The other officer explained the formalities?"

"Yes, thank you," said Papert. "I will see to all that myself, at once."

They were held up at the gates for a moment as someone

important arrived and the police on duty saluted. The visitor was an Englishman by his dress, not tall but broad-shouldered, spare in figure and carrying himself with an air of authority. He acknowledged the salutes of the men on the gate and hurried on; as he passed his eyes rested for a moment upon Papert, who recognized him. This was the same Englishman he had seen once or twice at the St. Pétersbourg and again once or twice at the Ambassador. He had been at the Gare du Nord also at the time of the riot; his taxi had pulled up just behind the Russians. In fact, it occurred to Papert that this Englishman had been hovering just within view quite a lot in the past three or four days.

"Some great one, doubtless," said Papert to his friend the constable; "who is he?"

"Somebody important from English police headquarters in London, so it is said. A friend of our Security Branch chief. He is also interested in Russians, they say; no doubt that is why he has come here this morning. I do not know his distinguished name."

Papert nodded indifferently and thanked the constable sincerely, with all the gracious turns of phrase which come so naturally to the French, for his great help and most kindly consideration for one in bereavement; the constable replied suitably and they parted.

Papert went straight to the café in the Boulevard du Montparnasse, where he received immediate confirmation of the constable's story and a description of the Russian with a gun which left him in no doubt at all that it was Yudin, though they did not know him by name. Yes, he had been in there before more than once, with a very neat gentleman with a fair beard and gold-rimmed spectacles and another man, a nasty little man like a rat. Incidentally, the gentleman with the beard, *"le monsieur barbé,"* had been in that morning asking for news of the tall one, had they seen him?

"And did you tell him?"

"But no, m'sieur. We said we could not remember, anything at all. But I think one of the customers told him that his friend had been arrested."

"That is so," said the waiter. "The poor madame in the red dress told him. She is a little——" He tapped his forehead, snatched up a tray of glasses and rushed away.

"So Chadai knows where Yudin is," said Papert to himself; he drank up his glass of wine and went out. Outside on the pavement he paused for a moment's indecision. The undertaker first, or Logan? "Logan first," he decided, "for he is alive and his time is limited. Vladimir, God rest his soul"—he crossed himself—"is in no hurry, for he has already entered upon eternity."

15

REMITTANCE MAN

PAPERT WENT to the Ambassador Hotel, persuaded Logan up to his bedroom for privacy and unfolded his long and tragic story. Logan, not so personally attached to Vladimir as Papert, was none the less shocked and furiously angry.

"The cold-blooded brutes! They murdered him for us, Alphonse. If we hadn't brought him into it——"

"I think we need not blame ourselves too much," said Alphonse, with the logic which seldom deserts a Frenchman even in his moments of profound emotion. "I think they would have killed him anyway, he knew too much; he said so, if you remember, the first time I brought him here to see you before we began to collaborate. Let it not lie upon your conscience, my friend. Myself, I am horrified, I am grieved, I am angry, but I have no sense of guilt. He let himself in for this, the poor Vladimir, and now he will never find his so amiable widow, at least not in this world. Do they have widows in the hereafter, Laurent?"

"I suppose so," said Logan absently. "They must go somewhere. Chadai——"

"I have not told you all my news," said Papert. Summarized, it was that Yudin had killed Vladimir and was in prison, though the police did not seem very confident of bringing the murder home to him. Chadai was still free, since he had called at that café in the Boulevard du Montparnasse that morning, also he knew that Yudin had been arrested, since one of the customers had told him about it. He might or might not know that Vladimir was dead; Chadai had only to go to Vladimir's lodgings and the landlady would certainly tell him. Finally, that Englishman in the grey suit who was always appearing somewhere in the offing—"For one thing, he was here in the hall below when the poor Vladimir brought in the suitcases full of blasting powder for you to take to the Gare du Nord, also he was at the Gare du Nord ten minutes later, I saw him myself"—this Englishman was someone high and important with the English police. "He walks into the yard of the Quai des Orfèvres as though he owned the place, the men on the gate saluting and way being made for him. He looked at me, our eyes met, but his expression did not change. He is a friend of our chief of the Security Branch, I was told, and has come from London because he is interested in Russians."

"Interested in Russians," said Logan. "Is he indeed? Interested in all Russians, or only in those who come from London? And, if so, why is he following us about, if he really is?"

They discussed Hambledon for some time without coming to any conclusion, since they had not enough facts to build a conclusion upon, and then Logan turned to another subject.

"I have been thinking things over," he said, "and I've decided that I shall have to go to London. I'm getting very sick of being chased round by Russian thugs and we aren't getting anywhere. Chadai and I could hunt each other round Paris for weeks and I should know no more than I do now. They are looking for something they think I have, that's all I know. What is it, where is it, and why do they want it so badly? The answer must be in London, Papert; my brother was in London and only left it to consult me."

Papert nodded. "Let us, then, go to London. I have never been in England, I shall be interested. Also, I shall practice my English, it is rusty with disuse. Then we will solve this problem, catch Chadai and cut his throat, and then come back here and resume our normal lives. It is good for everyone, the occasional change. Shall I pack for you?"

"It isn't quite so simple as all that. You must have wondered sometimes why I never went to England, Alphonse. There is a reason; it is that if I do so I shall forfeit my income."

"What? Forfeit your income? *Quel malheur!* I had sometimes wondered—forgive me—whether in your hot youth you had in some way annoyed your so incorruptible police, but this is worse, far worse. What a disaster! It is a risk not to be run."

"I didn't annoy the police, I annoyed my father, which was much more disastrous. He was a very serious man, Papert, very rigid in his views, unbendingly upright. There was a scandal in my family a generation earlier; one of his brothers, my uncle, did something quite frightful, though I never knew what it was. It cost the family no end of money to keep it hushed up, and my uncle was exported to the Argentine and never seen again. Then when I grew up with a lot of cheerful ideas about women, wine and song—there was a pretty chorus girl in it, I remember—Papa jumped to the conclusion that I was my uncle over again and took steps to avert the consequences. I have a very good allowance—he wasn't mean—and I can do anything or go anywhere except to the British Isles. If I put one foot ashore upon my native land, Alphonse, my income stops from that moment and never, never starts again."

"Incredible," said Alphonse. "Unbelievable. Staggering. What men of iron they were, your English forefathers. I have read about them in books but I did not believe. I was wrong. So you cannot go to London, my friend, it is out of the question."

"I'm not so sure," said Logan slowly. "If I went as my brother—no one knows he is dead except me."

"But his friends, his servants, his employees, his business acquaintances, that girl of whom you spoke whose flat was robbed, you will not know any of them even if they accept you without question, which I do not believe. There is the business itself, whatever it was——"

"Spices," murmured Logan.

"You will have to run it, and what do you know about spices?"

"Simple damn-all. But that doesn't matter a bit, because I am going to lose my memory." He smiled upon Alphonse's horrified look. "Why not? Men do lose their memories even in Paris, and look at the worries I've had. Quite enough to make me. I have been practising in the mirror the blank, lost, half-frightened expression, see? He turned upon Alphonse a face containing only anxious enquiry and a curious, rather unpleasant innocence. "What am I to do?" he asked in slow and careful French. "I do not know who I am, I have forgotten even my name."

"But the risk!" persisted Alphonse, bouncing in his chair. "The so deadly risk! A man may endanger his life or his liberty, that is reasonable; but to endanger his income, his beautiful adequate pension, that is sheer idiocy. Madness! You are completely, utterly insane."

"Listen, Alphonse. You know me, you know my brother is dead, you know we could double for each other, and yet, you won't believe this scheme possible. I shall be dealing with people who are *expecting to see my brother*, and do not know that I exist. Why on earth should any doubt arise in their minds? They look at me and they see Edward and that's that. If he is a little strange and doesn't recognize people, 'poor chap, he's a bit' "—Logan tapped his forehead—" 'you know. Lost his memory. Never mind, it'll come back if we don't worry him.' So they won't worry me. That'll be all right, you'll see in time."

Alphonse sighed deeply. "I see at least that you have made up your mind. How do you propose to start? Go to London and lose your memory there?"

"I don't think so, somehow. I did think of doing that, but a better idea has perched upon my brain. That Englishman that you spoke of, the man in the grey suit, the friend of policemen. If I cast myself upon him saying, 'I don't know who I am and why am I in Paris?' what will he do? Cherish me, surely. Brother Englishmen an' all that, he can't just courteously raise his hat and walk away, can he? What an escort to London, what a witness for me when I arrive! Money for jam, Alphonse, money for jam. There's only one drawback to this scheme; I shan't be able to take you. If I lose my memory, I shan't remember you, shall I?"

"I go," said Alphonse, rising gloomily to his feet, "the simple but dignified obsequies of our poor Vladimir await my attention. He has been financially successful lately, there is probably enough money to pay for it."

"Unless his landlady has come down on it before this," said Logan.

Alphonse threw him a startled glance and fairly ran out of the room.

Hambledon also was feeling discouraged and ineffective. Brachko was thoroughly dead, Yudin in jail and Chadai missing, even Tommy's detailed description had not enabled the Paris police to pick him up; probably, after the loss of his two companions, he had thought it wiser to go somewhere else. There remained only Logan at the Ambassador; if he had disappeared also, there would be nothing for it but to go back to London empty-handed. Not a particularly successful trip, this. Disappointing. He went to the Ambassador that afternoon and failed to see Logan, though the desk clerk assured him that Monsieur Logan was still in residence. This evening, perhaps?

But Hambledon spent a cheerful evening in the company of his friend from the Sûreté and cast care aside for the time being. Tomorrow would do for these wretched people who popped up and vanished again like rabbits in the gorse; all you saw was the flicker of a white tail and then it was too late. As for whatever it was they were pursuing, if indeed there was any such object in existence and the whole business was not the outcome of some personal vendetta directed against or by some person or persons unknown——

Hambledon realized that this line of reasoning was not so much a line as an unmanageable tangle, and thrust it out of his mind. The Bal Tabarin is not, in any case, the best place in which to think out problems.

The following morning, not too early, he walked up to the Ambassador, had a refresher at the bar and looked about for Logan, who presently came out of the lift to sit in a chair and skim through *Le Matin*. Just as Hambledon was making up his mind to go and speak to him, he threw down the paper and strolled out, so Tommy wandered after him. Logan stood on the edge of the pavement, apparently undecided which way to go; once or twice he brushed his hands over his eyes as though to sweep away cobwebs.

"Got a hang-over," commented Tommy to himself. "Out on the tiles last night, I suppose, like me, only I haven't got a hang-over. Or have I? No, definitely not."

Logan suddenly made up his mind, summoned a taxi and was driven away. Tommy, who had not been near enough to hear the direction, called up another taxi and followed. The course lay in the direction of the river; the leading car turned into the Ile de la Cité and drew up at the main entrance to Notre Dame.

"Sight-seeing or devotions?" asked Tommy, and directed his taxi to stop a few yards down the street on the north side of the great church. He paid off his man and strolled round the corner in time to see Logan look up at that amazing façade, shake his head and turn sharply as though he expected a car to be waiting just behind him. The taxi, however, had gone. Logan again employed his cobweb-clearing gesture, looked round at Hambledon and actually took a step towards him but changed his mind again and walked away towards the bridge to the left bank, the Pont au Double. Here he stood leaning against the parapet, looking down at the river below and a string of barges coming up-stream.

"What is all this?" Tommy asked himself. "Am I being led astray, or what? In this district, too," for, following the proverb, "The nearer the church the further from God," there are some of the liveliest quarters of Paris in the immediate neighbourhood of Notre Dame. However, he strolled on towards the bridge and crossed it leisurely. Logan looked at him, hesitated, made up his mind and ran to meet him.

"Excuse me—I do apologize, I do really——" Logan spoke in English.

"Certainly," said Hambledon cheerfully. "Please don't apologize, can I help you in any way?"

"I—— You are English, aren't you?"

"Completely."

"Oh, splendid. Well, I—the fact is—really, it sounds so silly I don't like to say it." He turned upon Hambledon an anxious enquiring gaze coupled with a curious look of innocence so unnatural as to be unpleasant in a man of his age. Hambledon was rather taken aback; it was a little like stopping a passerby to ask the way and meeting the blank gaze of an idiot.

"Please go on. What is it?"

"I," began Logan, "I've lost my memory, but I do know I'm an Englishman. This is Paris, isn't it? I don't know Paris well, but that is Notre Dame, isn't it; I mean, one can't mistake it."

"Quite right. This is Paris and that is Notre Dame."

"But what am I doing here?"

Hambledon broke into a laugh. "My dear fellow! How should I know? Business or pleasure or both?"

"I didn't know what to do and I was sure you were English; you will help me, won't you? Dammit. I feel so lost, I don't even know my own name."

"Haven't you any papers in your pockets?"

"Ah," said Logan, and produced a wallet and a passport. "Here it is. Edward John Logan. Logan? Am I Logan? It doesn't mean anything to me."

"Steady," said Hambledon, "steady. Let's look at the photograph. I should say that's you all right; in fact, it's an excellent likeness. British subject by birth, born in London in 1907, so you're forty-four years of age, aren't you? Address: Caroline Mansions, Regent's Park, London. That would be a block of flats, wouldn't it?"

"I don't know," said Logan miserably. "It's no good asking me. I can't remember anything whatever earlier than ten minutes ago. It's all a complete blank."

"Yet you recognize Notre Dame."

"I did, didn't I? Do you think I'll know everything again when I get home? I'm frightfully sorry to be such an infernal nuisance, but could you help me to get home? I don't know where I'm staying here, presumably I've got some luggage

—and a hotel bill to pay, unless I'm staying with friends——"
Logan's voice tailed off.

"Listen," said Hambledon, who did not believe one word of
all this but was more than willing to play. "Let's go on along
the Quai St. Michel here and pick up a taxi to another part
of Paris, go to a restaurant and have a cup of strong coffee
and a brandy. That might bring you round."

"I came here in a taxi," said Logan eagerly. "I remember
that. I was driving along in a taxi and the man stopped there,
at Notre Dame, and evidently expected me to get out, so
I did. Then I paid him—I suppose I paid him——"

"Don't worry," said Hambledon with a laugh. "If you hadn't
he would be here still, probably giving you a family history
of yourself which would surprise you."

"I must have paid him. I looked up at these towers and said
to myself, 'That's Notre Dame.' Then I looked round and
he'd gone. I saw you coming and nearly spoke to you then
because I thought you were an Englishman, but I thought
if I waited a bit my mind might come back, but it hasn't."
He grabbed Hambledon's arm. "Have I gone mad and don't
know it yet?"

"Nonsense," said Hambledon briskly. "Rubbish. Don't be
morbid. Temporary loss of memory is a thing which might
happen to anyone. Here's a taxi coming. No, he's engaged."

"What are those box things?" asked Logan, pointing to the
wide boxes upon the parapet of the river wall. "Are they
selling things?"

"Prints and old books and secondhand jewellery. Junk, most
of it."

"Never seen that before," said Logan decidedly. "Have they
been here long?"

"From time immemorial," said Tommy solemnly and waved
his hat to one of the old ladies who was a friend of his.
"Since the memory of man runneth not to the contrary. Hi!
Taxi!"

They drove to a restaurant in the Boulevard des Italiens,
since Hambledon thought they might as well be as near home
as possible while they were about it. Here they sat at a
table a little apart from the others, and when Logan began
to babble again Tommy checked him until the strong black
coffee had been brought and consumed. Logan's anxious
look did not lift, however, and Hambledon proceeded with
the enquiry.

"Now let's see what you've got in your wallet. Just a moment, I'll order the cognac. Waiter! *Deux fines, s'i'plaît.* Perhaps that will help us."

Logan laid his wallet upon the table. It was Edward Logan's actually, a good wallet of crocodile leather with silver corners and a small silver shield bearing the initials E.J.L. Hambledon pointed them out.

"Edward John Logan again, you see."

Logan shook his head. "If it was Obadiah Stigginbotham it would be all the same to me."

"Oh, come," said Tommy. "Be reasonable. Nothing could be the same as Obadiah Stigginbotham. Besides, you haven't got side whiskers. What I want to find in there is a card from your hotel, most of 'em hand one out to their customers with their room number written on the top right-hand corner."

Logan turned out the contents of the wallet upon the table and there indeed was a neat white card with the name in neat red lettering of the Ambassador Hotel, 16 Boulevard Haussmann, Tel. Pro 63.74., and a room number written in ink.

"There you are," said Tommy triumphantly. "What did I tell you? Home and dry is what you are. All you have to do is to return to the fold, the hotel porter will greet you by name and there you are."

"Yes," said Logan absently. "I wonder if it's a very expensive hotel. I don't seem to have much money here." He counted out just over seven thousand francs, which was about seven pounds in English money. There was also five pounds in English pound notes and, loose in his trouser pocket, a few English silver coins and two pennies.

"No sensible person would call the Ambassador a cheap joint, though I believe the George V and the Meurice might make it seem comparatively inexpensive."

"Once I get back there I could wire to London for some more money," said Logan more confidently.

Tommy refrained from telling him that, in these days, that was one thing which it would not be the slightest use his doing. In fact, the remark, so casually thrown out, impressed him and for the first time he began to wonder whether the fellow really had lost his memory. If this was an act it was a remarkably good one.

"I expect when you go back to the Ambassador you'll find you've got a wad of traveller's cheques waiting to be cashed, probably in the hotel safe. You look to me to be pretty well off, you know; expensive wallet, gold watch and all that."

"Here's the return portion of a railway ticket to London," said Logan. "I've got my fare home, anyway. But do you know," he added, turning on Hambledon a look of concentration so intense as to be almost painful, "what worries me is that I've no idea what I may have done. Don't you see? Suppose I'm a defaulting financier on the run and the minute I go ashore at Dover the police grab me. Suppose I've been involved in some drug smuggling—can't you understand? I've not only no memory, I've got no character either. Who is Edward John Logan, for heaven's sake?"

Tommy leaned back in his chair and looked at his guest. "Well, really," he said slowly, "you do think up some conundrums, don't you? In the first place, would a defaulting financier on the run take a return ticket? Answer, yes, he might with intent to deceive. I shouldn't think you're as bad as all that, you know; after all, Solomon Wulkans don't grow on every bush. You might employ a private enquiry agency to look into your past, of course, but why not go back to your hotel and simply read your correspondence? If there isn't any it might begin to look as though you had fled. On second thoughts, it's very unlikely indeed that you've committed any serious breach of our country's laws, because if you had you wouldn't be staying in an hotel, you'd be skulking somewhere *en pension*."

"Why?"

"Because hotels send a list of their guests to the police, and if there had been any sort of official enquiry after you from London you'd have been called upon by an *agent de police* long ago."

"Perhaps one did call," said Logan nervously, "and that's why I was in a taxi——"

"Oh, cheer up, brother," said Hambledon impatiently. "Be bold, be brave. What is all this fuss about? Do you feel a dark cloud of unspecified guilt inserting its filmy tentacles into the tenderest recesses of your immortal soul? No? Then why worry? Look, I'll come along to the Ambassador with you, it isn't far."

"Oh, thank you so much. I was hoping you would do that. Frightfully good of you. By the way, are you staying there?"

"No. No, I'm not, but I know where it is."

As they turned into the entrance of the Ambassador the wide glass doors opened as usual without any visible agency, being operated by a photoelectric cell, but the first encounter with this modern miracle is always a little startling and Logan shied momentarily before following Hambledon through them. The man on duty at the desk looked up and said: "Ah,

Monsieur Logan. Some letters for you," and gave him two with English stamps on them.

Logan thanked him and took them, looked at them and dropped them into his pocket. "By the way," he added, "did I deposit anything in your safe, do you remember?" He brushed his hands over his eyes in the now familiar gesture.

"Certainly, m'sieu. An envelope containing, as you told me, your spare money. Did you wish to have it out?"

"Please."

The man took a bunch of keys from a drawer and said that if m'sieu would care to come down he should have them. Logan turned to Hambledon and said: "You will wait, won't you?" in an imploring tone.

"Certainly," said Tommy affably. "In the bar."

Over a Dubonnet he told himself that it didn't really matter at the moment whether this fellow was shamming amnesia or really suffering from it; if he wanted to go to London he should be encouraged and helped to go there if Tommy had to escort him himself. Probably the best plan, it would ensure that he didn't get lost again. Questioning him about elusive Russians looked like being a sticky business if he really had lost his memory; if he was only shamming, Bagshott could be relied upon to disentangle him.

Logan came into the bar looking a little more cheerful and brandishing a long envelope. "It seems I shall not became destitute just yet," he said. "There's quite a lot of money here. What's yours?" He held open the mouth of the envelope and showed Hambledon a very sizeable wad of French notes.

"Yes, you don't look as though you'd starve yet awhile," said Tommy. "I suppose you cashed all your traveller's cheques at once when you arrived."

"Oh," said Logan, dashed at once, "shouldn't I have done that?" As a matter of fact, since Edward Logan had been in too much of a hurry when leaving London to wait for traveller's cheques, these French notes were Laurence Logan's own money. "What ought I to do; I can take them home with me, can't I? Or is there some rule I've forgotten?"

"I should consult Cook's," said Tommy. "They're more up in this sort of thing than I am. They've got an office in the Place de la Madeleine. You could book a reservation there on the train when you've made up your mind which day you're travelling. That reminds me, I must book mine soon."

"Are you going over soon?"

"Day after tomorrow, unless anything unforeseen happens."

"Oh. I suppose—no, dammit, I can't hang on to you as though you were my nursemaid."

Tommy felt that this was all being made much too easy, there must be a catch in it somewhere.

"Why? Do you think you'd be happier travelling with me rather than alone?"

"Infinitely. You can't imagine how uncertain this makes me feel; I'm almost afraid to cross the lounge in case I forget where I'm going."

"Well, look. I'm seeing a man this afternoon and after that I shall know whether or not I can travel the following day. If I find I can, shall I ring you up here to tell you?"

Logan overflowed with gratitude and said that would do admirably, and any time this evening would be all right, he wasn't going out again.

"What? Stay in the hotel all the rest of today on a lovely day in September?"

Laurence Logan shuddered slightly and said he wasn't running any more risks, thank you, and it was a nice hotel anyway, he had just noticed a place where they sold books.

16   RECEIPT FOR THE BODY

HAMBLEDON WALKED away, saying to himself that if this was some kind of trap he was well in it with all four little hoofs, but that it was interesting anyway. Perhaps this fellow Logan had the surviving Russian rather close on his tail and was enlisting Hambledon as a kind of bodyguard. But the Russian seemed to have disappeared.

Chadai, as a matter of fact, was following twenty yards behind Hambledon. He had had his beard shaved off by a barber who protested at being asked to perform such an outrage. *"Une barbe si fine, si distinguée, on ne doit pas se priver d'une si belle décoration du visage,"* but Chadai was adamant and off it came. The barber sighed deeply when he had finished and so did Chadai, for he had rabbit teeth and a retreating chin and the alteration was both startling and painful. He bought himself a pair of spectacles with wide horn rims and sidepieces; spectacles were a necessity because he was as blind as a bat without them. When he was dressed in a very French suit, a shirt with horizontal stripes, pointed-toed shoes and a wide-brimmed hat he experienced a slight shock every time he saw himself by accident in a mirror. It was no wonder that the French police failed to identify him from Tommy's description.

He had missed Logan earlier that morning but he saw him and Hambledon walking together like friends from the café in the Boulevard des Italiens to the Ambassador, and it struck him, as it had previously struck Papert, that this English-man seemed to have been standing, as it were, in the wings watching every performance of theirs for several days. Chadai therefore abandoned Logan for the time being and followed Hambledon instead.

Tommy went on at a sharp walk because he had a lunch en-gagement with his friend from the Sûreté and was almost late; when he arrived at the appointed restaurant the Frenchman was already there. They went to a table which had been re-served for them; Chadai was extremely lucky to get one place at a table reasonably within earshot. The conversation ranged from clay-pigeon shooting to hydrogen bombs, from the war in Korea to German rearmament, from food to wine and back again; it was not until the end of the meal that Chadai heard anything which really interested him.

"That Russian you identified whom London was asking for, one of the three you described——"

"Oh yes?"

"London must want him very badly; the extradition papers have gone through already."

"Quick work," said Tommy. "I think a Grand Marnier, unless you have any better idea? Have you sent him across already?"

"No, he goes tomorrow. We send him as far as Calais and one of your Scotland Yard detectives takes charge of him there. Wanted for murder, I understand."

"He is, yes, but I think they want to ask him a few ques-tions about another matter as well."

"I hope you get what you want, and you can always hang him afterwards, can't you. He is a killer, that type, if I ever saw one."

"It's a help to have even one out of the three," said Tommy. "The little one, of course, blew himself up, and the third seems to have disappeared."

"Sensible man. Perhaps you'll find him in London when you go back—when are you going?"

"Day after tomorrow. I'm travelling on the Flèche d'Or with a friend, man named Logan," said Tommy deliberately, watching the Frenchman for any reaction to the name, but there was none.

"Logan. The name means nothing to me," said the Frenchman with a laugh. "Another of your bad boys?"

"No. Oh no, I think he's all right."

"I was mistaken, then. I thought you brought out the name —bump!—like that to see if I knew it." Both men laughed, Tommy said that that kind of thing tended to become a habit and his friend agreed with him. "All the same, it is quite true that I have nothing against that name."

"Delighted to hear it," said Hambledon.

When they got up and left the restaurant Chadai still sat on over his coffee; it seemed to him that he had enough to think about for the moment. Yudin was being taken across tomorrow, this Englishman and Logan following the next day. Yudin was going to be made to talk and it was imperatively necessary that he should not. He must either be rescued or——

Logan must have the papers on him and he was going back to London. Day after tomorrow, that fellow said, on the Golden Arrow. So he would arrive in London at half-past seven on Friday evening. The banks would be closed; he would go straight to his flat, arriving there about eight if the train was punctual. Yudin was being handed over at Calais on Thursday, tomorrow. That Englishman, friend of policemen—for Chadai knew who the Frenchman was—who was he? He had known about the three of them being in Paris, he knew Brachko had blown himself up, he knew Yudin was in a French prison and that he was being extradited to London tomorrow.

Chadai's mind ran back over the conversation he had just heard. The French police officer, referring to Yudin, had said: "The Russian you identified, one of the three you described." So this man knew them all by sight.

This Englishman was not a policeman, he had not the look of one; besides, he was not tall enough. One of the things which had surprised the Russians was to find that English policeman had to be above a certain height, as though it mattered what size a policeman was; it was just like the effete democracies to pick out men for show instead of for their efficiency. Yet he was evidently in touch with Scotland Yard. He was probably a member of British Intelligence, in any case a man to be remembered and watched.

Chadai put Hambledon out of his mind for the time being, paid his bill and went out of the restaurant. The first thing on the agenda was the matter of Yudin. They would not take him across by night, nor in the Golden Arrow by day; one could not imagine a handcuffed prisoner sitting on one of the cushioned seats of that all-Pullman train. No privacy in a Pullman. They would take him, therefore, by the train of ordinary carriages which left the Nord at the same time as the Golden Arrow and arrived at Calais a little later, giving the Golden Arrow passengers time enough to go aboard the steamer first and grab all the best seats. The boat from England, by which the Scotland Yard man would be coming to meet Yudin, came into Calais at—at——

There is a British Railways office in the Boulevard des Capucines down which Chadai was then walking; he turned back and went into it to consult timetables.

The boat from Dover came into Calais at twenty minutes past 2 P.M. if it were punctual. The boat to Dover left Calais at four o'clock. An hour and forty minutes between the two, say an hour and a half. Much can be done in an hour and a half.

Chadai came out of the office and went on his way towards the Bastille area of Paris. This is not a nice district but many things can be bought there which are not on sale anywhere else. Chadai wanted a warrant card such as the Sûreté issue to their detectives, and he got it since even detectives have their pockets picked sometimes. He also wanted the name and address of a car owner-driver at Calais who would drive where he was told and forget all about the journey when it was done. He would not be required to take any part in any proceedings of any kind, let alone violence, dear me no, what an idea. He need never descend from the driving seat. It was only that in matters of delicacy it was sometimes a convenience to have a driver with a bad memory, was it not?

It is not usual to send anyone below the rank of detective inspector to France to bring home extradited prisoners, but Scotland Yard was a little shorthanded at the time, so they sent Detective Sergeant Johns. He had never been over before but his French was very good by English examination standards, and anyway the job was so simple he could hardly go wrong. He had only to go ashore at Calais, meet the Paris train which came in just after the Golden Arrow, receive from a French police officer the body of the prisoner and sign for it, handcuff the said body's wrist to his own and walk on board the Dover boat. He need not, so far as could be foreseen, leave the precincts of Calais Maritime Station at all and was advised not to, except in the company of the French police and at their request. No sight-seeing and getting lost, no wandering round after pretty girls. Compree?

Detective Sergeant Johns considered his superior's idea of a joke to be entirely beneath contempt and went ashore at Calais quite prepared to spend an hour and a half strolling round the Maritime Station observing with interest the lively activities of a French port. The Customs, the Currency Control, the trains, the engines, the porters—he had gathered that there was much entertainment to be had by watching the antics of French porters. However, the moment he had passed Customs, which in his case was just a matter of showing his warrant card, a smart dapper Frenchman who had been standing looking in at the Customhouse door came up to him.

"Good afternoon. You are the Scotland Yard detective who has come over to fetch——" The Frenchman quoted the name under which Yudin had been passing in Paris.

"I am," said Johns, and showed his warrant card which was, actually, still in his hand.

"I am *Agent de police de Sûreté Lacour*," said Chadai, giving the name which was on the warrant card he had acquired Paris the night before. He even showed Johns the card but carelessly obscured with his thumb the photograph of its original owner. "I came to meet you because we have just had a message through from Paris that the train your man is on will be late and there may be rather a rush for the boat. So, as there are a number of papers to sign, I was told to ask you if you would mind coming along to the police station first to get them done. I've got a car outside."

"Certainly," said Johns in his careful French. "It will be a pleasure."

He was mildly surprised to notice that the driver wore only ordinary chauffeur's uniform, but perhaps this was one of the many things they did differently in France. They drove fast into Calais town, giving Johns a twinge of not unpleasant terror to be driving on the wrong side of the road for the first time in his life, and pulled up outside the police station. Chadai got out, telling Johns to wait a moment in the car, please, and went inside. Johns was quite happy; even a foreign police station looked like a police station and was clearly labelled as such, and there was plenty to look at in the streets. What a thrill it is, the first arrival in a foreign town.

Chadai went inside and asked to speak to the Superintendent. He introduced himself, showed his warrant card with his thumb still over the photograph, and said he had a favour to ask. "It is this. I have just come from England with a prisoner to take through to Paris, they are sending a car for us from the Sûreté. I arrive and there is no car but a message to say they broke down and will be an hour—two hours—late. Here am I at the Maritime Station with a prisoner at the moment locked up by courtesy of the station authorities in a lamp room or some such place. It has, at least, no window and a strong door. May I bring him here, if you would be so courteous as to lock him in one of your cells for me until the car comes? It is at any moment possible that the station authorities may wish to use their lamp room or whatever it is for its lawful purpose, and——"

But certainly. The Calais police would be happy to do all in their power, and so on.

Chadai thanked them quite sincerely and said in that case he would go back to the Maritime Station and collect the prisoner. *Au revoir,* then.

He went out, got back into the car and said to Johns that the man in charge of the papers to be signed had gone out to lunch and not yet returned, he wouldn't be long.

Johns looked at his watch and said he must on no account be late in meeting the train.

Chadai looked at his, compared it with Johns', and said with perfect truth that there was plenty of time. It was then only twenty minutes to three; there was more than an hour before the train was due. "Suppose we go and have a little glass of something and then come back here, eh? It will pass a quarter of an hour."

Johns agreed, why should he not? He would have liked to suggest walking, instead of driving, in order to get into closer contact with Calais, but he felt a little shy of suggesting it; he was the guest. Chadai told the driver to go to a certain café of which Johns did not catch the name, but it would not have conveyed anything if he had. When they reached it and went in, Johns was a little disappointed; the place was shabby and dingy to his mind, empty or nearly so; he would rather have gone somewhere bright and cheerful to sit outside at a table upon the pavement as they do on the Continent. However, he felt again that he could hardly protest; perhaps after they'd had a drink he could suggest walking back to the police station, it wasn't far.

Chadai left him sitting at a table near the door and went to the bar to fetch the drinks himself as there was no waiter in the place. He came back with two glasses of red wine, gave Johns one, picked up the other and said: *"Salut!"*

Johns picked up his glass, said: "Here's mud in your eye," and translated it, *"Voici de la boue dans votre œil,"* and drank it off. Chadai laughed heartily, patted him on the shoulder and said something about "the other half, as you say in England."

Johns thought the wine pleasant but rather strong; he was no judge of wine, half pints of beer were his usual drink and not too many of them. He would just have this "other half" and then excuse himself from having any more; one did not drink on duty, a policeman would understand that.

Chadai came back with two more glasses, and this time Johns drank it more slowly. It had probably been a mistake to swallow the first one so quickly; one drank wine slowly, didn't one, to appreciate the flavour? He did not really like the flavour at all; he did not feel well, his head was singing and the room swinging round. The habit of discipline and a sudden terror of making a fool of himself brought him to his feet; he took two steps towards the door and fell flat on his face.

The bartender came forward and helped Chadai to carry Johns out to the car and dump him in the back seat; fortunately for them, the pavement was narrow and four steps covered the distance, for Johns was tall, solid and heavy. They pushed him in, Chadai got in beside him and the car moved off.

They did not drive straight back to the police station but went for a little tour round about the town while Chadai went through Johns' pockets and transferred everything they held to his own. His tie was taken off, also his boots and his raincoat. His hat was already squashed in a corner of the seat.

Chadai tapped on the window between him and the driver and the car turned towards the police station. When they arrived Chadai and the driver got out quickly, dragged out the inert form of Johns, conveyed it inside the station and dropped it on the floor. The driver went out at once and Chadai explained.

"Here is your prisoner; he has had a little wine, as you see. He is better like that. He is a tough, this type."

Johns looked it with his collar unfastened, in his socks and with his hair tousled, a bump coming up below his right eye where it had met a chair when he fell and his nose swelling where it had met the floor. The French police gathered round and looked at him.

"Be careful if he should wake up before I return," said Chadai, "for he is a fighter. He will also try to persuade you that he is an English detective; indeed, that is largely why they are anxious to see him in Paris."

"He is the right type, physically, for an English policeman," said the Superintendent, "admire for me his large feet. We will keep him safely for you, no fear of that."

"May I also have a receipt for him?" asked Chadai. "Just to regularize the position, as is proper."

He got his receipt, renewed his apologies and thanks, promised to be back within two hours at most and went out to the car.

"Maritime Station," he said, "and drive slowly. Don't go right up to the entrance, stop a little this side of it."

He looked again at his watch; the time was a minute or two to three. Excellent, the most difficult part of the business was over and had taken only forty minutes; there was still a good three quarters of an hour before the train came in.

Chadai took off the thin-soled boots with pointed toes which he had bought in Paris and put on Johns' regulation boots instead. This was a tiresome business, for they were at least two sizes too large and he had to stuff the toes with paper and pull the laces very tight; even so he felt that he would not so much walk in them as flap along like a penguin. He struggled into Johns' raincoat, took off his own tie and put on Johns' typically English one in its place, straightened out some of the more recent creases in Johns' trilby hat and put it on his head. The car stopped fifty yards short of the station entrance; Chadai got out and paid off the driver.

"By the way," he added, "there is a perfectly good pair of boots in the back of the car for which I have no further use. I am going on a walking tour in the Ardennes and such thin soles are quite unsuitable, I made a mistake in bringing them. You, no doubt, know some deserving poor man who will be glad to have them to wear on Sundays."

The driver, who had not spoken one word from start to finish of this expedition, merely nodded, let in his clutch and drove rapidly away. Chadai turned up his—Johns'—coat collar, pulled down the brim of his hat and strolled casually into the station. Half an hour to go before the train came in. Magnificent. He went to the left-luggage office and took out the bag he had left there earlier.

It must be emphasized that all of his clothing which showed, except the bottom four inches of his trousers, was not only English but also the dress which is practically a uniform for

English plain-clothes detectives. Also, he had not to deceive the British, who might notice small discrepancies, but the French. He awaited the train with entire confidence.

When it came in he stood back and waited until a police officer got out accompanied very closely indeed by Yudin and followed by a second police officer. Chadai took it as a well-deserved tribute to his changed appearance that Yudin's glance swept over him without a sign of recognition. It was true that Yudin wasn't very bright, but if he didn't recognize him no one would. Chadai went up to them.

"I think that you are the gentlemen who are bringing me a prisoner," he said in slow and careful French, copied from Johns. "I am Detective Sergeant Johns from Scotland Yard." He showed them Johns' warrant card with a quick official flip, as though anxious not to make a display of it before the other passengers streaming past them; if the French police did not have a chance to see the photograph that did not worry them, they had seen English police warrant cards before.

They all retired to a quiet corner, where the French hand-cuffs were taken off Yudin and replaced by the English ones from Johns' coat pocket. The other end of the handcuffs went round Chadai's wrist, after which he signed the receipt for the body and the official business was over.

"Now," said Chadai, "I think there is time before the boat sails, if you gentlemen would care to have a little drink with me, and perhaps our prisoner also?"

At this point something in his new escort's voice apparently struck Yudin as familiar, for he started perceptibly and stared at him incredulously. One of the French police noticed it.

"Your prisoner thinks it a good idea, anyway," he remarked. "See how his face lights up! I myself see no objection."

Yudin started again, but with pain this time, for Chadai had pinched him savagely in the wrist. They had their little drink and parted the best of friends at the gangway. There was a cabin reserved on board for prisoner and escort; they went down to it at once, Chadai locked the door and did not open it again till they reached Dover. The voyage passed un-eventfully, though there was nearly a regrettable incident when Yudin, robbed by excess of astonishment of the little tact he ever possessed, innocently asked Chadai if his face had always been like that.

At Dover things were even easier. Prisoner and escort went ashore among the first, and Chadai told a porter that a com-partment had been reserved for them on the train. It was a fairly safe guess, since a cabin had been reserved on the

steamer, and he was quite right, there was. Experienced offi-
cials noticed the two men walking curiously close together,
correctly deduced a handcuff link between them, and hustled
them on without further formalities into the train.

The boat train runs non-stop from Dover to Victoria, and
since Customs and Currency controls are passed at Dover
there are no impediments at Victoria to the exit of passengers
from the platform. One just gets out of the train and walks
away. Two men from a reserved compartment were naturally
among the crowd who did this; they had no luggage except
Chadai's small bag, which had provided them with a few
minor alterations in their appearance on the way up. Yudin
wore John's hat, for example; Chadai had a cap and a neat
black-and-red checked scarf. They walked unhurriedly along
the platform, down the stairs into the Underground and disappeared.

17   *THE KITCHEN SINK*

THE AFTERNOON PASSED peacefully in the police
station at Calais; Detective Sergeant Johns
slept the stertorous sleep of the drugged and no car arrived
to take him away. The sun sank in the west as usual, lamps
pricked the gathering shadows in the streets, Johns began
to turn in his sleep and the French police to be a little uneasy.

"Two hours," said the Superintendent thoughtfully. "That
fellow said he would be back in two hours, did he not? What
was his name, by the way?"

"Lacour," said the desk sergeant. "Lacour, from the Sûreté."

"That's right, Lacour. And the prisoner's name?"

"I don't know——"

"Then look up his papers," snapped the Superintendent.

"I haven't got them, sir. I understood him to say he had
given them to you."

"He told me he had given them to you."

The two men looked at each other for a moment, then the
desk sergeant's eyes fell and the Superintendent turned
away.

"We'll give him a little longer," he said. "Four hours' delay for a mechanical breakdown is not unprecedented." He went into his office and shut the door.

An hour later, at about the time when Chadai and Yudin were alighting at Victoria, Johns woke up. He had a blinding headache, a raging thirst and no idea how he came to be there, but he did know where he was: in a cell. A police cell, there is no mistaking them when once known. A printed notice pasted on the inside of the door further informed him that this was the police station of the town of Calais in the Department of Calais, France. Johns sank back upon the bed and held his head in both hands.

Presently he staggered to his feet and looked round for a bell; there did not seem to be one, so he knocked upon the door. A face came and looked at him through the grille.

"If you please," croaked Johns in his best French, "may I have a drink of water?"

The face disappeared and went to tell the Superintendent that the prisoner had recovered consciousness and wanted water.

"How does he seem?" asked the Superintendent. "At all violent?"

"No, sir, not at all. Quiet and miserable. One would say that his head ached."

"Give him some water. Two of you, not one alone. Be careful. We were warned that he might be violent."

Two policemen therefore entered Johns' cell and one gave him water in an enamelled iron mug while the other stood by in case of emergency. But Johns merely drank the water to the last drop, returned the mug with a word of thanks and added: "Would you be so kind as to tell me how I come to be here?"

"Brought in, like any other prisoner."

"What for?" asked poor Johns. "Drunk and disorderly?"

"You was certainly drunk," said one man and was about to continue when the other touched him on the arm and muttered something Johns could not catch. They both went out again, locking the door behind them.

Presently it opened again to admit the Superintendent and a sergeant. Johns, correctly guessing that this was a superior police officer, stood up and came to attention, a movement which made the Superintendent recoil slightly.

"Sit down," he said.

"Thank you, sir," said Johns, and collapsed rather than sat. The Superintendent asked him who he was; Johns told him and the Superintendent said he had been told that Johns would say that.

Johns blinked and felt in his pockets for papers which were not there. Of course, his pockets would be emptied when he was brought in.

"My warrant card and passport will be among the things I had on me, sir."

"You had nothing on you except your clothes."

"Then I've been robbed," said Johns, "and doped. Lord, how my head aches," he added involuntarily. "Beg pardon, sir."

"If you are an English police officer, what are you doing in Calais?"

Johns told him, adding details about the prisoner's name, time of arrival from Paris and so on. "I was met by a police officer named Lacour," he added. "We went to a café while we were waiting to see someone here—I suppose it would be you, sir?—to sign some papers. I don't remember anything after going into the café."

The Superintendent looked at him thoughtfully for a moment, turned on his heel and went out of the cell.

"There's something funny here," he said to his Inspector. "I may be mistaken, I often am"—a formula he always used when he was sure he wasn't—"that fellow might conceivably be a con man but I don't believe he's a thug. That's the English police manner; I worked with them during the war. I am going to ring up the Sûreté."

He did so, and the conversation was anything but satisfactory. No, the Sûreté were definitely not expecting a prisoner from England that day. Nor sending a car to Calais for a non-existent prisoner, naturally. Yes, they had sent a prisoner to Calais to be taken to England by a British police officer, what was all this about?

The Superintendent, beads of perspiration rising upon his brow, explained how matters stood with him. "Detective Inspector Lacour of the Sûreté, he showed his card and asked for a receipt which we gave him. Yes, Lacour."

The Sûreté said they would make enquiries and ring again, and the Superintendent utilized the time of waiting by ordering coffee to be taken in to the prisoner calling himself Johns.

The Sûreté rang up half an hour later and said that the prisoner from Paris had been duly handed over to a properly accredited British police officer at Calais and signed for, the receipt bore the signature of L. P. Johns, Det. Sergt. As for Inspector Lacour of the Sûreté, he was there in their office on duty at the moment and had not been to Calais for months. If there was anything more they could do to help they would be most happy, and in any case would be glad to receive fullest particulars about the officer calling himself Lacour, as it seemed at first sight to be a case of impersonation.

The Superintendent thanked them in a choking voice, rang off and stared at his desk for some minutes in silence, after which he sprang to his feet, rushed out to his car and drove himself down to the Maritime Station. The chief Customs official on duty at the port that day had gone home, but the Superintendent ran him to earth helping his children with their homework.

"You had a Scotland Yard man in on the boat from Dover today, did you?"

"The two-thirty boat, yes. He showed his card and I passed him through."

"Would you know him again?"

"Oh, I think so; it is not so long ago, it is——"

"Come with me."

He was whirled round to the police station and taken to the cell where Johns was drinking his third cup of coffee, eating sandwiches and convalescing fast. He sprang to attention when his visitors came in, and this time the Superintendent did not recoil.

"Is that the same man? Take your time and make certain."

"I don't need any time," said the Customs man with dignity; "that is undoubtedly the same man whom I passed through this afternoon. He looks as though he'd been in the wars; what have you thugs of police been doing to him?"

On the following day Hambledon and Logan came without incident to London and arrived a few minutes after seven-thirty in the evening. Logan said that he was going straight to the flat—"Perhaps when I am among my own things again I shall remember"—and told a porter to get him a taxi. Hambledon said that he would come along with him, "just to make sure you're all right," but in reality to see if Logan were recognized and accepted by the concierge, his man-servant Greene and anybody else who might happen to be about. A formality, of course, but this was the first opportunity Hambledon had had for checking Logan's identity.

The taxi pulled up at Caroline Mansions. Hambledon told the driver to wait and the concierge came running out to carry Logan's luggage.

"Good evening, Mr. Logan, sir. Very glad to see you

back. Greene told me this afternoon he'd had a wire saying you was returning. Very pleased about it, he was."

"That's that," said Tommy to himself, "this is Logan all right. Just wanted to make sure."

They went up in the lift, the concierge carrying the two suitcases, and Logan rang the bell at the flat door. There was no answer.

"Odd," said Logan thoughtfully, and rang again. "He's out, I suppose, but why, when he was expecting me? You did say he got the wire, didn't you?"

"Yessir."

"Oh well, something cropped up, I suppose. But why are we ringing at the door of my own flat?" Logan put his fingers in his waistcoat pocket, drew out a latchkey and opened the door. The sitting room was empty and there was no sound in the flat.

The concierge went just inside, put down the suitcases, was tipped and retired to the lift. Logan stood looking round him with a faintly puzzled frown, Hambledon hesitated in the doorway and there was a moment's awkward silence.

"Well, you'll be all right now, won't you?" said Tommy.

"What—oh yes, thanks, awfully, perfectly all right. I say, I don't know how to thank you for all——"

"Nonsense, it was nothing, happy to have been of service."

"We must meet again soon, will you dine with me one night? . . . Splendid, I'll ring you tomorrow or the day after, we'll fix up something."

"Delighted. I shall look forward——"

"I'll ring you——"

"Good night, then," said Tommy and turned to go.

"Good night," said Logan; as Hambledon went down in the lift he saw the flat door closing on a narrowing section of Logan looking eagerly about the room.

Hambledon went to Scotland Yard, where Bagshott was waiting for him; it was immediately obvious that something had upset the Superintendent.

"Hullo, Hambledon! Pleased to see you back."

"Thank you," said Tommy, "though I don't know that I've accomplished much. But what's biting you? There are careworn creases on that candid brow, there are——"

"That Russian we wanted, one of your three, he's got away from the French police."

"What? Oh, hell. How?"

"I have just been listening to a long story from the detective sergeant who was sent across to collect him," said Bagshott grimly. "He has only just left me; he came across on the same boat as you did."

"I thought he was coming yesterday. Where's he been in the meantime?"

"In the jug in Calais."

"In the——"

"And I had to send another of my men over to get him out."

"What——"

"You see, the French police had signed a receipt for him, so naturally they wouldn't let him go until someone else signed another receipt. So I had to send——"

Hambledon burst into a roar of laughter in which Bagshott unwillingly joined.

"Yes, I know it's funny, but what a set of damned fools it's made us look."

"Start at the beginning, Bagshott, for pity's sake."

"We sent Detective Sergeant Johns to Calais to pick up your prisoner and bring him over last night, but he didn't arrive. So we rang up Dover to see if they'd passed a prisoner and escort through the controls and they had. Besides, there was a reserved cabin on the steamer and a reserved compartment on the train, both of which had been used. My first thought was that the Russian had managed to overpower Johns and throw him out of the train, but it occurred to me to ask first for a description of the police officer seen at Dover. He turned out to have rabbit teeth and a retreating chin. Nothing like Johns. We tried to get the port authorities at Calais but the passenger offices were closed at that time. The next thing was an apologetic call from the Superintendent of the Calais police; they were desolated and so forth but there had been a mistake and apparently they had one of our detectives in custody." Bagshott gave Hambledon an outline of the French Superintendent's story. "So would we send someone over to identify and collect. We did so, and Johns' story was a very odd one." Bagshott repeated it and added: "Though, as you may imagine, I wasn't in a mood to find excuses for him, I really can't wonder that he was taken in. Even the French police, you see, accepted this fellow as genuine."

"Rabbit teeth, I suppose," said Hambledon. "Johns gave the same description as the Dover people, presumably."

"Certainly it's the same man. What's more, it's a member of the gang whom we haven't seen before, and he and the other Russian are now loose in this country."

"It sounds to me like the sort of scheme that leader of theirs with a beard would think up. Simple, direct and effective. I wish we knew their names; it's very irritating to think that Logan probably does, only he can't remember anything about them, or so he says."

"Don't you think this loss of memory is genuine, then, or do you?"

"It's a thing one just naturally tends to disbelieve, isn't it?" said Hambledon. "I am simply not convinced one way or the other. I've kept you informed as we went along, and nothing fresh happened on the journey to prove it one way or the other. Talking about Logan, Bagshott, it's an odd thing that his manservant wasn't there when he got home, although he was expected at that time. I didn't think anything of it at the moment, but since you tell me those two blighters are here in England—— Do you mind if I ring up Logan's flat?"

He did so and sat with the receiver at his ear listening to the bell ringing on and on, but no one answered it.

"I don't quite like this, Bagshott."

"I'll ring up that commissionaire fellow," said Bagshott, looking up the telephone number of Caroline Mansions. "They may have gone out, of course."

The commissionaire said that almost certainly Mr. Logan had not gone out again, he would have seen him. Would they like him to ring Mr. Logan on the house telephone?

"Please," said Bagshott, and there was a prolonged pause.

"If Logan's gone out," said Hambledon, "the manservant ought to be there by now."

"Are you there?" said the commissionaire. "I can't get no answer, sir, though I can 'ear the bell ringing. But we do 'ave complaints sometimes that the telephones 'aven't rung though I 'ave 'eard the bell. Would you like me, sir, just to run up to the door?"

"Please," said Bagshott again. "I'll hold the line."

There was another wait.

"Are you there, sir? I can't get no answer, though I rang the door bell several times."

"Thank you very much," said Bagshott. "Much obliged for all your trouble." He put down the receiver and looked at Hambledon.

"I like it even less," said Tommy.

Bagshott nodded, picked up one of his office telephones and said: "Car please, one constable and driver. I'm coming down at once."

At Caroline Mansions, Bagshott, Hambledon and the constable got out, and Bagshott asked the commissionaire if he had seen anything of Mr. Logan or his servant in the last few minutes.

"No, sir. Not a sign."

"You'd better come up, then. Bring your passkey."

Bagshot rang the bell at the flat door, gave just enough time for someone to answer it promptly, and told the commissionaire to open it. He did so, retiring round the doorpost as the door swung open, but there was no fusillade of shots or other violent reaction and Hambledon and Bagshott entered the room unopposed. It was all curiously quiet, and the commissionaire put his head into the doorway.

"Coh' scare the crows," he exclaimed, " 'istory repeatin' itself!"

The constable pushed him back, shut the door and stood outside it. Inside, the room was in considerable confusion and Hambledon and Bagshott were cutting the ropes from another naked man tied to a chair as the manservant had been on a previous occasion. Again there was surgical tape across his mouth, but this time the victim was Logan, not pallid with terror as Greene had been but scarlet in the face with fury. The moment he could speak he began to swear violently and most viciously, calling down upon the heads of his assailants punishments at once painful, humiliating and mutilating. Hambledon listened with great interest until Logan suddenly broke off and rushed out of the room by a door opposite.

"Greene! Greene—— Oh, just a minute. Keep still, man——"

The others followed to find Logan in the kitchen ransacking drawers for a sharp knife to cut bonds which attached Greene to the taps above the kitchen sink. He was sitting in the sink and his elbows were firmly tied behind him, one to each tap, but he was at least fully clothed. As soon as he was released and his mouth freed, for he also was taped into silence, he began to worry about Logan.

"Sir, sir, you'll catch your death with nothing on, your clothes, sir——"

"Oh yes," said Logan, becoming suddenly conscious, "my appearance is a little informal, you must excuse me. Very hot in here, isn't it?"

Hambledon looked behind him at the gas stove which had the largest ring turned fully on and flaring; across it was laid a short steel poker with an ornamental brass handle, and the steel part was white-hot.

"Should I, perhaps, turn this thing out?" he asked diffidently. Greene started forward, but Bagshott anticipated him and turned off the tap with a fork.

"Fingerprints," he explained. "Don't touch it."

"Our best sitting-room poker," moaned Greene, "completely spoilt."

In the meantime Logan had gone out of the room, presumably in search of clothes, and Hambledon wandered quietly after him. The short passage had five doors in it, for the kitchen, the bathroom and two bedrooms, with the door to the lounge across the end. Hambledon was in time to see Logan go in at the first door, switch on the light momentarily and come out again at once to try the room next door. This, evidently, was the right one, for he went inside, pushed the door to behind him and could be heard pulling drawers and opening cupboard doors.

"He didn't know his own bedroom," said Tommy to himself. "He couldn't have known I was going to see that, and he looked into Greene's room first. This is Greene's room," said Hambledon, glancing into it, for he was always thorough, "yes, it is. He didn't know his own bedroom, therefore this loss of memory business is perfectly genuine. I should have thought that habit would have taken him to the right door, but apparently not." He strolled on along the passage into the lounge, followed by Bagshott, to whom he repeated his observations in a low voice. "I lost my memory once for years, as you know," he added, "but I'd had a clout on the head and when I came round I was in a strange place, so there was nothing to recognize. This man's come home and still he doesn't know his own bedroom——"

18

THE PHOTOGRAPHER

GREENE CAME IN, uttered a cry of horror at the sight of the litter which strewed the lounge from end to end, and was about to start clearing it up when there came a shout from his master in the room next door.

"Greene! Greene! Where do I keep my socks?"

"Good gracious, sir," said Greene, scuttling out like a well-

trained rabbit, "where you always kept them, in the——"
A door shut.

"That remark could have been intentional," said Bagshott
doubtfully.

"But the door business wasn't," said Hambledon. "You
didn't see it. Well now, what is all this mess?"

The floor was strewn with what can only be described as
shredded garments; clothes which had been cut and torn
apart wherever a double thickness of material could possibly
have concealed anything, however small and flat. A bowl
of yellow chrysanthemums had been swept from the table
to make room for Logan's suitcase, which had had the linings torn out bodily and even the padded handles slit open.
There was a silver cigarette case on the floor among the debris;
Hambledon picked it up, opened it and showed the contents
to Bagshott. There were cigarettes in one side of it; upon the
other side, which was empty, an inscription in a fascimile of
handwriting.

" 'From Betty,' " said Bagshott, reading it. "Betty Alton, no
doubt."

"No doubt at all," agreed Hambledon, "but look at the
cigarettes. Russian, man, Russian."

They were, in fact, of the Russian type with a stiff tube
for a mouthpiece at one end.

"Plenty of people do smoke Russian cigarettes who have no
connection whatever with the country," said Bagshott.

"All your forefathers were called Thomas and your mother
came from Cincinnati," said Hambledon irritably. "Of course
it isn't conclusive, but taken with everything else, it's a
trifle odd. I'll have one, just in case your intelligentsia can
tell where they came from." He put one of the cigarettes in
his pocket and dropped the case on the table just as Logan
came in dressed in a lounge suit which fitted him like a
glove.

"That's better," he said cheerfully. "Greene, have I anything drinkable in this place? Sherry, yes, whiskey, very nice.
Port——"

"The port should remain a few days longer undisturbed, sir,
if I might suggest it. The earlier visit of that man to the flat
involved breaking a few we had left, and it was not until
early this week that I was able to obtain delivery of a 1927
Cockburn which is such as you would care to have in the house.
There is an Amoroso sherry, sir, and a Tio Pepe if these
gentlemen care for anything so dry?"

Bagshott, fidgeting slightly, said that he would have whisky, please, and might he speak for a moment to his constable. Logan said, "Please carry on," and Hambledon said that Tio Pepe was one of the few things which made life worth living. Bagshott opened the door and told the constable, still on duty outside, to go back in the car to Scotland Yard and send some fingerprint people. Greene served the drinks and the three men sat down.

"Now," said Bagshott, "what is all this?"

"I came in here," said Logan, "as Mr. Hambledon will tell you, finding it quiet here and Greene apparently out. I strolled round the room trying to make up my mind whether I remembered it or not and was actually standing on the rug there looking at that Wyllie over the mantelpiece when I heard a step behind me and there in the inner doorway was a nasty-looking fellow pointing a gun at me. Well, I knew it couldn't be Greene, so I ducked and threw that stool at him. I hit him in the face, too, but another taller fellow dodged out from behind him and they both came for me. Not to delay you with a long story, there was a bit of a brawl and they won. You saw the result. What is it, Greene?"

"If I might be permitted to clear up the room without disturbing you, sir?"

"You won't disturb me, and anyway I expect these gentlemen want your story; carry on. To finish my bit, they tied me up, having removed my apparel, and proceeded to tear it up in a rapid but painstaking manner, after which they disembowled my suitcases. Still unsatisfied, they came and asked me where they were. I don't mean that they asked me where they themselves were, they used those words: 'Where are they?' I said I didn't know what they were talking about and they didn't believe me."

"And did you really not know?" asked Hambledon.

"I have not the faintest idea," said Logan frankly. "I only wish I had. I explained that I'd lost my memory two days ago and they were most amused. They said they would help me to get it back, so they picked up the poker out of the fender and went out in the kitchen. Now you, Greene."

"About a quarter of an hour before you came home, sir, there come a ring at the door. When I answered it there was a gentleman—so to speak in the light of after events—outside who asked if Mr. Logan was back yet. I said Mr. Logan was not at home and he said he knew you was coming from Paris tonight. He said you had wired him from Paris to meet you here, and showed me the telegram; it was just like the one I got from you, sir. Well, ever since the time that other man got in and ransacked the place, I have been nervous about admitting strangers, but this man was quite different and looked quiet and respectable, quite the gentleman as you might say, and there was your telegram, sir, so I let him in."

"I never sent the telegram," said Logan.

"Of course not, sir, I know that now, but how was I to know it then? I held the door open and he came in; before I had time to shut it he grabs me by the throat and drags me away from the door while a second man comes in and shuts it after him. They pushes me out in the kitchen, lifts me into the—the sink," said Greene, his voice trembling with indignation, "and tied me up as you found me. Then we all sits quiet and waits till you come in, sir. I heard you speaking to someone and I was praying you'd brought some friends home, but no. The door shut and these two men waited till all was quiet and crept out on you."

"That's where my bit of the story comes in," said Logan.

"Of course," said Bagshott. "Please go on, Greene."

"Well, I could hear them talking to the master, sir, and there was tearing noises and that for a long time. After a bit they came back into the kitchen and the rabbity-faced one, the one who rang the bell, had the sitting-room poker in his hand. He laid it across the gas ring there and lit up, then he looks at me and says: 'Your master doesn't want to talk,' he says, 'but when I want people to talk, they do,' and he looks at the poker getting hot. Well, reely, I felt quite faint to think of it, when just at that minute the telephone rings."

"I nearly went mad," said Logan. "There it was ringing away within a couple of yards of me and I couldn't do a thing. I wonder who it was."

"Me," said Hambledon. "Please go on."

"It rang a long time," said Greene, "but when it stopped those two blackguards looked at each other and grinned. One of them wrapped one of my dusters round his hand and goes to pick up the poker, when the other telephone goes. The house telephone, sir," said Greene, addressing Hambledon, "it has a different ring. So they puts down the poker again and looks at each other and the tall one says something in some foreign tongue. Well, that telephone stops and it isn't but a minute before there's someone ringing and ringing at the front doorbell. Well, that seemed to scare them off; the rabbity one picks up his coat what he'd taken off and puts it on again and they both walks out of the kitchen."

"They came back in here," said Logan, "looking at the door as though they thought it would jump out and bite them.

Then they went close to the door and listened and I heard the whine of the lift going down. They didn't wait after that; the rabbity one gave me a dirty look and they opened the door quietly, crept out and shut it after them. Ten minutes or so later you gentlemen came in, and if I'm as pleased to see Saint Peter when my time comes I shall be surprised."

"Descriptions of them, please," said Bagshott. He was sure of what he would get and was not disappointed: the cold face and angular form of Yudin and the rabbit jaw and retreating chin of Johns' misleader.

"There's one thing, gentlemen," said Greene hesitantly.

"What is it?"

"The smaller gentleman, when he was talking English to Mr. Logan in the other room, his voice sounded like the man with a beard who came before. Of course it wasn't the same man, but——"

Hambledon banged the table and Bagshott saw it at the same moment. "Of course!" said Bagshott. "Beardie without his beard," said Hambledon. "No wonder he wore one, with a face like that."

"This would be one of the Russians you told me about, would it?" said Logan. "The ones I got mixed up with in London before I went to Paris? No wonder I lost my memory. Automatic defence mechanism, you know. I just couldn't bear the thought of them, so my inner commissionaire, if I may so fancifully put it, just threw them out and slammed the door."

"That's it," said Hambledon, and added to Bagshott, "I occupied some part of our journey today in bringing Mr. Logan up to date with his recent history."

"I was enthralled," said Logan. He paused, shuffled his feet, looked embarrassed and finally blurted out: "Miss Betty Alton. I say, do you happen to know—I mean, did you gather—in short, what sort of terms are we on, do you know?"

"Terms?" said Tommy blandly.

"Dammit, man, am I engaged to her? That's what I want to know."

"I haven't the slightest idea. She spoke of you with the greatest respect——"

"Not unmingled with awe," said Bagshott.

"She said you were very kind but she thought you'd gone away and didn't mean to come back——"

"Because you were disgusted with the company she kept. Her brother Stephen, she meant."

Logan looked blankly from one to the other and then turned

on his manservant, busy gathering up rags from the floor and stuffing them into suitcases.

"Greene! Any light on this subject?"

"Never heard you mention the lady's name, sir."

"Oh, lor'. And all I know about her is what you've told me and this," said Logan, opening the cigarette case to display the inscription.

"Umf," said Hambledon. "Very awkward. You have my sympathy. Do you——"

"Greene!" said Logan.

"Sir?"

"So far as you know, I'm not married, am I?"

"So far as I know, sir, no."

"Thank goodness. I beg your pardon, Hambledon. You were about to say something when that frightful thought came upon me."

"Nothing important, I was only going to ask if you liked Russian cigarettes."

"No, I don't. Beastly things. One puff too many and the last layer of burning tobacco comes down that tube and fills your mouth with glowing ashes."

"I merely noticed that those are Russians in that case."

"Yes, I know, that's why I haven't smoked them."

"Perhaps Miss Alton does," said Bagshott, getting to his feet. "I don't think we need worry you any more tonight. We know who we're looking for now; I mean, we know what the bearded man looks like now. You won't be going away again yet, I suppose?"

"I don't think so. I must go along to my office in the morning and see if I can recognize my typist. Have I a typist?"

"You have a very charming secretary," said Tommy Hambledon.

"Oh, have I? Perhaps she'll be able to wake my ideas up—she's not Miss Alton, is she?"

"Lord, no. Miss Davie, Miss Nancy Davie. By the way," added Hambledon, "have you a solicitor? Most people have."

"That's an idea," said Laurence Logan, inwardly quailing, for if Edward had told anyone about his twin brother, it would be his solicitor. "I'll look through my papers and find out."

Several days passed during which nothing in particular happened; possibly Chadai was nursing the black eye he acquired when Logan hurled a stool at him. Tommy Hambledon saw or telephoned to Logan frequently upon one excuse or another, also the police kept an unobtrusive eye upon him. Logan's principal worry appeared to be the business; he said that he seemed to remember less and less about more and more, that pepper was all very well in the pepper pot but out of place in one's hair, that for all the good he did by going to the office he might as well stop at home and that if the place were sensibly reorganized Miss Davie would be the head of the firm and he would be the office boy. "Then I could give notice and she could engage someone else," he said wistfully. "How I hate pepper, and the smell of cinnamon makes me sick."

"Put her in charge, then," said Hambledon. "Give her a a power of attorney or take her into partnership."

"It's an idea," said Logan. "I might even do it."

On the next day Bagshott rang up Hambledon and said: "Can you come over? We've got something at last."

Bagshott's detectives, plodding patiently on the trail of the men who tortured Alton and murdered Cutler the driver, had uncovered a friend of Alton's who was a photographer by trade. They interviewed him in the early stages of the enquiry and he admitted readily that he had known the late Stephen Alton. Yes, Alton came to see him occasionally, why not? The last time he came was some time before his death, two months before at least. The photographer was only sorry he could not help them more. No, Alton had not come upon any business, merely as a friend. The police gave it up for the time but they had their doubts about him; the photographer's shop never seemed to attract much custom and yet the man appeared to be making a comfortable living. Nothing rouses the curiosity of the police so quickly as a manner of living which is too good for the ostensible income, but they had nothing against him.

When the Alton case seemed to be bogging down into one of those unexplained mysteries the police dislike so much, Bagshott sent a couple of men to interview the photographer again, in the hope of picking up some fresh crumb of information, however small.

"When my men got there," said Bagshott, "the girl who minds the shop was out, but the door was unlocked, so they went in. There was nobody about and everything was quiet except for the sound of someone moving about; he knocked something over and it broke. The noises came from under the shop floor, so they went through to the back of the house, where they found the cellar stairs going down behind the larder. They went down them and opened the door at the bottom to find the cellar lit by a dim red light and Rodwell, that's the photographer, very busy. They switched on the main light and there in full view was a nice heap of one-pound treasury notes, still wet, on the bench before him. Quite good ones, too," said Bagshott kindly. "Rodwell had made a wonderful job of them. The cellar was very nicely fitted up as a laboratory and he had been experimenting in photographically printing in different colours as required."

"Glorious Technicolour, in fact," said Hambledon.

"Well, with a difference. Anyway, they brought him in. He's a cheerful little squirt and when he saw the game was well up and he was in for a long stretch in jail he asked if it would make his sentence any lighter if he told us about something else. We said that of course we could make no promises and it depended on the value of the infor——"

"The usual blah-blah," said Tommy.

"He said it was about the Alton case——"

"When you asked me first about Alton, I didn't tell you the whole truth," said Rodwell. "It might have meant me giving evidence in court and goodness knows what all, and I don't like publicity. But now I look like getting it anyhow, it don't matter so much. Alton came to see me about two months before he went west and I never saw him again, that's quite true, but he didn't come just as a friend, there was a little business he wanted me to do."

"What was that?" asked Detective Inspector Ennis as Rodwell paused.

"Did any of your bright boys know what that boxlike piece of furniture behind the door was for?"

Ennis looked at the detective sergeant who had arrested Rodwell.

"A sort of camera for taking microphotographs of documents, sir. They are quite common in banks these days for storing records and so forth in small space."

"Them little things," said Rodwell contemptuously.

"But this one was much larger," said the sergeant.

"Carry on, Rodwell," said Ennis.

"Alton had some sheets of drawings he wanted me to microphotograph, so I did them. Come out well, too. Seven sheets altogether in black ink on white paper. When I'd done them and processed them and they'd come out of the drier, Alton took and looked at them with a magnifying glass. 'These'll enlarge up to any size, will they?' he asks, and by way of answer I put them in the projector for him and threw them up on a screen. Lovely, they were; I was pleased. Plain as print, you could read every word; that is, anyone could who knew the language."

"What was the language?"

"German. Not that I know it, but I can recognize it. There was words like '*von der*' and '*ausgang*'—well you know they're German, if you get me——"

Ennis assured him that they did.

"Well, then Alton asked me if the negatives would fade or anything and when I told him they wouldn't he tore up the drawings—it did seem a shame, too—and put the bits in an old biscuit tin and set fire to them. When they were all burned to ashes he broke up the ashes into powder, emptied it down the drain, and pulled the plug. Then he paid me what I asked, took his film and went away, and I never saw him again from that day to this."

"How big was the strip of film?" asked Ennis.

"Sixteen millimeter—that's about half an inch wide—by two and a half or three inches long. That's all."

"So now we know what we're looking for," said Hambledon contentedly, "which is always such a help, and it's something the Russians don't know, they are still looking for the originals. You remember Betty Alton told us that when the Russians first searched her flat they talked about 'the papers' and 'a packet, not so small.' No wonder they couldn't find them."

"Stephen Alton could have hidden a tiny strip of film like that anywhere," said Bagshott. "Slipped it down between the floor boards in the flat——"

"No. The floor of that room was carpeted to the walls, if you remember, and he hadn't time to go into any other room when the Russians bounced in on them. Let us clear our minds," said Hambledon. "Alton had come to the flat straight from Heirons' office, where he had expected to meet the Russians and do a deal. He would have them on him to show them. He wouldn't show all the strip, of course; he probably had a bit of one cut off ready, or adhesive tape stuck on them or something. Anyway, he bolts to Betty's flat and there the film disappears. Alton hasn't got it or the Russians would have found it on him; Betty hasn't got it or she would have told us, I'm sure of that. It isn't in the flat, because Alton didn't have time to hide it. Therefore the Russians are right—Logan's got it. And he's lost his memory."

"You mean Alton slipped it to Logan somehow. But Betty

says they never met until Alton was being held up by a man with a gun."

"Women don't know everything, incredible as it may seem," said Tommy. "Logan's pretty deep in this somewhere; he and Alton may have been in this together."

"A thing so small," said Bagshott thoughtfully, "might have been planted on Logan without his knowing it."

"Slipped in his pocket when he wasn't looking? And the next time he took out his handkerchief it came too and fluttered unnoticed to the pavement among the feet of passers-by. Don't be so depressing, Bagshott."

"I never understood what that unfortunate devil, Muntz, was doing on Alton's cabin crusier. Who arranged the meeting in mid-channel, and why?"

"Because Muntz didn't trust anyone, poor wretch. We knew he had escaped from Russia with something very extra-special in the way of inventions and we were trying to help him. But whenever anyone approached him he simply fled. He found for himself a man in Rotterdam who was doing a bit of smuggling, and his organization chartered Alton's boat to meet the ship. Poor Muntz was convinced that any German scientist out of Russia who landed in England openly would just be thrown back without a hearing—the Fuchs case, you know—so he wanted to land illegally and make his contacts before any questions were asked. When I think that we had a destroyer hanging about off the Scheldt on purpose to bring him across, it's really rather sad."

"About this strip of film," said Bagshott. "The next move is to go through Logan's flat until we find it."

"If it's there."

"As you say. The sooner the better. I think I'd better have a search warrant just in case there's any——"

"Non-co-operation? Look, Bagshott, I'll go along there right away; he may have found it and not know what it is. Or he may be out. I'll ring you from there."

HAMBLEDON WENT at once to the flat in Caroline Mansions and found he had missed Logan; Greene said he had just gone out. Something anxious in the servant's manner drew Hambledon's attention and he asked if anything were the matter.

"Not to say 'the matter,' sir, only he's so changed. He doesn't seem like the same man. He was always so regular and methodical, sir, you could set the clock by him as the saying is. Breakfast eight-fifteen; as the quarter sounded from the church clock across there his bedroom door'd open and he'd walk into the lounge. Leave the house for business at a quarter to nine and back again in the evening at twenty-five past five. Unless he went out somewhere, which wasn't often, it was bed at a quarter to eleven. Whereas now it's up any time in the morning, maybe seven o'clock if it's fine, or maybe lying in bed till eleven and his breakfast on a tray——"

"He's had a severe mental upset, you must remember. It's a serious shock to lose one's memory. If he's not quite so easy as he was, you——"

"He's not so easy, that's true," said Greene, and added unexpectedly, "but he's a lot more 'uman."

"Oh. Well, that's something. Tell him I'm sorry to have missed him, will you? When do you expect——"

"You might find him, sir, if you was to give yourself the trouble to walk down to the White Swan. He's taken to going there most evenings for a game of snooker, and he'll drop into a tobacconist's on the way and have a yarn with the man who keeps it; he's travelled a lot, they tell me. Been in some queer sort of legion of the French Army when he was young, though he's as English as you or me."

Hambledon's mind went back to the moment when he and Bagshott had released Logan from his bonds on the evening he returned from Paris. He had cursed fluently in his anger, which was natural; what was more surprising was that he had used expressions which are more common in the French Foreign Legion than in England. An allusion to camels as near relations of the accursed is not an English habit.

"No doubt Mr. Logan has travelled extensively himself. It would amuse him to find someone who knew the same places that he knew."

"Indeed, no, sir. He has told me several times that the only disadvantage of being a London businessman is that one has so little opportunity for travel. Since I've been with him, sir, he's never had more than a few days in Paris, and not even that, of course, during the war."

"Of course not." Hambledon received directions for finding the White Swan and walked thoughtfully away. Any man who, like the tobacconist, had once served in the French Foreign Legion might well have stories to tell which were worth hearing, and perhaps Logan satisfied at second hand an inborn but abortive wanderlust. As for exotic swearwords, some men collected them, like postage stamps, for their aura of foreign travel.

Hambledon reached the tobacconist's on the corner and glanced in as he passed the door; the shop was empty except for the ex-legionnaire behind the counter, but there was a second door leading into the side street. Hambledon turned the corner to see Logan barely twenty yards ahead and lengthened his stride to overtake him.

But it was immediately obvious that Logan was not quietly strolling along for an habitual hour in a favourite hostelry; he was alertly interested in something or someone ahead of him, and at the same moment when Hambledon quickened his pace, Logan did the same. He also was following someone, and now he was almost running.

Hambledon looked beyond Logan at a tall man who was walking away from them both along the pavement; his back looked familiar, and suddenly he turned his head; it was the tall Russian who was arrested in Paris and rescued at Calais. An expression of horror came over the Russian's face and he broke in a run; so did Logan. Yudin, however, had long legs and twenty yards' start; he tore along the road towards a small green van which was standing at the pavement, scrambled into the driver's seat and started the engine. The van began to move just before Logan reached it, but he put on a spurt, swung himself onto the back of the van and scrambled in; as he did so the doors, which had been open, swung together and were closed from the inside.

"I must see the end of this," said Hambledon, and by one of those miracles which occasionally happen even in London an empty taxi came towards him to be hastily signalled, turned, and ordered to "follow that green van."

There was no difficulty about this; the van was not travelling particularly fast and was scrupulously correct in its behaviour at crossroads and traffic lights. Hambledon leaned forward and spoke to his driver.

"You passed that van just before you picked me up, do you remember?"

"Yessir. Driver ran up in an 'urry an' 'opped in quick, I saw him."

"That's right. Was there anyone else in front, in the seat beside the driver?"

"No, sir. Only the one man on that van."

"Thank you," said Hambledon, and leaned back reassured. Logan had only one Russian to deal with, and it was possible if not probable that the Russian did not know he had a passenger. There would be a partition behind the driver, so that he could not see into the van, but the abrupt arrival of fourteen stone or so should have been more than noticeable. However, the van went steadily on and so did the taxi. They threaded their way through the maze of squares between Marylebone Road and Oxford Street and then turned east. New Oxford Street, High Holborn, Newgate Street, Cheapside, Poultry, with the taxi practically hanging onto the tail of the van, till, at the point where Old Jewry runs into Poultry, they had their first piece of bad luck. A car driven by a thruster came out of Old Jewry across their bows and stopped because there was no gap at the moment in the stream of traffic going west; by the time he had moved on and released them the green van was well ahead; in the swirl of traffic where six main roads meet at the Mansion House they lost sight of the van altogether.

"Any idea where he went?" asked Tommy, anxiously peering over the driver's head at the maze of car lights, street lights, traffic lights and omnibuses which all appeared to be dancing a complicated quadrille, for by this time night had quite fallen.

"I did think as I saw 'im going round to King William Street, sir, but I can't be sure."

"Leading to London Bridge," said Tommy, remembering the Polish ship on which Stephen Alton had died. That was tied up to a wharf opposite the Tower of London, and foreigners tended to return to a district they knew. "Yes, try that."

The taxi cleared the traffic roundabout and shot down King William Street; on the wide roadway of London Bridge, under the tall lamp standards, a small green van was steadily forging ahead.

"That looks like 'im, mister."

"Tallyho!" answered Hambledon, much to his own surprise, for he was never a hunting man.

"Yoicks!" said the taxi driver appropriately. "Whatever that means," he added as the river Thames passed majestically beneath them.

"He may turn here," said Hambledon as they neared the South Bank. "Don't overshoot——"

"He's turned left," said the driver, and also swung into Tooley Street. "Slowing down, too."

"Keep back, don't overtake."

"Left again, here we go round the mulberry bush."

The green van turned down Morgan's Lane—was it named after a pirate?—and right into Pickle Herring Street, which runs along beside the river.

"He may stop along here," said Hambledon. "If he does, turn up the next road to the right and stop round the corner."

The green van did stop, and rather abruptly, at big wooden doors in a high wooden fence. Yudin leapt out and ran towards the doors as the taxi swept past and round the corner out of sight in Potter's Fields. Hambledon thrust a pound note into the driver's hand and ran back round the corner; already the green van had disappeared, and even as he looked first one great door swung shut and then its fellow, a moment's pause while presumably a key was turned, then a grating thud as of an iron bar dropped into place.

Hambledon put his hands in his pockets and sauntered along the road; on his left were small houses and shops closed for the night, on the opposite side was a continuous line of strong wooden fencing six or seven feet high, some with barbed wire along the top and some without; inside these fences were the wharves upon the river. The road was practically deserted at that time of night and obscurely lit with infrequent street lamps, though Hambledon could see above the fence the lean necks and bulbous heads of tall floodlights for use when the wharves were busy at night; it would be bright enough down here then. He crossed the road to the gates by which Yudin had entered; there was a white square upon one of them which proved to be a card nailed on. "This Wharf To Let," he read, "Apply Messrs. ——" So-and-so, at an address which conveyed nothing to Hambledon.

"So the Russians are trespassing, as one might have known they would, and these wharves don't stay unlet for long, since a printed card is used instead of a painted board." He reached up—there was no barbed wire here—got his fingers over the top and tried to heave himself over, but the vertical planks gave no foothold and were slippery with damp and dirt. Hambledon managed to get his eyes above the top for long enough to see the green van inside, but he could not quite pull himself up. He dropped to the ground again and looked about him.

A woman came round a corner along the street and turned into a house; the slam of the door was plainly audible. "If only I'd kept the taxi," thought Hambledon, and with the thought he heard it drive off. Two girls came out of a house almost opposite; when they saw Tommy standing in the shadow of the fence they giggled, nudged each other, and ran away. It was very quiet there, only the distant roar of traffic which never ceases in London but only rises and falls with the passing hours, and the long deep note of a ship's siren on the river answered by the higher lighter "toot-toot" of some smaller craft. From one of the upper windows opposite there floated down the sound of a baby crying; as though it were in some way a signal, three cats ran out in the road and started to fight.

"This won't do," said Hambledon. "I didn't come all this way to referee cat fights. If there were a telephone box handy I'd ring up Bagshott."

But there was no telephone box within sight and he could not remember having passed one recently. Still, there must be one not far off, certainly in Tooley Street. He made up his mind and began to walk back quickly by the way they had come. There was something coming towards him from Morgan's Lane, not a vehicle nor merely a pedestrian; Tommy saw it as it passed under a distant light—it was a thing he had not seen for a very long time, a street organ. Hambledon stood where he was and waited for the oncomer, for an idea had come to him. When the man drew level Tommy stopped him and said: "Would you like to earn a quid?"

"Whad-jer think, mister? Show it me."

Hambledon did so.

"Whad-jer want me to do for that?"

"Lend me your barrel organ a minute."

"Mister, for a quid you can 'ave the"—something—"thing all night."

"I want to stand on it," explained Hambledon, and gave him the note.

The man peered at him. "That's O.K. We all 'ave our 'obbies, and if yours is standin' on barrel organs I dessay it's 'ealthy. Mister, for a quid you can jump on it; I've 'ad enough for one day."

"Bring it along here," said Hambledon, and led the way to the door labelled "This Wharf To Let."

The man followed, pushing the organ and talking all the time. "Mister, if anyone tells you as there's money in this game you refer 'em to me. I 'ired the —— thing this mornin' from an I-talian in Clerkenwell for ten bob a day and what 'ave I took? Blinking seventeen an, two-pence 'a-penny that's what. I arst yer, can a man live on seven an' twopence 'a-penny a day? Push the thing till I ache, pull the thing till me knees give out, stop and turn the 'andle and what do I get? Gerraway, that's what. 'Ere's a penny to move on, get crackin'. Got no ear for music, folks 'aven't, these—— Want it up against the fence, do yer?"

The monologue ceased suddenly as the man watched subsequent proceedings with astonished eyes and his mouth hanging open. When there was no more to see he took up the handles once more and trundled his organ briskly along the road and round several corners until he came to a public house where he was known. He left the organ beside the pavement, went inside and stood himself several drinks in quick succession.

"Flush of money tonight, aren't you?" said the bartender.

"Ah. Gen'leman gimme a quid to stand on me organ."

"To *stand* on your *organ?*"

"Thas right. You wanner quid? 'e says. I wanner stan' on your barrel organ. Mister, I says——"

"Don't believe it," said another customer.

"Gimme another," said the organ-grinder. "Gimme two. Thish gen'leman 'ere don't believe it. For why? 'Cause 'e couldn't do it, thass why."

"Course I could, but who'd want to do such——"

"You gimme a quid," said the organ-grinder, "an' you can stand on me organ yourself. *Any* gen'leman as gives me a quid can stand on me organ——"

"You're sozzled," said the customer, and the bartender nodded. The organ-grinder drank up the second of his latest purchases and asked for another.

"Not tonight," said the bartender. "You push off 'ome, you and your organ."

"I'll 'ave another. I'm goin' t' 'ave another. I can pay for it, can't I? I've got plenny er money——"

He was propelled through the doors, which closed behind him, and appeared unkindly to recede as he staggered backwards across the pavement and came to rest against his barrel organ, to which he clung. A policeman strolled up from nowhere in particular and said: "Best be getting along home, hadn't you?"

The organ-grinder looked up, focused his eyes upon the policeman and broke into a grin.

"You gimme a quid and you can stand on me organ."

"That'll do," said the constable, assuming it to be mere impertinence. "Move on, now."

"Better men than you glad to stand on me organ."

This might be impertinence but it was a little unusual. "What is all this?" and the organ-grinder told him.

"Stood on your organ and then went over a fence? Where was this? In Pickle Herring Street; how long ago?"

" 'Bout an hour. Hour an' a 'alf, maybe."

"Come and show me," said the constable, and led the way with the barrel organ yawing and pitching behind him. Before they reached "This Wharf To Let" he had to lend a hand with the pushing, but the dignity of London policemen is, as everyone knows, innate and unaffected by circumstance.

"You're certain this is the place?"

His companion pointed a shaking finger at the notice.

"Yes, I see." The constable thought for a moment and then drew himself up by his hands to look over the fence. There was a small van on the far side by the edge of the wharf; it had no business to be on a vacant wharf unless, of course, the caretaker had given permission. He knew who the caretaker was and where he lived in a street near by. The constable let himself down again and addressed his companion, who was languidly draped against his organ.

"You stay here, see? I'll be back in a minute."

When the constable returned with the caretaker and the key, they had first to remove the organ-grinder, who was sitting on the ground with his back against the door, fast asleep. Even then the organ proved useful, since the caretaker had to climb the gate to undo the iron bar which Yudin had dropped into place. Constable and caretaker went in, shutting the door behind them.

"That van's got no business to be 'ere," said the caretaker. "I didn't give no permission for no one to put no van in 'ere."

They examined it; it offered no evidence except the name and address of the owner; Chadai had hired it quite normally for the evening on the pretext of wanting to move a few chairs. They left it and walked about the wharf which, apart from the intruded van, was as bare and empty as a hungry dog's dinner plate five minutes later.

"There's no one here," said the constable, throwing the long ray of his torch about him.

"There's something out there, look," he added, pointing at a dim object in the middle of the river. "Looks like a launch of some sort without lights."

"You're right. Not under way, neither, just drifting. Tide's falling; she may go miles, but they'll be run down as sure as——" He paused, curved his hands about his mouth and bellowed: "Launch there, ahoy!"

"Maybe there's nobody aboard," said the constable, "just come adrift on her own."

"There is someone aboard, can't you 'ear? Tryin' to start the engine. They've got 'er, too."

The launch engine broke into an uneven sputter and steadied; a dim light appeared and a figure could be seen at the wheel. The boat got under way and moved slowly upstream on the further side. It passed the wharf, turned in a wide sweep under Tower Bridge, and was lost to sight.

"If that is them what was ere," said the caretaker gloomily, "they've been and gone."

The policeman agreed, but at that moment they heard the engine stop once more. The launch came into view again, nearer the wharf this time; as it drifted past there could be heard the sound of men's voices raised in anger.

"Spot of bovver," said the caretaker. "Now, if the River Police was ever where they're wanted——"

The launch lost way, stopped, and began very slowly to swing round in the current.

"Someone," said the caretaker, "ought to go out an' give those pore beggars a tow 'fore some'un comes along an' cuts 'em—— Gorramighty!'

The boat they were watching burst suddenly into a bright sheet of flame.

NEXT OF KIN

LAURENCE LOGAN came out of the tobacconist's side door and turned towards the White Swan, thinking that he had had nearly enough of London and wanted to go back to Paris. So long as he kept up this pose of having lost his memory, he could not even have Papert in London, for if he really had he would not remember the Frenchman. Something would have to be done to speed up this business; no one had even seen the Russians since they had bolted out of his flat the night he returned from Paris. He looked up, and there, twenty paces ahead and walking away from him, was Yudin. That is, it looked like Yudin's back, his carriage and his walk; of course it might be someone like——

The man ahead suddenly looked round, and Logan saw his face. It was Yudin. A look of terror passed over the Russian's face and he began to run away; Logan, forgetting all Hambledon's warnings, immediately gave chase. The green van moved off, but he made a spring, pulled himself up and fell headfirst into the van. Even as he did so Chadai, who was crouched waiting for him, hit him on the back of the neck with a cosh and Logan subsided into unconsciousness.

The doors swung together at the back; Chadai caught them and fastened them shut. They had one small oval window in each door through which Chadai watched with interest Hambledon stopping a taxi and setting off in pursuit. Chadai recognized him at once; this was the Englishman who had been with Logan in Paris, who was friendly with the French police and who knew so much too much about three Russians. Well, if he wished to gate-crash this party they would try to give him an adequate welcome.

Accordingly, when the big doors of "This Wharf To Let" closed behind the green van and Yudin came to help lift out the prisoner, Chadai sent him to sit in the driver's seat out of sight and himself waited with the van doors open a little so that he could hear as well as see what should come. He heard footsteps outside, quiet but plainly audible, followed by a scrabbling sound as a head appeared above the fence, outlined against the lighter street. There was an audible grunt and the head disappeared; Chadai waited but there came no more scrabbling noises. Evidently the Englishman had decided that he could not climb the fence and was considering what to do next. At last there came the sound for which Chadai waited—quick footsteps walking away.

"Yudin!"

Yudin came running round the van.

"That was the Englishman I told you about. He followed us in a taxi. He looked over the fence."

"Was he alone?"

"I think so. He has gone away now but he— Listen!"

The rumble of a vehicle being wheeled towards them; it stopped and there was the sound of voices, though the words were inaudible. The trundling noise started again and came nearer, accompanied by a grumbling monologue in a man's voice; the words were indistinguishable until the speaker reached the gate and they heard the last sentence. "Want it up against the fence?"

Chadai pushed Yudin round the corner of the van out of sight and himself ran on noiseless feet to stand close to the fence in deep shadow with his face down and his hands concealed. Tommy Hambledon, astride the fence, looked down and saw nothing; he swung the other leg over and dropped down. In the moment of instability as his feet touched the ground Chadai, within a yard of him, uncoiled like a spring and struck him on the back of the neck with the cosh. Hambledon slid to the ground in a heap; Yudin put his head round the van to see what was happening and Chadai held up his hand for silence. They remained motionless, like a pose in *tableaux vivants*, until the organ-grinder outside the fence left off staring, took up the handles of his organ and wheeled it briskly away.

"There you are,'" said Chadai. "Both of them. Simple."

They bundled the inert Hambledon into the van beside the equally uninterested Logan and drove to the edge of the wharf. There was a sort of shallow slot cut down the face of the wharf in one place, just deep enough to shelter a vertical iron ladder from being crushed or swept away by a ship coming alongside. The van was backed to the head of this ladder; at the foot of it there was a fairly large petrol-driven launch of the type which has one roomy cabin amidships, the engine and wheel in a small cockpit aft and petrol tanks in the bows with filler caps projecting through the deck. The launch was tied up fore and aft and there was a couple of feet of oily river water between it and the foot of the ladder; she was pulling away with the falling tide.

"Go down and tighten those ropes, Yudin. Pull the boat as close in as you can, then we can lower them straight down."

Yudin went. He knew nothing whatever about boats and did not want to, and he was terrified of falling into the water. However, he managed this simple operation fairly well except that when he twisted the rope round the cleats he added a knot which no seaman would have approved.

"There's a length of rope in the cockpit," said Chadai's voice from above. "Bring it up."

They lowered their prisoners down, one at a time, dragged them into the cabin and laid them on the floor. Yudin lit a hurricane lamp which hung from a hook in the cabin roof and asked if he should light "the other lamps outside, the red and green ones."

"No, of course not. They are only used when the boat is moving. We are staying tied up here. I told you that before."

"Yes, but I did not know we did not want lights."

Logan, having been the first to suffer, was the first to recover. He groaned, rolled over, shielded his eyes from the light, sat up unsteadily and looked round him. He saw a bare cabin, for the furnishings had been stripped for replacement, two portholes with short stout planks nailed across them, and the smiling faces of Chadai and Yudin, who seemed pleased with themselves. There was also a large twelve-volt battery in one corner.

"Good evening," said Chadai. "I thought we could talk here undisturbed, which would be pleasant. Your watchdog here refused to be left behind, so we brought him along too."

Logan looked again and saw that he had a companion in misery; Hambledon was lying behind him on the floor.

"He still sleeps," said Chadai. "It does not matter, I think we need not disturb him. When we have done with you, you and he can share the battery, one foot of each. I should think it would do for both."

"I have not the faintest idea," said Logan slowly, "what you are talking about."

"That battery on the floor there which normally actuates the starter of the engine on this boat. It also provides current for the lights in here; I must ask your indulgence for the paraffin lamp. The battery is large and heavy; we disconnected it, all ready to tie to your feet when you go overboard at the end of this interview. We think that will keep you down; we made a little mistake in the case of Alton. I understand that his carcass was recovered. Your disappearance will be a more complete mystery. Your friend can accompany you. Stand up!"

Logan rose slowly to his feet.

"You contemptible thugs," he said.

"You will now tell us where you have put the papers."

"What papers?"

"You know. Those your friend Stephen Alton stole."

"I don't know anything about them, and if I did you should fry in Hell before I told you."

"You may do a little frying before you reach Hell. Lighted matches applied to the toes have been known to make strong silent men positively loquacious."

"Listen," said Logan. "I have never seen your papers, I know nothing about them and I don't know where they are."

"You are lying. These are the papers which Stephen Alton stole from the German, Muntz. Alton had them on him when he went to your woman's flat; afterwards they were out on him nor in the flat. You took them to Paris with you; since they were neither in your luggage nor on you when you came back from Paris, it follows you have given them to someone or hidden them somewhere. You are now going to tell me where they are."

"Once more I tell you——"

"Once more I tell you not to lie. We know better; you have been closely followed ever since you left London."

"You blasted fools," began Logan, losing his temper, "you woodenheaded idiots, you are all wrong. You always were and you always will be, you—you——" Words failed him in English and he slipped into French; when that proved inadequate he went into Legion French, which is a sort of mixed grill of six or seven European languages with a few Asiatic words thrown in. He swore at the Russians in every tongue he knew; Yudin's face remained completely impassive but Chadai's showed surprise and even unwilling admiration.

"I must congratulate you," he said when Logan at last ran out of breath and epithets. "For a quiet London businessman you are a wonderful linguist. Even Legion French; one would swear you had served in it."

"I have, you stupid oaf," roared Logan. "I've lived abroad for years. You've slipped up, you fool. First you let Muntz get away, then you failed to get the papers from Alton, and finally you chase the wrong man. It was my twin brother your tame thug there murdered on the Dunkirk train ferry, you pig-faced baboon. I don't know if he ever had the papers or what he did with them. I hope he threw them into the Channel, going across. Go home and tell your bosses how clever you've been and I hope they boil you in oil!"

Chadai believed him, for the Russian was no fool and the accents of truth are unmistakable. Besides, here was the explanation of how Logan had apparently escaped on the train when Yudin, a man of experience in such matters, had been certain that he was dead. There was a brief silence during which the boat, which had been imperceptibly heeling over, dropped suddenly and lurched again, and there came from above them the squeaky groan of ropes slipping under strain. Chadai realized what was happening and ordered Yudin to go and slack off the mooring ropes. "The tide is falling," he said, "we shall be hanging on the ropes before long."

Logan burst into a roar of laughter. "You will, indeed you will! This is a dress rehearsal for the great day, isn't it?"

"What great day?" said Chadai, who was not really listening to him.

"When they hang you both at Pentonville."

The launch seemed to slip down at the bows and settle more comfortably upon the water; Yudin, unable to loosen granny knots under strain, had simply cut the rope with his knife. Footsteps and scrambling noises overhead told those in the cabin that he was now going aft to deal with the rope at the stern, and Chadai resumed the discussion.

"It would appear," he admitted, "that if what you say is true, and I am inclined to believe it, it is just possible that you really don't know where the papers are. Not that that will make much difference to you, because you must realize that you have got to die anyway, you know too much. You will, however, die more painlessly. There is your sleeping watchdog, too; it's hardly worth while waking him before he enters upon a longer and sounder sleep——"

There was a half-heard exclamation from Yudin outside; the launch dropped suddenly and at once lurched forward. Chadai began: "What the——" and Yudin burst in at the door with a gush of unmistakably agitated Russian.

Chadai addressed Logan formally. "You will please excuse me a moment; my brilliant deck hand has set us adrift. It is only to start up the motor and bring her round to the wharf again." He took down the hurricane lamp. "Forgive a temporary darkness; he has also dropped our electric torch overboard."

"What a pity you disconnected the battery," said Logan as the cabin door slammed; "you have to crank her and I hope she breaks your arm."

It was totally dark in the saloon; Logan heard and felt Hambledon sit up, and spoke to him at once.

"So you've wakened up, though I don't know that you've gained much by it."

"I've been lying doggo ever since they brought us in here. Logan, there's a copper pipe runs along the side here, low down near the floor. It may be the petrol pipe—this way. Get down and crawl towards me; I don't want you stamping on my fingers, I shall want them in a minute. Yes, here it is. Come over here; got it? That's right. Now try to get your fingers behind it and pull. There's a union about halfway; if we can break it——"

From outside came a mechanical "clankety-clock" as Yudin, urged on by Chadai, wound the starting handle. The motor coughed, hesitated, fired twice and stopped again while Chadai, like the Red Queen, cried: "Faster! Faster!"

"This is sort of panelling, isn't it? Try kicking it in, so we can get our fingers behind the pipe——"

The inner skin of the cabin wall did not stand up to kicks, but it was difficult in the dark to break it back in the right place near the pipe.

"I've done it," said Tommy, and tugged at the pipe. Several of the holding clips gave way and at the same moment the engine burst into life, was throttled down and began to run sweetly.

"Quick," gasped Hambledon. "Come here. Got it? Now, heave!"

Three-eighths-inch copper pipe is quite strong but it will not stand up to being wrenched by two strong men with their lives at stake. It came away from the wall, resisted two more attempts and then broke at the union so suddenly that Hambledon and Logan rolled over backwards. There was a splashing sound; an intensely cold liquid ran over their hands and the saloon filled with the smell of petrol.

"Done it!" said Tommy. "That'll stop his engine."

It did; the engine consumed the contents of the carburetor and came to a stop. Angry voices floated in from the cockpit and Yudin resumed operations with the starting handle.

"Now what?" said Logan.

"I am hoping Chadai will think that perhaps there's a tap

in this length of pipe and that we have simply turned it off. Then perhaps he will come in to see, and we will assault him. He'll have to leave Yudin up topside in case anything comes along."

"And if he doesn't come down?"

"Better still, for sooner or later somebody will come alongside and rescue us, and I hope it's the River Police. This is, after all, the Pool of London, and they can't have things drifting about— Listen. They've stopped cranking. To the door, Logan! Here it is; yes, it is locked. There's a Yale sort of lock as well as a— Logan, he'll have the hurricane lamp in one hand and the automatic in the other and there's that high step to negotiate. The moment he puts one foot over," said Tommy, talking faster and faster, "grab him and pull him forward. Sling him forward and jump for the door—are you ready—here he——"

The door clicked, the door opened outwards and Chadai's hand appeared holding the hurricane lamp; just above it was his other hand, holding the automatic. He shouldered the door wider open; Hambledon and Logan, flat against the wall on either side of the door, were not to be seen until he put his head inside, and he could not do that, encumbered as he was and the boat rocking, until he had put at least one foot over the high threshold. He did so and instantly four strong hands seized him and jerked him violently forwards; his other foot caught on the high step and he fell heavily onto his face. Even as Logan and Hambledon leapt for the door the hurricane lamp crashed to the floor, flame leapt from the top of the glass and in an instant the saloon was one flare of fire.

They stumbled out, singed and dazzled; the door swung and slammed as from inside there came the single heart-shaking yell of one who dies in a petrol fire and after that, silence.

Hambledon looked at the lock but it was fastened, and Chadai, inside, had the key——

They rushed up the few steps to the cockpit and already the flames were breaking through the roof. Yudin, demented with terror, was crouched on the coaming gibbering. He was terrified of the river, but behind him there was fire.

"Come on," said Logan, and pushed him.

"No, no, no!"

"Oh, let him burn," said Hambledon callously. "Come on, we must swim for it." He tore off his shoes and coat.

"No," said Logan obstinately. "He murdered my brother and he's going to hang."

"What a moment to argue ethics," said Tommy. "Man, those tanks for'ard will explode in a minute. Chuck him overboard."

There were three almost simultaneous splashes. Yudin kicked and struggled, so Logan, who knew something about lifesaving, knocked him out and they towed him away between them, swimming hard to get away from the blazing launch. A triangle of lights bore down upon them; a searchlight picked them out and the River Police dragged them out of the water. Yudin was laid gently down.

"Be careful of him," said Logan. "I suggest handcuffs."

"We'll look after that. Anybody on board that launch?"

"Don't get too near," said Hambledon. "The tanks——"

There was a deep explosion, and with it there rose from the launch a great bubble of fire which burst, hurling in all directions gouts of burning petrol which fell upon the river and floated, little blazing islands upon the dark water. Round the launch there spread a wide pool of leaping flame in the middle of which the boat could clearly be seen, sinking by the head. Her stern came up, the screw came out of the water, she slid forward and went down like a stone.

"Exit the First Murderer," said Logan contentedly.

"The first? Then where's the second?"

"Here," said Logan, pushing with his foot the dripping form of Yudin. "He'll be all right; we only knocked him out because he struggled."

"We'll get you gentlemen ashore," said the River Police, for Hambledon had given his name. "Dry clothes first, questions afterwards."

Hambledon rang up Scotland Yard while he and Logan, wrapped in blankets, were awaiting the arrival of dry clothes from their respective homes.

"You know," said Logan when the telephoning was done, "you lay so still I thought they'd killed you."

"I thought it best," said Tommy. "I never believe in inviting trouble, but by heck I nearly gave myself away when you brought out that bit about your twin brother. So that's why you didn't know which was your own bedroom."

"I beg your pardon?"

"At your flat. I didn't quite believe in your loss of memory till I saw you go into Greene's room in mistake for yours."

"That convinced you? How odd, I don't even remember doing so."

"But why this memory business at all? I can understand your passing as your brother to the Russians, but——"

"On account of my father's will," said Logan, and explained that he was merely a remittance man whose income would stop for good if he returned to England. "I meant to clear up this affair without being too much in the limelight and then retire to France and die at a more convenient moment—as Edward, that is. As Laurence, I should then be all right so long as no one knew I'd been in England. I hadn't worked out the details, but that's the general idea. I had to lose my memory to cover the fact that I didn't know anybody and hadn't the foggiest ideas about the business. If only you'd been really unconscious——"

"I do apologize, but how was I to know? However, the really important thing is still as dark as ever. Did you find among your brother's things a strip of sixteen-millimeter film about three inches long or a little less?"

"No. No, I don't remember noticing anything like that. Why?"

"Because the wretched Stephen Alton, who caused all this trouble in the first place, had those plans, designs or what-have-you microphotographed and destroyed the original papers."

"And the Russians didn't know that!"

"No. They were looking for something much bigger, so it's just possible they overlooked it."

"Yes," said Logan, "I suppose so. Well, I've got all my brother's things at the flat; you'd better come and hunt for it yourself, if you will."

Their clothes arrived almost simultaneously with Superintendent Bagshott, who was given a brief résumé of the whole story during dressing operations. He listened in silence until Logan had finished.

"I was reading the other day," said Bagshott, "an article in some paper about certain savage tribes who always destroy twins as soon as they're born. I think there is something to be said for the custom. I suppose you realize that you've probably rendered yourself liable for heaven knows what penalties for impersonation?"

"I haven't signed any cheques," said Logan quickly.

"Oh. Well, I'm glad you had that much sense."

Logan looked pained, Tommy laughed, and they drove together to the Caroline Mansions flat in a rather chilly silence. Here, as Logan let them in with his latchkey, Bag-shott said to himself that this was the first time he had entered that flat to find everything perfectly normal. Greene came in at the further door and gave Logan a letter which had come by post, and it was addressed to Edward J. Logan Esq.:

Dear Logan,

I gather you are now returned from Paris; Cogsworth told me he saw you yesterday. As I am sure you do not wish to remain intestate any longer than is unavoidable, would you care to make an appointment with me about drafting a new will?

Yours sincerely,
H. C. R. Fenchurch

Laurence Logan drew a long breath of profound relief, folded up the letter and put it back in his pocket. So there had been no need for his loss of memory and careful impersonation. Never mind, it had been rather fun. He broke suddenly into a wide and cheerful smile, for was he not Edward's next of kin?

"Well, now," he said, "shall we get on with it?"

With Greene helping, they sorted out every single thing which Edward Logan had taken with him and Laurence Logan had brought back; his toilet things, the Penguin book he had been reading in the train, his wallet and diary and, once more, his unfortunate ill-used suitcases. They sent Greene to bed and searched minutely until, at twenty minutes to three in the morning, Hambledon sat down heavily in a chair and said: "Well, that's that."

"Edward may have lost it and never knew he had it," said Laurence. "Or didn't know it was of any importance and threw it away. Or destroyed it on purpose. I may even have lost it myself. Have some more beer. No, have some Scotch, I'm going to. Lord, I feel as though this day has lasted for weeks." He yawned widely and poured out drinks for the party.

"I suppose," said Bagshott, "you didn't throw out anything from your brother's effects which you regarded as rubbish? Odd screws of paper, empty cigarette packets, any debris of any kind?"

"My good man," said Logan, who did not like Bagshott particularly, "you didn't know my brother. He did not harbour debris, consequently there was none for me to throw away. Talking about cigarette packets," he added more genially, feeling that he had perhaps been a trifle rude in his own house, "there's that beautiful silver cigarette case Betty Alton gave Edward. I must send it back—meant to before, but I've been rather dodging the lady. She——"

Hambledon came out of his chair in one movement. "The case—where is it?"

"Here," said Logan, opening a drawer. "Why, I——"

Hambledon snatched it rudely and opened it; there were six cigarettes still remaining.

"Russians, made with a tube," he said rapidly, and slit one open with his pocketknife. "There were seven, but I pinched one the other day." He slit open a second. "We had our doubts about you, you know"—he opened up a third—"it wasn't much to go on, but they were Russians——" He cut open the fourth cigarette and a narrow strip of film sprang out of the cardboard tube and uncoiled itself upon the table while they all stood round and stared at it.

Eventually Hambledon picked it up and held it to the light with Edward Logan's ivory-handled magnifying glass to help him. After a moment he laid it down again and put the glass over it as though it might otherwise attempt to escape.

"That's it," he said, "that's it. An expensive bit of film, gentlemen, don't you agree? For what that tiny strip contains Muntz died in the North Sea, Alton on the river and Logan in the train; the car driver Cutler in London, Vladimir and the rat Brachko in Paris. Chadai was burnt to death tonight, and one of these days Yudin will hang by the neck until he also is dead."